THE CULT OF ELLE

MACABRE FAIRY TALES BOOK 1

J.S. DOUGLAS

Macabre Fairy Tales Book 1
The Cult of Elle
by J.S. Douglas
Copyright © 2023 by Julia Shaw
All Rights Reserved
Published by Julia Shaw
ISBN-13 979-8-9865796-3-4
ISBN-13 979-8-9865796-4-1
Cover Design by Zoe Perdita of Rainbow Danger Designs
Interior layout by Zoe Perdita of Rainbow Danger Designs
Editing by Amie Belcastro
First Edition

For: Captain
Thank you for listening to everything I've written for fifteen years. I wish I could have read this one to you, too. I miss you, buddy.

PROLOGUE

Lady Elle Marchand sprawled on a chaise lounge; her honey-colored hair disheveled as it rustled against moss-green pillows. A summer breeze tugged at the simple beige shift that covered her alabaster limbs. Closing her viridian eyes, Lady Elle focused inward, pulling at the energy and matter that composed her body.

The chaise's worsted wool pillows blackened and curled as her skin glowed red with the molten heat of creating something new. A steaming, fist-size mass bulged above her right breast. For a few moments, it pulsed with prismatic color, the lump forming a rippling sack of skin, like a tumor growing at incredible speed. Then, a beak emerged from the throbbing mass. Earthly color washed over the shape as it found its form. At last, a common chaffinch hopped from foot to foot on Lady Elle's chest.

This small piece of her physical form leapt, leaving a blackened dent in the woman's chest. As it flapped its wings and gained altitude, the small crater in Lady Elle's chest smoothed over, skin knitting itself together and returning to milky white. Lady Elle accomplished this miraculous healing with a moment's thought, most of her mind now taken up with controlling the chaffinch swooping over the garden wall and flying across the surrounding farmlands.

Searching for prey, Lady Elle ignored the vineyards filled with flowering grapes, waves of young barley and wheat, small earthen homes, and the dark forest. The chaffinch's sharp eyes spotted the gilt-covered carriage bumping along the King's Road. The conveyance kicked up dust as it transported Lady Elle's stepmother and two young stepsisters. Catching a thermal, the small bird glided past the carriage and followed the road to its natural conclusion, King Charmant's castle.

The imposing stone of the castle's outer and inner baileys did not block the small creature. As it swooped past the walls, a surge of energy thrummed through the animal, causing Lady Elle to lose control over the form. Another chaffinch, the single observer of this phenomenon, almost fell out of the sky in surprise as it watched Lady Elle's minion flash with prismatic colors, then plummet as it transformed into a lump of steaming matter once more.

Crumpling her face in concentration, Lady Elle reformed her bird before it hit the ground. Recovering and righting itself, her chaffinch swooped toward the small French castle, seeking a place to rest and observe.

It had taken years for Lady Elle to master the ability to hold a form in the face of the opposing power held beneath the castle. She'd sought this energy source for over a century, had convinced her adoptive father to move them to this location once she'd discover the power. He thought it his idea to return to his childhood village. But Elle knew better. Gentle persuasion coaxed him to settle down next to this force.

Once they'd settled, she turned to the challenge of capturing the power. Before she could step near it, she spent years perfecting her ability to maintain a consistent shape in its face.

In that way, the bracelet locked onto her wrist helped. It made her true form inaccessible to her, keeping her stably in the body of an earthly creature, rather than her true, unearthly shape.

Back on her chaise, Lady Elle shook her head slightly.

Dangerous thoughts, she mused. *If I were not trapped in this human form, I would not be seeking the power to return to myself - or to my true home. I would have been able to access that power over a century ago.*

Pulling herself from the brink of maudlin speculation, Lady Elle returned her focus to the mission at hand. She perched her little bird on the edge of a parapet and left a tiny portion of her energy and attention with the small creature. Then, she switched focus to her other small spy, a brown and gray dunnock gripping the greasy shoulder of the Noamhite tribal leader, the chief of her cultish followers.

Twenty travelers stepped through the deepest parts of the woods, careful to remain concealed.

Four youths, little affected by the Change, acted as scouts. These men ensured the fifteen tribal elders and one Changed One stayed out of sight.

The Changed One was once a man, a former tribal chief, who had made the full transition into a water-dwelling, tentacled creature whose appearance most matched Lady Elle's natural form. Her proudest creation, she would be damned if she didn't return home without him by her side.

Focusing her keen bird's eyes, Lady Elle recognized this section of forest. Flapping her wings and hopping from perch to perch, her little bird burst through the leaf cover and peered past the expanse of trees ahead. Sharp eyes caught sight of the outer gate. They would be at her chateau before sundown.

Working her bird form back down to the men, she spoke to them through its little beak. Elle's contralto voice announced, "You will be at my chateau by sundown. There, you must eat, bathe, and rest. You may not get another chance before transcendence."

Nineteen men fell to their knees and bowed, faces pressed into leaves, sticks, and mud. The Changed One could not kneel, though he did flatten himself as completely as possible.

Addressing the least human among them, the tiny brown bird said, "As for you, my faithful old friend, refresh yourself in the pond here and then make your way to the castle. One of my men will escort you. There you will find a lake in which you can rest until the time comes."

The nightmarish tentacled mass looked up at the bird, its unblinking luminous eyes showing a depth of expression only Lady Elle could read. It opened its mouth and fluted a hushed thank you through the flaps of skin cascading down its face.

The journey had taxed her oldest acolyte, but now that she had a chance to access the power source, she knew the pilgrimage from Britannia would be worth it for him. The rest of her followers might perish upon contact with the energy of her world, but she felt deep down in her cartilage that the Changed One would make it through.

"Carry on," she instructed, perching her bird back on the lead man's shoulder. Her followers stood and resumed their trek.

Returning her mind to her main form, Lady Elle stood. On the brink of success, she felt dull and uninspired.

Interacting with these humans is the difficulty, she told herself. *They are too predictable.*

Then, remembering how simple tribal women living in a Britannia fen trapped her on this earth and in this form over a century ago, Lady Elle straightened.

Not all of them, she reminded herself. *I shall not repeat that mistake.*

She swept into the grand chateau, not sparing a glance for the two attendants standing discreetly on either side of the garden door.

"Ready the carriage. Fill it with three men and two footmen. Leave room for me. It is time to put our plan into action."

The attendants' strange faces twisted, and their eyes shone with fierce joy. Both men bowed and then took off running toward the front of the house.

Calling another attendant, Elle readied him for the arrival of her reinforcements.

Finally alone in the hall, she looked down at her frock. Beige and draping, the garment could look sensual if she tightened it, or nondescript if she loosened it. No one outside of her small coterie saw her in much else. Tonight, that would change.

She closed her eyes and emitted an intense vibration, shaking her body so rapidly that any small dirt particle loosened and dropped from her person. Then, she focused on the matter comprising her current form. Reshaping it, reshaping herself, she stretched her body, creating height, some slight curves, a small bosom, and, most importantly, a dazzling gown. The fabric now enveloping her arms concealed the bracelet that trapped her in this human form. Her hair curved itself up into a shining mass of honey-brown curls accented by glowing jewels. Around her neck grew an ornate necklace, sparkling in the afternoon light.

Stretching her form and moving her mass around left little available substance for her feet. The tiny, doll-size extremities looked more like tentacle tips than a human foot. Pondering her feet, she refocused her energy on two objects she'd made long ago, from a different time. They were once part of her but had remained in a different shape for so long that she'd forgotten about them.

From the dusty attic above, two tiny, doll-size silver shoes squirmed out of a trunk, kicking the lid open with unnatural force. The footwear squeezed between the floor and the door and clicked their way down the stairs. Promenading through the flagged hall, they found Elle and stilled. She picked them up and rubbed off the dust.

"You will do," she told the shoes, putting them on her feet and then exuding water from her substance, rinsing off any last vestiges of dirt and leaving puddles on the stone floor.

Her attendants returned, having changed into the livery she'd designed for them. Bowing, they informed her in croaking voices.

"All is ready, my lady."

"Excellent," she said, her deep voice echoing in the hall. "Let us begin."

CHAPTER 1

Prince Marceau Charmant flexed his hands, his frustration mounting.

When will these introductions be over? he wondered.

The prince stood on aching legs atop a stone dais at the end of the tapestry-hung great hall. The graying king sat on a cushioned throne next to the prince, watching the spectacle unfold. Charmant looked at his father and rolled his hazel eyes. The older man smiled slightly, showing graying teeth through his dry lips.

He is enjoying this too much, thought the prince, turning back to the great hall in time to greet yet another guest.

The herald announced a young woman and her father, the latest guests to be presented. Holding her curtsy longer than necessary, the young woman glanced up at the prince flirtatiously through long lashes. Prince Charmant greeted them with a smile and a small bow of his own. His father nodded, and the two stood.

While Charmant's mind had drifted as the herald read their names, he had dutifully memorized the guest list and knew the man was a baron. The king had invited all the eligible ladies in the land to attend the first three balls of the summer in their castle. Though the information was not included in the invitation, every attendee knew the king wished his son to marry.

This is why the young lady in front of him, indeed every woman on the guest list, dressed in finery more suited to a princess. The many jewels encrusting the various guests nearly blinded him. Each newly announced woman jingled with gems when they curtsied. The prince's stomach churned as covetous eyes sized him up with each of the herald's announcements.

It is a strange sensation to be the belle of the ball, he mused.

The prince's dressers had also garbed him in finery, though he did not flaunt his wealth with jewelry. Instead, he wore a silk tunic cut to fit his tall frame. Simply belted, a gilt-edged cape flowed over the ensemble. Beneath the silks, his fine-woven wool stockings clung to well-muscled calves. While his father wore long-toed shoes, the prince eschewed the style. The youngest of six, he had been sent to learn how to soldier before his father called him home. His soft leather shoes were cut for comfort rather than style. Thin gold encircled his brow. Though small, the gold circlet gleamed against his black hair and tan skin.

The king dismissed the young lady and her father with a gesture. Charmant sighed. The baron and his daughter were some of the least tiresome of all the attendees he'd met. At least they hadn't launched into a speech or poem.

Prince Charmant glanced up at the slit windows cut into the high walls. Hope warmed his chest when he saw the fading light.

The introductions must be coming to an end with the day, he thought.

Facing forward again, he watched as another man, this one trailed by four young women, made his way to the dais. Forcing a smile, the prince shifted his weight to ease his aching muscles.

Can I endure three more days of this nonsense? Prince Charmant wondered as he smiled and bowed. He glanced at his father again. The king's face cracked into a broad smile as he greeted his subjects.

The family in front of them went through the motions, each girl presented to the prince like a rare gift. Charmant's eyes went to the herald, watching as the man rolled up the paper.

Bowing and smiling at the people in front of him, the prince listened as his father dismissed the party. Turning, Charmant began to bow to his father.

Perhaps I can escape to the gardens for a moment before the ball begins, he thought, envisioning the cool air against his sweaty skin.

A throat cleared on the threshold, and the herald let out an undignified groan.

Charmant shuffled back into place, his feet and calves making their complaints felt. His eyes went wide as a dazzling beauty entered the great hall. Pale blue silk and white iridescent fur accented her diminutive frame while subtly showcasing her curves. Two men of noble bearing accompanied her, their stomping strides clumsy compared to her dainty steps. She walked as if she were dancing down the long hall.

One of her attendants stepped over to the herald and whispered in his ear. The man's strangeness juxtaposed with the luminous woman struck Prince Charmant as odd. The attendant stood squat with bowlegs and a straight back. His clothes looked as if they were cut for a larger, leaner man, though they bore the arms of a noble house.

Charmant paused in his assessment of the man. The heraldry emblazoned on his tabard indicated the de Noelles Marchand family, with one addition. The heraldic symbol exhibited four fleurs-de-lis positioned in a diamond shape, with two curving tentacles embroidered beneath.

Though the de Noelles Marchand chateau sat within a day's ride, Prince Charmant had never met all the residents. Being the youngest of six, he had never expected to marry. A soldier's life took up the past five years. On top of that, while the castle had been his childhood home, he'd never played with the de Noelles Marchand girls, who were several years younger than him. Now that he considered it, he knew of just two girls, and they had been introduced to him already. Though the sisters hardly seemed of age to visit court, he judged this exquisite creature older than them.

She must be my age, twenty? Perhaps? Beautiful yet wise enough to rule.

After his days of soldiering, he yearned for a woman with sense and wisdom, as well as beauty.

Refocusing on the herald and the lady's attendant, Prince Charmant tried to read the man's lips, but it was impossible. The darkening hall made his face difficult to discern, and the man appeared to suffer from a malformation of the lips. It appeared as if his mouth opened far wider than it ought, gaping along an inhuman slash.

It must be a trick of the evening light, Charmant told himself as he stared. The opening for the man's mouth was not only elongated, but he could not ascertain where the gray-hued skin ended, and the lips began.

Squinting in the glowing rushlights and failing sunlight, the man appeared as a frog turned human.

The herald nodded and stood straight, playing a fanfare on his horn. He announced the lady as Elle Marchand. Charmant's mind went blank, and his heart pounded as Lady Elle walked forward on flashing silver feet. She brought a luminosity to the room, appearing to glow even as the light dimmed. Around her, servants lit more candles, accenting the woman's beauty.

Curtsying low in front of the prince and king, Lady Elle looked up, her brilliant emerald eyes sparkling in an unblemished face. Her pink lips spread into a broad, artless smile.

"Your Majesties," she acknowledged in a clear, musical voice.

"My Lady," the prince said, bowing to her. His heart beat in his throat as he stared. He needed to dance with her, know her, and hear that voice again. She sparkled, radiating brilliance. A jewel glimmering in his great hall, waiting to be plucked.

Stepping down from the dais, he offered the lady his arm. She placed a delicate hand on his forearm and smiled up at him. Roses and musk drifted from the lady's neck. Without thinking, the prince leaned closer and sniffed, his eyes fixed on her decolletage.

The king stood from his throne, his favorite courtier helping the frail man from the dais.

"You are a vision, Lady Marchand," smiled the king, bringing the prince back to himself. "And I am sure my son would enjoy escorting the loveliest lady in the land to the ball. Alas, propriety has already chosen our companions for us."

Lady Elle removed her hand from the prince's arm and curtsied again. One of her attendants offered an arm and walked her to the screened off portion of the great hall behind which stood the rest of their noble guests.

Prince Charmant straightened, heat rising to his face. His arm tingled where the lady had touched him, sending shocks through his body.

What is happening to me? he wondered. No stranger to lust, this yearning felt different.

The king clasped Charmant on the shoulder, jolting the prince back to reality.

"Come, my son, let us refresh ourselves in privacy."

They walked to a private room just off the great hall. The small refreshing room usually held one noble and an attendant. The king sank into the single chair in the room and beckoned his son inside. They shut the door on the attendant.

The king sighed and reached out a shaking hand. Charmant took it in his own, noting the leech marks on his father's wrist. The blemishes brought him back to earth, to his father's needs, and to those of his people.

"I saw the way you looked at Lady Marchand," the king stated. "Old Marchand, her father, was rich as Croesus. She is young and healthy. I had intended to advise you to marry the dowager Queen Blanche, but if Lady Marchand strikes your fancy, she may be a better match. Her wealth does not come from raising rents or imposing taxes on villages already decimated by plague, as does ours.

Her wealth comes from ships filled with spices and jewels. Also, she has never tried to have children; presumably, Queen Blanche has tried and failed. What say you, could you marry a merchant's daughter?"

Charmant gaped, his heart plummeting. "She is a merchant's daughter?"

"Yes. Old Marchand helped my cousin, the former king, build many of our kingdom's towns and brought commerce to our dwindling population. A good man. Good enough to be knighted, then marry a noble lady."

Charmant took a deep breath and pondered the issue. Not a romantic like his father, he turned his mind to practical considerations. His kingdom was hemorrhaging wealth. Many of the surrounding villages and much of his own family had been killed by the plague. He and his father were the lone survivors of the illness that had ripped through the castle, killing his mother and five siblings, along with most of their servants.

"If she has the dowry you anticipate, and if I continue to find her comely, I am certain we can make a match," Charmant assured his father. "After all, we came into royalty by God's grace. Who am I to discount a woman who came into nobility because of His plan?"

"That's my boy," the king beamed. He paused, eyes searching his youngest son's face. "Forgive a romantic old man, but she does seem to strike a certain feeling in you, does she not? When I told you about her merchant father, the color drained from your face."

Charmant smiled, touching his father's hand. "I suppose I do find her quite beautiful. There is something about her, something I cannot name."

"True love?" asked his father.

The prince shook his head. "I do not know what you and my mother had, father. I do not know how that feels. I do not know if I will ever feel it. You had something special, something that I believe few find - perhaps it is something one sees or feels once in a lifetime."

Squeezing his father's hand, the prince smiled again. Tears ran down the king's face.

"I miss mother, too," Charmant said.

The king sniffed, wiping his face with a free hand.

"Attend to me, my son. Help me remove this heavy crown from my brow and wash the evidence of my grief from my face. Tonight must be a joyful evening, one in which you will find a wife."

Charmant hefted off his father's golden crown and bathed his hands, face, and feet. He helped the older man up and called the attendant. He did not want to be the one to assist his father in evacuating his bowels.

After completing his own ablutions, Charmant joined his father and the ball's attendees in a procession to the ballroom. The king led, and Charmant gave his arm to the neighboring dowager queen, Queen Blanche. The lady's reputation of beauty and grace preceded her, and Charmant had been interested to see how she showcased her loveliness.

Instead of a dark hood, the lady wore a sheer linen head covering that hinted at chestnut locks, with a few sly curls slipping out and framing her creamy, unlined face and dark eyes. A tall woman, her eyes aligned with the prince's as he took her arm. He had been pondering the rumor that she had a stepdaughter in delicate health and wondering if the young lady would be a better match for him than this older widow. But, when he caught her eye, his mind blanked.

Queen Blanche had a power, a force she communicated through eye contact alone. Charmant now understood why she remained ruler even after her husband's death over a decade ago.

Licking dry lips, Charmant looked away from the striking woman.

I will have to avoid those eyes, he thought. A shiver ran through him, one he tried to conceal by straightening his spine and plastering his most charming smile across his face.

With a nod from the king, the doors swung wide.

Together, Charmant and the queen walked into the glittering ballroom.

Thousands of candles and rushlights reflected off mirrored surfaces, causing the enormous room to glow brighter than the morning sun. Enhanced by profusions of white and yellow roses, the room shone even as the true sun dipped below the horizon.

That evening, Charmant danced with every woman in attendance. They and their families knew that he sought a bride and each lady made herself agreeable to him. Many of the ladies dressed in dazzling jewels, had daring headpieces and charming manners. But Prince Charmant's eyes kept drifting to the slight figure standing on the side of the dance floor.

Lady Elle Marchand's porcelain skin glowed in the candlelight. Bejeweled honey-colored hair framed her sweet face and viridian eyes.

No other man danced with her. Instead, she stood like a beautiful sculpture beneath the largest profusion of candles and waited for the prince.

When the prince finally ran through the many women with whom decorum forced him to dance, he approached Lady Elle Marchand.

"Would you dance with me, my lady?" he asked.

She smiled up at him and gave him her delicate hand.

They whirled and twirled on the floor, making the dance look effortless to those around them. Every time their bodies came in contact, the prince felt lit from within - as if stoking a fire that would burn him up. He had never felt this kind of passion in his twenty-two years of life.

When the song ended, Prince Charmant bowed, and Lady Elle curtsied. Then she walked away, leaving motes of brilliance in her wake. Charmant blinked several times, trying to blink away the dots of light that sparkled around Lady Elle. When he looked again, she had disappeared.

CHAPTER 2

A few hallways over, a young servant unbarred the heavy cellar door. Heaving at the wooden monstrosity and cursing its solid, metal banding, he managed to swing it open, revealing worn stone steps.

Here, the cool earth kept the temperature just above freezing. The best wines were stored in the enormous cellar, along with root vegetables, cured meat, and anything else that needed to be stored in a cool, dry place.

The servant used his candle to light the two rushlights lining the passage, then made his way down the stairs into the cavernous room. Partygoers were imbibing quite a bit of wine, mead, and ale, and the cellarman feared he had brought up too few wine casks. Normally an ale tester, this servant had been tasked to bring up more wine to ensure drink flowed freely among the merrymakers.

He walked into the large room and began the process of filling two small casks to carry up the stairs for footmen to serve at the ball. Busy with his task, he didn't recognize the sound of scraping shovels until the vessels were full and the enormous barrel stopped up. Only when he lifted the casks did it strike him that pre-lit rushlights illuminated the room. Pausing, he followed the path of a few lit rushlights down to the northern wall. There, a torch flickered, casting dancing shadows across the room.

"Louis, Hugo, is that you?" he grumbled. "You two had better not be siphoning off the ale or skimming a rind of cheese. The Steward will pitch a fit if you are caught."

The scraping sounds stopped, and he listened for a moment longer. Above him, the muffled melodies and the thump of feet obscured any further noise.

Containers growing heavy in his burly arms, he called again, "I could use some help, if you two are done with whatever it is you are doing."

A songbird chirped next to his left ear. Turning to look for the trapped animal, the servant's mouth widened into an "O" of surprise as the swinging end of a spade slammed into his face. He fell, his head cracking against the large wine barrel, and his arms dropping the two casks. Blood smeared across the metal-banded oak container as his body slumped into the dirt.

A filthy man stood over the servant, his flat face and wide mouth expressionless. He let the dirt and blood-caked shovel fall from his long, suction-cup-lined fingers. Squatting down, he pulled the servant's body to the northern end of the cellar. He dropped the body next to the pile of stones and dirt he and his two companions had dug out of the base of the wall.

The other men set down their shovels to lift the body behind the earthen pile. To them, this body was yet another piece of debris they would have to remove from the cellar.

"One of us must take his place," croaked a tall man. His lip-less mouth reached from cheekbone to cheekbone, opening inhumanly as he spoke. Wide, luminescent eyes dominated his face and the most common protrusion on a human visage, the nose, had flattened to two holes impaling gray skin. Sweat from their exertions gleamed off his bald pate and dripped down to his neck, collecting around the gill slits that flapped open and closed while he talked.

The two frog-like men looked at the third man in their crew. The Change had not completely altered him. His long-fingered hands looked human, and an arched nose still graced his countenance.

His mouth, though. His mouth had elongated beyond the bounds of normal human lips. Where once all had been symmetrical, now the right side of his lips extended to the base of his cheekbone, giving one the impression that he'd been horribly mutilated. Yet no scar tissue or other sign of injury befouled his visage. Instead, the smooth skin on his face ran right up to the opening, eliminating the appearance of lips and simultaneously making his features look both lopsided and disfigured.

Soon, they knew, the man's mouth would stretch symmetrically, slicing itself open to the cheekbone on the other side of his face. After that, his nose would melt and expand until his visage looked like his companion's - a pale frog's face on a human body. But for now, he could pass as a castle servant.

The man caught the two Changed men's looks and nodded. He crouched and began to strip the servant's body.

CHAPTER 3

C harmant walked through the crowd of nobles, hoping to find Lady Elle. Sparks of light still danced in his eyes as he scanned the crowd.

Before he could get to the doors at the end of the ballroom, a great gong rang. Charmant sighed. Propriety dictated that he accompany Queen Blanche to the feast and then sit with her and make conversation for seven interminable courses. He bent to fate and went to find the queen.

Course after course of trout, peacock, heron, venison, and boar filled his belly as he made polite conversation with the beautiful queen.

They talked of her kingdom, which stretched to the ocean's shore. She told him of the great castle in which she lived, all alone. Something about her made Charmant uncomfortable. Her laugh was too brittle, and she shunned any mention of her only child, a stepdaughter.

At the beginning of the conversation, Charmant gorged himself on his favorite fish in saffron sauce. However, as the evening wore on, he watched as the queen appeared to eat, but her food never seemed to diminish. Feeling brutish for his larger appetite, he found himself slowing, chewing delicately, and only tasting foods that he would have enjoyed in generous mouthfuls moments before.

By the time the servants laid out the third course, Charmant ran out of things to say. He tried to ask after her stepdaughter. Surely the girl was of age to attend court. Her father had died several years before and her mother a year or two before that. But the queen could not be moved to speak on that subject.

Falling silent, he made his way through course after course, his eyes straying around the table. Trying to recite the names of each noble to himself, he could not find Lady Elle, though he saw her stern stepmother and young stepsisters. He'd watched for her throughout the meal and, though guests and servants filled the room, he hadn't seen her sit down.

Where is she? he wondered, scanning the room.

"Looking for someone, Your Highness?" asked Queen Blanche. Her lips stretched into a smile, but her black eyes pinched together at the corners in annoyance.

He avoided looking into those cold eyes, instead staring at her unlined forehead as he replied.

"No, indeed, my queen. For who could compete with your fascinating company?" he stretched a false smile across his face as he spoke.

"Oh, you are as charming as your name," she told him, stroking his arm. It took all of his self-control not to smack her hand away.

"You are too kind, my queen. I look forward to enjoying your company at tomorrow's ball, as tonight has been such a success."

The queen twitched her lips up a bit more, but her eyebrows crinkled in confusion. Surely, she noticed the sarcasm in his words. Though, anyone who tried to compliment him by calling him "as charming as his name" lacked an understanding of subtlety.

He needed to get away from this woman.

The last course served, Charmant took a polite bite of each dish, then stood and bowed to the queen. The close air. The heat and smoke. Her cold company. All of it made his skin itch.

Without another word, he strode out of the great hall and back into the ballroom.

Where is my lady? he wondered. Flicking his eyes through the few guests who had eschewed the feast, he did not see Lady Elle.

The back terrace, he thought, jogging to the open doors. Barred shut when the ballroom was not in use, these doors had been open for the last three days, admitting artisans and servants alike to decorate the enormous room.

It reminded him of the days when his mother threw festival and holiday balls, flinging the doors open as artisans, milliners, and others came and went from the castle to prepare for a feast or gathering.

He stepped onto the terrace, squinting through the gray, predawn light. A hush swept over him, contrasting with the clatter and laughter indoors. Standing against his castle's stone wall, the prince breathed, inhaling the scent of dewy earth and rich foliage. A delightful smell wafted across the expectant air. The scent of roses and musk.

Charmant's skin prickled with goosebumps as he peered around the terrace, searching for his lady. Far in the distance, the horizon softened with golden light, illuminating the world enough for him to see her.

Lady Elle stood against a great column on the northern corner of the terrace.

She looked even more beautiful and mysterious than she had in the bright ballroom. Her skin appeared almost translucent. As Charmant approached her, he could see the blue veins running just beneath the surface of her skin with curious clarity.

"Hello," he said, stopping several steps away from Lady Elle.

It took every ounce of willpower to keep his arms at his side. The passion he had felt during their dance welled up inside him, burning his breast and making his once chill skin hot and flushed. His arms yearned to hold her, and his lips thirsted for her kiss.

She turned; her large green eyes glazed with a white substance. He was reminded of his falcon's eyes, how they blinked horizontally as well as vertically. That second eyelid a thick, semi-transparent window into an unknowable animal's soul.

The impression remained for a mere moment. Then, her eyes flickered into focus.

Charmant took an involuntary step back, his skin shivering with goosebumps.

Lady Elle's guileless green eyes widened in concern.

"Your Highness, are you quite well?"

The depth and musicality of her words soothed him.

"Yes," he wrapped his arms around himself and looked into those forest eyes. They were again wide and green, framed by dark lashes. He smiled at her, dismissing the phenomena as a trick of the changing light.

"A chill breeze must have passed over me," he reassured her.

Lady Elle nodded, turning to watch as dawn transformed the dark orchard and gardens in front of them from blackness to a sparkling tangle of green, white, red, and brown. The rich scent of flowers and earth coming alive once more wafted over them, lifting Charmant's heart.

He breathed through his nose, smelling Lady Elle's rosy musk melding with the rich fragrances dancing around them.

"The dawn is beautiful from here," she breathed. "But I suppose it must mark the end of our evening together."

"Oh," murmured Charmant, his lips curling into a smile. "I believe we may see one another again."

She looked over her shoulder in that dreamy light and said, "Whatever could you mean, Your Highness?"

Heat raced across his skin, burning him up and sending vibrations through every extremity. Taking four rapid steps, he loomed over Lady Elle, running a finger across the silky fabric of her dress. Each warm fold increased his passions, flooding his mind with a desire to explore her with fingers, mouth, and more. He wrapped a strong arm around her stomach, pulling her backside into him.

"I believe I will call upon you in the morrow," he whispered into her ear. "Your mother is unlikely to refuse my proposal."

Elle pivoted in his arms. She tilted her head, so their faces were almost touching and pressed her womanly frame against him with full force.

"So, you would have me as your own. As chattel?" she spat, glaring at him with flashing emerald eyes. Her cheeks glowed pink, adding to her beauty.

Charmant's head swam, and his arms loosened. He tried to take a step back on shaky limbs. Passionate blood continued to pump through him, keeping his muscles tight. Binding her in an unwanted embrace. His body would not let him release this woman.

"Is that not why you are here?" his dry throat closed around the words. No woman had ever spoken to him this way. Want warred with chivalry within him, her words adding a layer of confusion to his already muddled mind. Dizziness swept through him. He clutched at Elle's bare arm for support.

A voice from behind him hit like a whip.

"Unhand her," it cracked.

Charmant yelped as his arms turned ice cold. He dropped them and took two steps back. His hands burned where they had touched Lady Elle's skin. Examining his palms, he saw blisters forming.

He looked back at the person who had spoken. Draped in voluminous midnight blue silks adorned with one enormous jewel at the shoulder, Lady Elle's stepmother stood regally, an ancient willow among saplings. Thin lips set in a stern expression, her still-youthful aquamarine eyes glared into the prince's face.

Charmant turned to her and showed her his hands.

"Witchcraft," he said.

The lady's eyes widened with fear. Her hand rushed to her mouth.

"No, no," purred Lady Elle from behind him. She walked over to the woman in blue and laid a gentle hand on her arm. "Providence provided immediate retribution for touching a lady who was not ready for such energetic advances. Do you not find that strange happenings occur at dawn when the Lord above looks down upon the world with fresh eyes?"

Charmant glanced at his hands. They bubbled with blisters. He looked back at Lady Elle and her stepmother.

"What..." he started. Fog filled his head, muffling his thoughts.

"Mother, I am perfectly safe with the prince. Do not be concerned," Lady Elle told the woman. Then she took two quick steps forward and clasped Charmant's hands in her own.

"We must be going. We shall see you at the next ball, Prince Charmant. Thank you for an illuminating experience."

Prince Charmant stood stunned. He allowed her to slip away, hooking her stepmother's arm in her own and leading the lady back into the castle with a dancing step.

He didn't know how long he stood, staring at the closed door. When he finally came to himself, golden light filled the world, bringing the terrace and the surrounding landscape into glaring relief.

He looked down at his palms once again. Not a hint of a blister upon them. He rubbed his hands together and watched as dust motes floated off each palm, dancing into the morning air.

"Witchcraft," he told the morning air, "but who is the witch?"

CHAPTER 4

After a long sleep, Prince Charmant awoke to afternoon light streaming into his room. Finding his washbasin cold, he bathed quickly in the chill water, scrubbing off the sweat of the previous evening. Though clean, he found his body unrefreshed. His skin itched from head to foot, as if dried sweat and dead skin still covered him. He dressed in his softest, most comfortable clothes, clothes barely appropriate for a lord - much less a prince. The loose fabric floated around him, leaving the itchiness unabated.

Giving up on feeling comfortable, he thought ahead to that evening and the next ball. He would have to get ready soon. But first, he wanted to talk with his father about Lady Elle.

The prince slipped on soft shoes and walked down the hall toward the king's bed chamber. Lost in thought, he wondered. Who was the witch? Lady Elle or her stepmother? He thought of that dark, stern figure glaring down at him and her daughter. Lady Elle's words echoed in his mind.

Providence provided immediate retribution for touching a lady who was not ready for such energetic advances.

Was that how her stepmother explained the use of magic to her?

Had she beguiled the young woman into believing that everything magical was simply Providence protecting her? Or was the beautiful Lady Elle some kind of sorceress?

He could not believe that someone so beautiful would do evil. It must be her mother or one of the evil-looking servants. Not the beautiful young woman. After all, did not beauty and goodness go hand in hand?

If the culprit was Lady Elle's mother or one of her strange servants, he had a duty to take her away from such evil.

He looked up and realized that he had continued walking instead of stopping at his father's door. He backtracked and told the young servant at the entrance to announce him.

The boy standing watch at the king's chamber flicked his eyes up to the prince's for a moment before casting them down. He bowed, and stammered, "His Majesty has not yet awakened. I am to admit no one until he wakes, Your Highness." He bowed again; his head so low it almost touched the ground.

Charmant did not know this child. He could be the son of one of the servants who had died in the plague - or he might be a previously untrained villager brought from a local town for service. The boy maintained his bow, head low and body shaking.

"Very well, thank you for letting me know," murmured Charmant, making his voice gentle in spite of his agitation.

Charmant turned to find three bowing men. He could not see their faces, but they were clothed as dressers. His skin twitched and his stomach growled.

"You will have to wait," snapped Charmant. "I must walk and have a meal before I dress for this evening's festivities."

"Yes, Your Highness," the three men intoned in croaking voices as Charmant strode out of the hall. He paused to look back at them. Their bowlegged, straight-backed posture reminded him of something, but his foggy mind couldn't quite discern what.

He walked into the great hall, finding it filled with servants making ready for the ball. The castle steward, Octave, stepped to the prince's side and bowed.

"We have set out your meal on the terrace, Your Highness. M. Martin is eating there as the king has ordered his meal sent to his room once he wakes," Octave straightened from his bow. Though Octave and Charmant were the same height, the steward always hunched in the presence of royalty. Only when commanding the rest of the servants did he stand at his full, imposing six-foot stature.

Charmant nodded and passed through the ballroom, now abuzz with servants, artisans, and performers all trying to make themselves and the vast chamber ready for the evening's festivities. Everyone paused as he and Octave walked through, the whole room bowing as he pushed through the terrace doors.

His father's most trusted counselor, Monsieur Elouan Martin, stood and bowed as the prince sat. Octave loaded up two plates for Charmant and stepped back. The prince looked at Octave's impassive face. The castle steward was one of the few servants who had survived the plague, and Charmant knew the man better than many. Octave rocked from heel to toe very slightly as he stood, a sign of anxiety.

He wants to be in motion, directing his staff and not standing here serving breakfast, thought the prince.

"You may go, Octave. This meal is sufficient, and my father would not forgive me if I kept you from supervising the preparations." Charmant flashed the man a smile.

"Thank you, Your Highness." Octave's smile showed in his voice. He bowed and left in a rapid walk.

"That was kind, Your Highness," Elouan commented, redistributing his large belly before taking another bite of bream in wine sauce.

The smell of fish this close to waking agitated Charmant's already frayed nerves. Taking a breath through his mouth, he peered down at his own plate. As always, Octave knew his breakfast tastes. Bread, butter, three boiled eggs and a small dish of nut and fruit-filled croquants sat in front of him. Picking up a croquant, he sniffed deeply, banishing the fish smell. He dipped the biscuit into a glass of chill white wine and took a bite.

"I could feel his nerves. He wanted to return to his post, I have everything I need to enjoy my meal, and I dislike eating around nervous people. Additionally, I wanted to speak with you privately."

"What can I do for you, Your Highness?" Elouan quickly swallowed his bit of food and mopped his face with a cloth.

"I wish to know everything about Lady de Noelles Marchand, her daughters, and the de Noelles line."

"Ah," Elouan stated, his voice going flat, "your father mentioned you were interested in her stepdaughter, Lady Elle Marchand."

"I am."

"I must warn you against the match, Your Highness. Lady Marchand is not of noble blood."

"Yes, my father told me that she is a merchant's daughter, but that her wealthy father became nobility when he was knighted. Additionally, he married into nobility."

"Indeed," Elouan nodded, his jowls jiggling with the motion, "but there is more to it than that. She is a foundling, adopted by Marchand. We can have no knowledge of her bloodline."

This information gave Charmant pause.

"If you wish to marry wealth and nobility, Your Highness, may I suggest pursuing Queen Blanche? Her lands border ours, and it would be a strong alliance indeed."

The prince's heart sank. After his evening with Queen Blanche, he wanted nothing to do with her. If possible, he would prefer never to see the woman again. His dislike of the woman must have shown on his face, for Elouan continued.

"It is said, my prince, that her people are among the healthiest in the land. It is said that many of her villages are brimming with wealth and good fortune," Elouan raised an eyebrow. "Our people could benefit from the health and wealth in her lands."

"I see," Charmant clenched his jaw. "I will have to spend more time with her this evening. I fear Lady Elle Marchand had my heart last night. Perhaps I overlooked the queen too hastily."

Elouan nodded. "I hope you will, Your Highness. I think you may find the queen to be the loveliest in the land."

Standing from the table, Elouan sketched a brief bow. "I must attend your father."

Charmant ate a last bite and took a final sip of wine. His skin itched, and he felt more jittery than when he'd sat down.

"I should be getting ready," he told Elouan's large back. What he really wanted was an evening off and a swim in the lake. He squinted up at the sky, taking stock of the sun's position. Perhaps he could spare a few more moments for a refreshing swim and then speed his dressers along. He needed a wash, and the dip would cool his infernally itching skin.

Making up his mind, Charmant stepped down from the terrace and followed the path that cut through the gardens and into the orchard. In the green dimness, he felt whole once again. These trees had grown here since his childhood, and he could walk among them with his eyes closed, knowing the position of each root and trunk.

The path he followed disappeared, splitting into three footpaths. The left path led to the family graveyard, the middle to the inner bailey, and the right to the lake. A fourth, faded path hooked a sharp right and led to the front doors of the castle, but he and his siblings were the only people who had ever used that walkway. The front doors were reserved for residents and guests. The servants and fruit pickers used the main walkway that led from the back of the castle to the orchard.

Charmant gazed up at the swaying branches, heavy with flowers and ripening fruit. After the insanity of these three balls had concluded, servants and villagers would fill the orchard to pick plums. Later they would harvest apples, pears, and figs. The orchard would teem with people all summer long.

He heard a rustle from his left and looked over to see two men walking through the orchard. They appeared to be workmen and carrying a bundle between them.

Perhaps some servants were harvesting early fruit for the ball. It would be difficult to discern which plums were ripe and which still needed more time, but that was the servant's job, not his. Charmant dismissed the men from his mind. He had more important things to think about.

CHAPTER 5

Arriving at the lake, Charmant stripped his clothes and waded in. The cool water lapped at his skin and cleared his head.

He dove, gliding like a fish through the crystalline water. Bursting back into the warm summer air he lingered, absorbing the scents and sounds surrounding him. Lapping water, the soothing hush of tree leaves, and the mineral scent of fresh water calmed his jitters.

Brisk strokes took him to the lake's center, where he floated on his back and gazed at an uninterrupted blue sky. The unblemished cerulean expanse served to wash away the final fog of his confused mind.

Stretching his limbs and exposing his bare chest to the late afternoon sun, he decided he would erase the ladies of the de Noelles Marchand clan from his mind and focus his thoughts on the cold but rich and marriageable widow, Queen Blanche.

"Or perhaps some other overlooked rich and noble woman," he told the sky.

Lady Elle appealed not because of her looks or mysterious nature. Instead, he believed the decision to pursue her was simple, based on passion and desire. Perhaps, given her station, he could keep her as a mistress once he had married another.

Floating in the water, dreaming of beautiful Lady Elle, was simple. Playing politics and considering which match would best suit the needs of his people, that was complicated. No wonder his father had left the job to him.

Flipping onto his stomach, Charmant made for the shore. He dipped his head below and prepared to swim hard, to shake off the last vestiges of uncertainty.

Something grabbed his right ankle, squeezing tight.

Charmant's eyes popped open. He kicked and squirmed and twisted underwater. The bottom of the lake lurked many feet below him, but mud and silt clouded the water. Peering through the murk, he glimpsed five finger-like tentacles gripping his ankle. The water slid past his skin, the light from above dimming as the monster yanked him toward the muddy disturbance below.

Rushing water filled his ears as the prince clamped his mouth shut, his lungs aching as he thrashed. Panicking now, he kicked out with both feet. His still-free left foot connected with something cartilaginous. Encouraged, he tried to strike the area again but found no purchase or leverage.

Folding his body down into a crouch, Charmant used his hands to follow the tentacle to its source. A mass of tough, slippery skin met his fingers. He grabbed at it, yanking desperately. His fingers slipped, landing on a slit - perhaps a gill? Pushing his hands into the crevice, he pulled with all that he had.

The tentacles released his right foot and a dark cloud burst through the dirty water. Through the murk, he glimpsed two luminous orbs.

Charmant's lungs ached with desperation. His heartbeat thudded in his ears as he twisted up toward the lake's surface and used all his strength to propel himself skywards. Breaking through the water, Charmant flailed and gasped. Trying to breathe and launch himself toward the shore simultaneously slowed his overall progress, but he couldn't stop moving away from that repulsive thing.

Reaching the shallows, Charmant's legs wobbled, and his feet slid. He used hands and knees to crawl through the soft, sticky muck of mud, silt, dead leaves, and animal dung lining the lake's edge. Looking around, he searched for a servant, a poacher, anyone who could help him. The lake, usually teeming with people, lay in silence. All the castle servants and surrounding villagers were occupied, readying themselves for another evening of feasting and dancing.

At the bank, Charmant dragged himself to his feet and stumbled across the narrow beach to the bush on which his clothes lay.

Could that thing get out of the water and chase him? He did not know and determined not to wait and find out. Yanking on his breeches and tunic, he jammed his feet into his boots. About half of his clothing lay strewn across the bush, but he refused to take the time to get fully dressed. The servants would just have to see him in a state of muddy dishabille.

Scooping up his additional clothing, he glanced back at the lake. Now calm, the placid blue water looked just as inviting as it had when he'd dived in. Covered in drying mud, Charmant itched for a cool dip in the lake he'd known as a child. If he could go back in time, he'd spend the afternoon in the water with his brothers, ignoring nanny's call from the shore.

But this place was no longer the idyllic reservoir of his childhood.

Losing sight of the blue expanse, Charmant turned his mind to the castle.

I must tell someone of the beast in the lake.

He paused, now fully in shadow, his mind whirring.

Who? Who would believe me? My father? He may believe me, but his health wouldn't take the strain. The huntsman? What is he to do about it? Go fishing? A priest? He would believe me taken by the Devil. That is no way forward.

Fear, sweat, and mud dripped from his pores as he pondered. No one could help him, no one who might be able to rid the lake of its new occupant. Perhaps, instead of raising the alarm, he would make enquiries. Talk to the fishermen. Fein interest in the lake's stock. That sort of thing. It would have to occur after the balls, of course.

Hastily dressed and stinking of lake mud, Charmant jogged back to the castle. Glimpsing the low afternoon sunlight, he quickened his pace. He still needed to make it to the dais in time to greet their guests.

CHAPTER 6

Deep in the cavernous cellar, frog-like men worked with pick, shovel, and bucket. Lip-less men with slashed mouths and elongated fingers hauled dirt-filled pails away from the cellar door while still others, dressed in the castle livery, brought barrels of wine and beer to the great hall for the upcoming feast.

Every servant to a man walked with bowlegs, talked in guttural tones, and hauled their burdens with rod-straight backs.

One man stood apart, directing the dig and ensuring clansmen in castle livery gained access to the food and drink they needed. From the eyes down, his face had completely undergone the Change. Below his eyes lay a frog-like face and gills slashed into his neck. Long, cartilaginous arms ended in hands with tentacle-like fingers covered in pseudopods. No one could see his legs, but when he moved, sinuous motion made one think of a sea creature rather than a land-dwelling man. On his left shoulder rested a small chaffinch.

When a servant stopped to ask him a question, the leader did not open his mouth to respond. Instead, his gills emitted fluting noises that only a clansman could understand. Through this strange form of communication, he made it known that the men must haul timber to shore up the tunnel sides. They had three days to make as much progress as possible, before the true leader of this affair would inspect their progress.

CHAPTER 7

Prince Charmant hurried to the dais as the chapel bell rang its last note. He stood at his designated spot, favoring his left foot. His right ankle burned where the tentacle had gripped it. A dresser stood with him and adjusted his clothing, making sure everything fit correctly and ensuring hose covered up the angry red marks encircling the prince's ankle.

"You do not need to rush. The king is not here," he told the boy.

When he had returned to his room after his swim, Charmant's usual dressers were nowhere to be found, nor were the bowlegged men who attempted to attend him earlier in the day. Instead, Octave had to attend to Charmant himself, accompanied only by a kitchen boy.

Charmant did not know what the household would be like tomorrow. Octave was losing his grip on things. He vowed to wake up earlier and do what he could to ensure the household held together through the chaos of the balls. Throwing balls was his mother's domain. The men of the house had no idea what they were doing.

Even now, as he looked out at the great hall, he observed cracks in the servant's handiwork. Many of the domestics wore dirty, stained clothing. Their faces were dirt streaked and sheened with sweat. Three balls in a row would run them ragged.

"His Majesty, the king," announced Octave.

Charmant bowed, then looked up to watch as an attendant helped his father onto the throne. Garbed in heavy fur, the king's ashen face appeared even grayer than usual.

If this was what the king looked like after one night of merrymaking, Charmant could not imagine how the man would manage to attend the final ball.

The great hall's doors opened, and attendees came forward to bow before the king. Charmant plastered a smile on his face and greeted each guest. Most, including Queen Blanche, had made merry the evening before. Many of the ladies seemed no worse for wear. He supposed they had planned and anticipated these balls the moment his father announced them in the spring. They were ready to display themselves, even if he felt less ready to pick a wife with every passing moment. The calm and determination he'd discovered on the lake fled the moment that thing had wrapped around his ankle.

Lady Elle and her family were announced. This time, she, her stepmother, and her two stepsisters came in together, attended by men wearing the usual de Noelles coat of arms.

Remembering the coat of arms Lady Elle's attendants wore the night before, Charmant's ankle twinged. Were the tentacles he saw on the previous evening just a trick of the light? His stomach flipped, and his hands clenched with nervous uncertainty. Why was everything so confusing with this family and this woman?

He kept his face a careful blank, trying to hide his trepidation. As he greeted the ladies, Elle caught his eye. She gave him a radiant smile, her face aglow with youth, joy, and beauty.

Charmant's skin turned hot. Not just on his face but all over. His body responded to Lady Elle's innocent beauty even as his mind told him he must consider other women - particularly the icy Queen Blanche.

Returning Lady Elle's smile, he saw Lady de Noelles Marchand glaring at her adoptive stepdaughter. Charmant's heart sank as he wondered what it must be like to live in a house filled with jealousy, anger, and possibly witchcraft.

Lady de Noelles Marchand turned her gaze to Charmant, and her face lost all color. Glancing from him to Lady Elle, an expression of dismay mixed with hope flashed across her visage. Narrowing his eyes, he glared at the formidable lady.

What are you hiding? he wondered to himself.

CHAPTER 8

T hough the servants were run ragged, the ball was a masterwork in craftsmanship. The king had hired an ingenious artisan who decorated the ballroom with stained glass panels of purple, red, and yellow, behind which torchlight shone. These panels lined the ballroom walls, casting swathes of colored light upon the room. While the artisan used three colors exclusively, he considered every permutation and challenge the revelers could encounter.

Yellow panels were employed in the dancing portion of the ballroom. The cheery, golden hue attracted merrymakers to the dance floor. Guests of all types and ages were seen on the golden ballroom floor that evening, married women, widows, and maidens alike galloped and laughed with male and female partners.

The red section highlighted the delectable feat. Wine flowed and, indeed, the entire meal seemed to be composed mainly of hoofed animals in rich red and brown sauces.

Purple panels created natural conversational areas, allowing guests who wished for a private discussion to relax and talk. The deep, purple-tinged light created intimacy in a space in which one would otherwise feel exposed.

Prince Charmant met Lady de Noelles Marchand, Lady Elle's stepmother in the latter section.

All evening, Charmant strived to do his duty. He spent time with Queen Blanche, asking her questions about her kingdom and listening to her answers. He danced with the queen, complimented her, and did his best to focus on her lovely face while avoiding her intense eyes. He worked hard to find her touch more pleasing, though each play of her fingers reminded him of that slithery, horrible tentacle wrapping around his ankle.

Each time the queen glanced away from him; the prince's eyes betrayed him. They were ungovernable that night, flicking from the woman before him and scanning the room for Lady Elle.

More often than not, Lady Elle sat alone in a chair positioned at the edge of yellow and red. The orange light did not become anyone but Lady Elle, who looked as if lit by the last rays of a blazing sunset. Her porcelain skin glowed golden in the yellow light, and her soft red dress perfectly complimented the transitional hue.

Charmant's body yearned for Lady Elle. His ears felt scorched by Queen Blanche's trilling, and he wished they could be soothed by Lady Elle's musical voice.

Finally, he could stand the queen no longer.

"I must take my leave, my Queen. I have been neglecting all the other ladies for your fascinating company, and I must do my duty. Noblesse oblige," he smiled.

"You are as charming as your name indicates, Your Highness," she told him as he bowed out.

Charmant barely held back from rolling his eyes. Did she forget she had used that complement the previous night? The observation that his name meant "charming" was one that every sycophant who had ever attempted to get into his good graces had made. And now she had made it twice in just as many days.

Before these balls had begun, he'd wished his father would make the match for him. Now he understood that there were some ladies in this world who were intolerable. No wonder his father wished him to make the choice.

His jaw hurt from the brilliant, insincere smile he'd kept on his face since the moment he and the queen joined company. Bowing to the woman now, he replied, "Thank you, and you are as lovely as everyone says, Your Majesty."

Once away from the queen, Charmant felt his body relax. He danced with a few ladies to give the appearance of even-handedness, then he made a beeline for the chair in which Lady Elle had lingered for most of the evening.

It sat empty.

Glancing from one lighted space to the next, he could not penetrate the gloom in the purple space.

Perhaps Lady Elle is in there, he hoped.

So, he went looking for the lady who made him burn with desire. As he searched, he discovered Lady de Noelles Marchand. She sat in a comfortable chair, a full goblet of wine resting on a nearby table.

Charmant bowed to the lady. She began to stand, and he waved her back.

"No need to stand on formalities. We are all nobles here, Lady de Noelles Marchand."

The lady sank back into her chair. She said nothing, looking at him with the expression of one who had bitten into a sour grape.

"May I sit with you for a moment, my lady?"

"Of course, Your Highness. You may do anything you please," she muttered.

Charmant sat down, unsure of what to say or how to start a conversation with a dour woman who may also be a witch.

What do I want to get out of this conversation and why am I drawn to her family? he wondered.

A servant walked over and placed a goblet of honeyed wine on the table next to him. The prince did not look up, but the lady did. Her face darkened further at what she saw.

Charmant glanced at the servant in time to see his bowlegs and straight back. Nothing more. Perhaps woman was simply ornery. Or drunk.

Time to find out, he decided.

"I am glad you and your family returned to the castle this evening. My father told me how much your late husband helped our family and our villages."

"Indeed?" she asked, one eyebrow raised.

"Of course. We value your noble lineage and kindness to the people. I hope that perhaps your family and ours can come together again in these dark times."

"We are here to serve, of course," she murmured into her wine cup. Another bow-legged servant bearing a wine pitcher swooped in, waiting for her to put down her goblet so he could refill it. The prince glanced up and jerked back. In the deep purple, the attendant's flat face and wide mouth appeared to leer at him.

Lady de Noelle Marchand looked from Charmant to the servant. She sighed.

"You," her voice dripped with irritation.

The servant stood stoically. Charmant could not tear his gaze away from the inhuman creature. He watched in horror as the servant blinked. First, thin eyelids covered his cornflower blue eyes. Then, when he opened them again, a white film coated the two orbs. This pallid secondary eyelid moved sideways and Charmant could once again peer into the man's eyes.

Bile rushed up the prince's throat.

Lady de Noelle Marchand rolled her eyes at the servant.

"Fine," she said, wiggling her cup. "More."

The attendant bowed and poured.

Charmant stood with such violence that his chair toppled. The contents of his stomach were going to come up at any moment. Holding a hand to his mouth, he ran as far as he could and retched into a stone urn.

When he finished emptying his stomach, he stood over the urn and tried to catch his breath. A dainty hand reached in front of him and handed him a lace-edged handkerchief.

"Thank you," he whispered, using the pristine cloth to mop his sweat-soaked forehead.

Charmant turned and found himself face-to-face with Lady Elle.

"My lady," he wheezed, the word torturing his now burning throat.

She curtsied, then smiled up at him, her brow crinkled in pretty concern.

"Are you alright?" she asked.

"I am sorry, my lady. But your stepmother. Her attendant," he could say no more. His stomach squirmed at the memory of that flat face and the double-blinking eyes. He shoved his hands behind him so that she would not see them shaking.

"They are rather strange, aren't they? My stepmother's attendants."

"They are inhuman," he spat.

"No, Your Highness. I do not wish to contradict you, but they are very human. My father found them in Britannia many years ago on his travels. He saved them from dire circumstances, and now each member of the tribe serves our family for a set number of years. To show their gratitude. Most have odd mutations that are common among their own people, but all are human."

"His eyes," quavered the prince, "when he blinked."

"Yes, many of them have that strange second eyelid. It reminds one of a hawk or a falcon. One gets used to it. Indeed, when one is as sheltered as I and my sisters, one feels as if the second eyelid is the norm and our eyes are strange."

Lady Elle's rich voice soothed his trembling hands and leaping stomach.

"Your eyes could never be strange, my lady. They are like emeralds set in porcelain."

Charmant smiled down at Lady Elle.

"Child," commanded a voice from behind her.

Lady Elle turned and curtsied as her stepmother appeared from the gloom.

"Oh, Prince Charmant, I am sorry, I did not see you," said Lady de Noelles Marchand. She made a perfunctory curtsy.

Charmant's face flushed. When he had sat with this lady, he believed he could make her slip up and admit to witchcraft. Instead, the sight of her servant caused him to flee. Even now, sweat pooled under his armpits at the memory of her attendant's face.

"We must be leaving, thank you for a wonderful evening," Lady de Noelles Marchand's cold voice rang out.

"Oh, surely you are not leaving yet," he protested, glancing at Lady Elle in desperation. He had wasted the entire evening with Queen Blanche, and he yearned to spend time with Lady Elle.

"We must leave. The girls need their beauty sleep. Perhaps you could use some rest as well, Your Highness. Your father has already departed." Lady de Noelles Marchand raised an eyebrow.

"Goodbye Your Highness," smiled Lady Elle. "If you would like, I can ask a servant to mix a soothing tincture. It always works for me when my stomach is sour."

"That would be kind, thank you, my lady," Charmant replied.

"Yes, have one of her tinctures," muttered Lady de Noelles Marchand in a flat voice. "She always seems to know what people need."

With a final curtsy, they were gone.

CHAPTER 9

Under the influence of Lady Elle's tincture, strange dreams populated Charmant's dreams.

Indistinct at first, his mind filled with the rustling of skirts, slick silk rubbing against his bare skin. His breathing grew labored as the room filled with a thick miasma. Green gems multiplied in the haze. First, two, then four, then eight gems, all the color of Lady Elle's eyes. The brilliant green spots gazed at him, blinking in and out of existence with a speed and randomness that blurred his senses. Below each set of green, pink mouths opened, gasped in ecstasy, then shut and faded, only to be replaced by a new mouth or another set of jeweled eyes.

Hands explored his legs, his manhood, his chest. In his aroused state, he arched his back, tensing for the finale. Instead of Lady Elle's luminous face floating before him, her stepmother's dark, glaring eyes hove into view. His body convulsed and spent itself, but Charmant's pounding heart hitched in fear and confusion.

Waking, he sat up and tried to catch his breath. The candle at the base of his bed had extinguished, but a few shafts of yellow morning light seeped in through his narrow window.

Peeling off the sweat-soaked blanket, Charmant stumbled to his feet, propelling himself away from the bed until he crashed into the closed bedroom door. Swinging it open, the prince gasped at the cool, scented air of the hallway. Staring at the solid castle walls, his nose filling with the scents of thyme and mint, his world slowly righted itself.

"Just a dream," he muttered to himself, taking in a deep lungful of the dusty, warm air.

"May I help you, Your Highness?" asked a quiet voice on his right. Charmant startled, his heart leaping to his throat. His head whipped around. A young man, a servant, stood near his door.

"Water," he croaked, his dry throat rasping on the word.

The servant bowed and walked away.

Charmant sagged back into his room, leaning against the stonework as his questions about Lady de Noelles Marchand flooded his mind once again. Was Elle's stepmother invading his dreams? If so, she most certainly put a spell on him. And if she boldly practiced witchcraft on a prince, then who knew what magicks she performed on her sweet stepdaughter?

Charmant came out of his thoughts, and he found himself pacing his bedroom floor.

"This will not do," he told himself.

Forgetting that he had already asked for refreshment, he washed his face and hands in his cold basin and pulled on his hose.

As he completed his brief ablutions, the servant entered his room carrying a heavy basin of fresh, rose-scented bathing water, a small wine jug tucked between his right arm and ribs, and a thick towel draped over his left arm.

Charmant waved him in. The splash of cold water had cleared the cobwebs from his head. His parched throat and clammy skin told him that he could bathe himself more thoroughly. Stepping back from the basin, he waited as the man hurriedly replaced it and draped a fresh towel on the table beside it. Then, the man uncorked

the bottle and poured wine into the goblet resting on Prince Charmant's bedside table.

Wetting the towel, the prince bathed himself in warm water,
taking occasional sips from his goblet as he luxuriated.

The servant bustled around him, relighting the banked coals in
his hearth.

The prince watched the man rushing around his room. The
servant looked much like every other, short, brown-haired, with rough
skin and stooped shoulders. The prince did not know him. He knew
few of the servants in the castle as the plague had taken many when it
had killed his mother and siblings.

Charmant's hands slowed as he wiped away yesterday's grime
and last night's sweat. He wondered about the man. Had his family
served the Charmant family before he, Prince Marceau Charmant,
had gone soldiering? Had this young man, a servant, suffered at the
hands of the plague just as he, a prince, had done?

Enough of this melancholy, thought Charmant.

The early morning light streaming through his window told him
he would have a chance to fulfill his promise and help with the
evening's preparations.

Donning one of the worn shirts he'd used during his soldiering
days, he left the bedroom without a word to the servant. The prince
molded his face into a haughty, noble expression. He knew the
expression still needed work. His face tended to relax into a cheerful,
somewhat cheeky smile. But today, he made an effort. He'd need to
order servants about, and he couldn't be caught off guard while
doing so.

Stepping into the great hall, Charmant almost walked into
Octave.

"Good morning, Octave!" said the prince. "I am here to assist in
any way that I can. It is the final ball, after all. Everyone must lend a
hand."

Octave turned, his lips and eyebrows arched in pleased surprise.

"Why, Your Highness, that is a kind offer. But, as you can see, Lady Marchand and I have everything well in hand."

Charmant stepped back in surprise.

"She is here?" he asked in a hoarse whisper.

Octave's smile disappeared. "Yes, Your Highness. She said her mother sent her. Apparently, last night you discussed acquiring the family's help?" The steward now sounded uncertain.

Charmant remembered the conversation with Lady de Noelles Marchand. It seemed the strange woman took him at his word and sent Lady Elle to lend a hand. Perhaps he was wrong about her. Maybe the dream had been just that, a dream, and the woman was simply a noblewoman who wanted the best for her daughters.

"Of course," reassured Charmant. He put a hand on the man's shoulder. "The widow Lady de Noelles Marchand's late husband has helped our family in the past, and I discussed partnering with her and her family in the future. I did not believe she would immediately begin the partnership, but it is welcome news if they are helping you. Do you require my assistance?"

"No, indeed, Your Highness. Thank you."

"Then I will not keep you," Charmant told the faithful servant.

As Octave walked away, Charmant looked around the room for his lady, barely registering the many bowlegged, straight-backed strangers working in the hall. His breath caught when he spotted the woman in charge.

Lady Elle glimmered in the morning sun. Somehow, she struck him as more beautiful in her everyday frock than when she had appeared in an elaborate, bejeweled ballgown.

A modest beige dress covered her body while hugging her curves. The dress color resembled her peaches and cream skin, making it seem from afar that she wore nothing at all. When he squinted, he made out the dress outline. The skirt gave it away. Fabric draped over her legs and feet, concealing them from view, though Charmant could imagine the firmly muscled and well-formed limbs which allowed this woman to shimmy from place to place like a dancer.

Too busy talking to two of her frog-like servants, Lady Elle had not yet noticed Charmant. The prince remembered his reaction to her servants the night before, and took a deep breath, determined to avoid a repetition of the previous evening's nausea.

You have witnessed worse grotesqueries on the battlefield, he told himself. With this thought in mind, he straightened his spine and strode over to Lady Elle.

"My lady," he bowed.

"Your Highness," she curtsied. "Is it not a lovely day?"

"Indeed," he replied. "Though you are more lovely than any day I have yet witnessed."

Lady Elle blushed at his remark.

Charmant glanced at her two flat-faced attendants. They stared back at him with bulging eyes, failing to look down or bow in his presence. Normally, he would scold servants for being so impertinent, but he could not face looking at the men for more than a moment's time.

Something inside him screamed, *what if they blink?*

Flicking his eyes away, he returned his gaze to Lady Elle, smiling at her beauty. The morning sun made her luminous skin and delicate features radiant. The air around her seemed to sparkle as dust motes twinkled in the golden light.

The great hall was windowless in the traditional sense, but three narrow holes cut into the ceiling vented smoke, and allowed sun to filter in. This, coupled with two large skylights his father had installed just before the festivities, allowed the morning sun to spotlight Lady Elle to her best advantage.

"Thank you for coming to help with the final preparations. It has been a long time since a woman filled the role of house manager. We men are sorely lacking a woman's touch around here."

"It is my pleasure, Your Highness."

"Can I help in any way?" asked the prince.

"I need the use of one of your rooms to prepare myself for this evening's festivities," she told him.

"Of course, I shall see to it that you are made very comfortable," Charmant declared.

The lady smiled, her eyes flicking back to her attendants. Clearly, she had much to do. Prince Charmant saw his presence caused her to pause when she could be completing her tasks before dressing. He bowed again.

"Thank you, my lady. I look forward to dancing with you this evening."

She curtsied.

Striding away, Charmant found Octave once more. He told the servant to make a guest room ready for Lady Elle so she could prepare for the ball. Octave grinned, his smile one of relief.

"I have already done so, Your Highness. And, may I just say, Lady Marchand is a great help. She and her strange house staff have been a true blessing during a moment when we were stretched thin. Thank you for obtaining her assistance."

Prince Charmant smiled. Warmth filled his belly as he thought about the future. Lady Elle was as efficient as she was beautiful, and her odd servants got along with his men. She would come with an enormous dowry. And, he admitted, he desired her so much that it drove him to distraction.

He made up his mind. After the festivities, he would take Lady Elle to wife.

CHAPTER 10

L ady Elle watched as the prince left the great hall.

Good, she thought. *If only I could rid myself of that meddling steward and his staff.*

Warmth rose within her, making her form shimmer.

You must maintain this charade long enough to find the power source, she reminded herself. It was difficult. Before she had been ensnared by those human women, she traversed the universe, destroying entire continents with her faithful Changed Ones. With just one thought, she could command her minions to do her bidding, wreaking havoc to one world while bringing a seed of life to another. Centuries ago, when she was an immature child, her changeable will brought grief and joy to many intelligent species.

Back then, planets and the species on them were her playthings. Until she was captured by one such species here, in this wretched place.

Elle's face turned up in a grimace of determination.

One day, she would again conquer worlds with a flick of her mind. But she could do nothing in her current trapped state. She needed the prince. She needed his castle. She needed to follow the plan.

Sufficiently calmed, she held her shape firm in her mind and turned, beaming as the idiotic castle steward approached.

CHAPTER 11

"I have found her," the prince exclaimed, bursting into his father's rooms.

His exuberance was met by a pallid face peeking out of an overabundance of quilts. The family doctor sat next to the bed, peeling fat leeches from the king's gray skin. The room smelled of herbs, incense, and old sweat.

"Father? Are you ill?" asked Charmant. Ever since his mother and siblings died, his father had felt that he, too, was at death's door. Sometimes his despair left Charmant feeling unmoored in the unremitting stream of duty. Today, it made him feel impatient. The king had succumbed to fatigued from the back-to-back balls he had scheduled. Charmant doubted his father was actually ill.

However, he tried to imbue his heart and voice with sympathy. After all, had not all of the king's work and planning paid off?

The king licked his lips. The doctor paused in his ministrations to provide the king with a sip of a dark liquid. Making a face, the king drank the concoction and asked, "What is it, my son? What did you say?"

Charmant smiled at the old man. Perhaps the news of an imminent engagement would revitalize him. The prince closed the door behind him and walked to his father's bedside.

"I have found the woman I will marry, father," Charmant told the king. "As long as you approve, of course. But I believe you will do so. She is the fairest, most graceful lady in all the land."

"It is not the Queen Blanche, is it, my son?" asked the king with a worried tone. "I know that Elouan advised you to pursue her, and it is good advice. But there is something about that woman..." he waved his hand, "I cannot describe it. She turns my spine to ice with her smile, then warms me with her charm."

"No, father," Charmant smiled. "Not Queen Blanche, though some call her the most beautiful in the land. No, I believe you know who I would like to wed. You suggested it before the first ball."

The king smiled, "The young Lady Elle Marchand, then?"

"Yes, sire. She has caught my heart. And, more importantly, I believe she will make an excellent queen and mother. She is assisting Octave in ball preparations as we speak. I but hinted to her mother last night that our families might make good partners, and Lady de Noelles Marchand sent her here to help. The young lady is exceeding Octave's wildest expectations. She is perfect."

"Excellent, excellent," sighed the king, licking thin lips before stretching them into a smile. He sat up, peeling the last fat leech off his own arm and handing it to the doctor. "I am sure we can arrange a marriage contract. She will bear you many sons and bring wealth to our house."

He reached out with shaky hands. Charmant stepped forward and grasped them.

"Ah, my son, this will be an excellent match. And she makes you happy?"

The prince nodded.

"Good, good. We shall have the ball this eve and then finalize the marriage arrangements on the morrow."

"Thank you, Father."

The king swung his feet over the side of the bed. His doctor dropped the last slippery leach into a jar and rushed to the king's side. Before the older man could stand, the doctor pushed a goblet into his face. The king rolled his eyes and choked down the tincture. Then, wiping his lips with the back of his hand, he struggled to standing.

Seeing his father's inflamed, varicose vein-striped legs, Charmant mentally kicked himself for dismissing his father's lassitude. Glancing at the king's grimace of pain, Charmant held out an arm for his father to grasp. The older man wrapped a leach-pocked arm around his son's muscled, youthful limb. Despite the pain the king displayed, he gripped his son's shoulder and squeezed. His mouth turned into a genuine smile.

"This *is* good news, my son. Excellent news. After all that our family has suffered - after all that the Charmant name has endured..." he trailed off. "Well, it is good news indeed."

A rush of warmth flowed through Charmant's veins as he basked in his father's joy. He walked the king to a dressing stool and helped him sit down.

"Leave me now, my son. I must ready myself for the festivities. I believe I am relieved of all ails at this moment. It shall be a grand finale to our merrymaking."

Charmant grinned, bowed, and walked out - almost skipping.

CHAPTER 12

Lady Elle closed her eyes and looked outdoors through the gaze of her chaffinch. The sun cast afternoon rays and dust clouds showed the carriages making their bumpy way to the castle. Her men were returning from another foray into the orchard, depositing dirt and stones behind the trees closest to the family graveyard.

She opened her eyes and cast about for Octave. He was nowhere in sight.

Good

She strode over to the door leading to the cellar. Opening it, she had no trouble walking down the unlit steps.

The storage room looked like any other larder-cum-wine cellar. Barrels lined one wall, wood shelves filled with joints of meat, vegetables, cheese, and other comestibles lined the other.

The one odd feature was the blanket-covered back wall. The dark blanket flapped and billowed, allowing chill air to rush into the already cold room.

Lady Elle ducked behind the blanket, her skin remaining smooth as a wall of icy air struck her. Beyond the blanket ran a tunnel, shored up by wood beams every few feet.

Something inside of Lady Elle pulled her along. She felt an irresistible tug in her abdomen as she walked down the uneven dirt ramp. The power pulled at her form, making her shape vibrate. She let the power drag her, let it mold her as she moved, her legs turning to something closer to her true form, allowing her to slither comfortably along the path.

About one hundred feet in, the tunnel ended. Two frog-like men dug methodically. One used a pick, the other a shovel. A third and fourth man packed the dirt from the excavation into buckets, ready for removal.

They all stopped when they saw her, each man's enormous eyes glinting white in reflected light. Then, all four men collapsed to their knees, bowing and pressing their faces to the dirt.

"Move," commanded Lady Elle. Her voice had thickened and deepened, filling the tiny chamber with sound.

The men, crawling on hands and knees, lined up in single file to make way for their goddess.

She walked to the end of the tunnel, placing her hand on the packed dirt. Her body shrunk. All feminine curves disappeared until she stood, a stick thin, hollow-faced, long-armed, tentacle-legged figure. One arm jabbed through the wall of clay and rock, pushing down toward the force that drew her to this castle in the first place.

The power source sucked at her, so strong she believed it could take her home. She stretched herself further, her human clothing disappearing as she lengthened. Her single unchanging attribute, a deep black bracelet encircled one twig-thin wrist. The blackness sucked in light and yanked at her skin.

Wincing, she tried to pull herself into a javelin of skin and cartilage. Tried to push through the dirt and access the power source. But the bracelet imprisoned her in human form. She could not touch the power she craved. Not while she wore the bracelet.

First things first, she thought. *My followers will finish the tunnel to the power source while I find a way to get rid of the bracelet.*

She had an idea of how to do it, an idea that might result in her stepmother being hanged for witchcraft. The thought pulled at her heart with fierce joy.

It is nothing less than that woman deserves.

Lady Elle retreated from that dark place buried in the earth. She re-formed into the womanly shape that so fascinated the prince. Extruding water, her body shed dirt, pouring it into rivers of mud that dribbled down the slope. Once again, her skin formed into the traditional garb of women on this hellish planet.

"Dig," she instructed her minions. They scrambled to obey.

Turning, Lady Elle pulled against the force that drove her down, down, toward the hidden power source. She had work to do.

CHAPTER 13

That evening's ball was more spectacular than the previous two.

The decorations portrayed the sky, both in the daytime and in the evening. Rows upon rows of candles hung on one side of the ballroom. Below the candles, rushlights burned in their sconces. So much light filled the room that it looked as if the sun were shining on all the partygoers. However, as one progressed through the ballroom and into adjacent, screened-off spaces, the light became sparser, with candles mapping out constellations in the darkness.

Naturally, the daylight section was the main hub of the merrymaking. However, as was clear from the previous evening, the king and his artisans understood the proclivities of the nobles. Some wished for privacy, while others thrived in the glaring candlelight.

Charmant found Lady Elle clothed in silver and standing on the precipice of night and day. Her backlit figure glowed as he approached her. The intricate embroidery and stunning jewels decorating her dress sparkled and shimmered.

"You look as if you were plucked from the sky above, Lady Elle. You are a vision to behold."

"Thank you," she breathed in her musical voice.

That voice and her beauty stirred the prince, causing his heart to beat rapidly and his skin to grow hot and tight. His usually steady hands shook with nerves and excitement as he offered them to the lady.

"Will you dance?" he asked, his words coming out in a rush. His face flushed at the brashness of his voice.

"Of course, Your Highness," she beamed, placing a silver-gloved hand on his arm.

He led her to the dance floor, his skin twitching with nervous energy. He wanted to sweep this girl into his arms, tell her they were to marry, and then take her abed. But something stopped him.

Charmant's mind wandered back to that first night when he had held Lady Elle without her permission. His eyes darted around the room, finding Lady de Noelles Marchand glaring at them from across the dance floor.

Why does she glare at us when she sent Lady Elle here to help? He wondered. *Perhaps that is the expression she always wears.*

"I wish to know more about you, my lady," Charmant murmured as he bowed, and she curtsied on the dance floor.

"I, too, would love to understand you more thoroughly, Your Highness," she replied, looking up at him through her lashes.

Charmant smiled and eased into the well-practiced motions of the dance. They fell into step with the circle of dancers and tiptoed, jumped, bowed, and curtsied to one another in the prescribed manner.

His joints loosened and his hands steadied with each step. Performing motions he had practiced since toddlerhood calmed his heart and helped him to forget about his dance partner's glaring mother.

Lady Elle's face maintained a studied blank expression. She danced with grace, her motions lithe, but they did not seem to bring her joy.

Is her mother's stare making her nervous?

Charmant looked up from the dance for a moment to search for Lady de Noelles Marchand. She had disappeared. Glancing about the room, his limbs grew heavy and slow.

Turning back to his dance partner, the prince found he almost stood on top of her toes.

Charmant stumbled backward, trying to make room, and stepped on another dancer's foot. In the tumult, he noticed Lady Elle's unchanging expression. She simply skipped back from the melee and stood, watching.

Embarrassed, Charmant excused himself.

"I will be on the terrace, Your Highness," Lady Elle whispered as she curtsied.

Charmant left the ballroom, withdrawing into a side room to wet his burning face and sip some wine.

Refreshed, he told one of the castle servants to accompany him to the terrace. The man balanced a tray of drinks and nibbles as he followed the prince.

Upon exiting the ballroom, Charmant and his servant found the terrace empty. Lady Elle's silver-clad frame walked along the garden path, nearing the orchard.

"My lady!" Charmant called after her. She disappeared beneath the trees.

The prince stepped down from the terrace onto the path to follow. Before he could hurry after the lady, he spied a gleaming object stuck between two stones. He leaned down and wiggled out a tiny shoe, no longer than his pointer finger. It sparkled silver as he held it up to the moonlight.

He paused in his pursuit to stare at the tiny object. It was much too small to fit a woman - even a young woman. It could possibly fit the foot of a baby or a doll.

A doll shoe, he told himself, *or a shoe from the days of her infancy. Perhaps she keeps it as a token of luck or love. And now she has dropped it.*

He closed his hand around the precious object and jogged to the orchard. Blackness shrouded the trees, an invisible wall.

"Lady Marchand?" he called, peering into the gloom.

Nothing stirred.

"Lady Elle!" he shouted.

Not a leaf moved.

He stepped into the darkness and felt swallowed whole. The thick leaves above rustled, allowing a brief trickle of silver light to transform the evening mist into amorphous specters. When the leaves stilled, pitch black settled around him again.

Fear clutching at his throat, the prince back peddled, stepping out of the tree line and into the normalcy of the summer moonlight glimmering over the decorative garden.

Perhaps, he thought, *rather than walking in the darkness, she found the right-hand path and is even now re-entering the castle.*

Charmant turned his steps to the garden and made his way around the castle, following a path that paralleled the trees. It led him to the front doors of the structure. Relief washed over him as he spotted Lady Elle's silver form stepping into her coach. The footman closed the door displaying her family crest.

He puffed out a sigh as her carriage swept her away. While Lady Elle's safety allowed him to relax, exasperation of another sort filled him.

Why did she leave? Did her stepmother come out ahead of me? Has the entire family left?

Looking down at the shoe in his hand, certainly flooded through him once more. Her lost trinket gave him a reason to visit Lady Elle beyond pressing his suit. He would visit their chateau in the morning.

The prince straightened his back and shaped his face into a practiced, haughty expression. Walking up to the footman who had escorted Lady Elle to her coach, he asked, "Who just left?"

The servant bowed and said, "The Ladies de Noelles Marchand, Your Highness."

Charmant nodded. Her stepmother forced Lady Elle and the girls to leave.

She will not be able to escape when I visit tomorrow, he decided.

"Please call my valet," he told the servant. "I am in need of brushing."

The footman bowed and ran to the doors of the castle. He whispered to another servant, one of the de Noelles Marchand attendants, and the man loped away.

With the object of his desire gone, weariness dragged on the prince's limbs. He decided to follow the example of the de Noelles Marchand ladies and retire early.

CHAPTER 14

Prince Charmant felt something warm and wet around his manhood. He looked down and smiled at the honey-gold hair spread over his groin. He lay back to enjoy the sucking sensation. Sparks of iridescence floated across his field of vision like dandelion puffs. The ceiling above his bed retracted, revealing a star-spangled sky.

The prince gasped in pleasure as coolness washed across him, replaced rapidly by a new sensation. Intensity rippled through his body and a curvy figure blocked the twinkling stars. The woman rode him now, hair cascading across her face as she bucked.

"Oh, Elle," he moaned.

The lady glared through her hair and he realized she was not Lady Elle at all, but her grim-faced stepmother staring down at him with two white glowing orbs in place of eyes.

CHAPTER 15

Charmant awoke, screaming and sweating.

He fought his blanket, thrashing until he managed to peel it from his soaking skin. The hot, humid room reeked of sex. Charmant swung his bedroom door wide and allowed a dry, scented breeze to rush in. In the dark hallway beyond, a single rushlight illuminated the slumped sentry sitting at his father's door. The man's snoring vibrated the air.

Back in his room, sleep eluded the prince. He stared at the dark mass of blankets and mattress, his skin twitching at the memory of the dream.

He wanted a swim. A moonlit splash would be just the thing to wash away the stink of the nightmare. But when he considered walking into the lake again, contemplated braving that stygian orchard, a shiver prickled across his skin.

Instead, the prince dislodged the candle from the end of his bed and strode down the hall to the rushlight. Lighting the candle, he returned to his room and used cold washbasin water and a clean towel to scrub every inch of skin. He scrubbed and rubbed until his skin glowed pink in the candlelight.

Then, he dressed himself in riding clothes, struggling with the boots. Usually, dressers helped him don the infernal things. Finally garbed for riding, he searched around his room for Lady Elle's shoe. He found it where he had left it the night before, on his nightstand.

Picking up the delicate object, he stroked it and watched the silver cloth gleam in the candlelight. He imagined all the moments this tiny thing had given his lady comfort. Perhaps it was all she had left of a favorite doll. If so, he vowed to employ an artisan to recreate the doll for her and measure out a matching shoe. Perhaps they would duplicate Lady Elle's favorite doll for their first daughter, giving the child the same happiness his lady felt when she received this shoe.

The sparkling trinket combined with his freshly scrubbed skin and the cool air rushing in from the hallway served to calm the prince. He tucked the tiny keepsake into a pouch and tied the pouch to his belt.

I will take the short ride to my lady's home and return this treasure personally.

He smiled as he envisioned Lady Elle's pleased reaction to his visit. And her "yes" to his proposal of marriage. He would not force her through a contractual obligation but would instead beg on his knees for her to marry him just as the men do in romantic stories. The gesture would win her affection. He knew it.

Pale morning light squeezed between the shutters, making patterns on his bedroom floor. He heard the sentry's snores stop abruptly, then heard the sound of two men murmuring and the squeak of an opening door.

The prince stepped into the hall to see Octave and the sentry peering in at his father. Likely trying to assure themselves that the king had not died while the man guarding him slept.

Charmant cleared his throat and both men jumped back, their eyes going wide when they saw who addressed them. Both servants bowed.

The prince walked past them and looked in on his father. He smiled as he watched the king's peaceful face peeking out over his heavy furs. Stepping back, he motioned to the two men to shut the door.

"Octave, I am leaving to visit the Chateau de Noelles Marchand. Ready my horse and have Cook pack a basket for my ride. I shall stand watch over my father. Now, go."

The men looked at each other, a mixture of relief and consternation passing over their faces. Then, they scurried off.

Charmant leaned on the wall next to his father's door, listening. The hall stood still and quiet. Most of the household had yet to wake. He knew from experience that someone would be in the kitchen, however. Day or night, the kitchen never slept.

While he waited, he pulled out Lady Elle's shoe. He placed it on one finger and raised it up so that the candlelight caught its glimmering surface. The well-worn shoe had such finely woven cloth that he could not discern the warp or weft. Swirling stitches ran from point to heel, each swirl reminding him of the tentacles his lady's servants had initially worn during their first meeting.

"Blessings be upon you, Your Highness," rasped Elouan in a sleepy voice.

Charmant watched him approach from the far end of the hall. Someone had rushed him out of bed. The normally fastidious man still wore elaborately stitched breeches from the previous night's festivities, with a plain sleeping tunic covering his chest.

"And you, Elouan," smiled Charmant.

"The sentry woke me when you sent him on his errand. He wanted to be sure the king was well taken care of."

"Of course, I thank you."

"There are fewer servants in the castle at the moment. The servant's quarters seem to have been partly taken over by the de Noelles Marchands' strange attendants. While I am grateful for their use, I wish they would leave the castle."

"Yes, I find their appearance, well, off-putting," confided the prince. "But, as I am to marry Lady Marchand, we will be housing any servants that come with her. While I do not enjoy their strange appearance, I know they will be welcome help to our staff. My father has shared how difficult it is to keep servants these days, with so few healthy villagers to maintain our lands."

Elouan sighed and nodded in agreement.

"If only we could find a way to prevent this plague from afflicting our lands, the way that Queen Blanche has done."

"Queen Blanche has ended the plague in her villages?" Charmant asked, his eyes widening in shock. Why had the woman not mentioned this incredible feat?

"No, not in all of her villages," admitted Elouan. "She told the king that the lands immediately surrounding her castle and the castle itself are disease-free. We will need to send a delegation to verify her claims and, if they are true, find a way to obtain such immunity for our own people.

"Perhaps there is an elixir or spring near her castle which contributes to the health of her subjects. If so, it is possible that the wealth you obtain in your marriage to Lady Marchand may enable the king to buy immunity against plague."

Charmant's heart gave a leap.

"Can you conceive of having such immunity," he cried in excitement. His mind raced, imagining offering freedom from plague to his father, his wife, their children, her family. The image in his mind of Lady Elle's stepmother stopped him short.

Perhaps not her. She may not be around to haunt my dreams much longer.

CHAPTER 16

"Faustine," Elle hissed.

Lady Faustine de Noelles Marchand looked up from her breakfast, the food turning to ash in her mouth. Slowly, she took a sip of watered wine and then wiped her mouth with a napkin.

"Yes, Elle?" she asked.

"Release me." Elle lifted her right wrist. On it writhed the obsidian bracelet.

Faustine stared at the wringing darkness, watching it twitch as Elle held out her wrist. She forced her eyes to Elle's face. The girl was smaller than usual today. Faustine lifted her feet and looked at the floor. Mice circled her chair, sitting on their back legs and staring up at her with beady eyes.

When Elle spoke next, their tiny voices echoed her words.

"I will be a princess soon. My followers are even now preparing my way home. Removing the bracelet will allow me to leave you and your family forever."

The mice surrounding Faustine started to climb the chair legs, their tiny paws digging into the wood as their mouths repeated "leave forever."

Faustine leapt from her chair, running to the far end of the small room.

"You know I want you to leave, Elle."

The thing in girl form nodded. She was even smaller now as a crow formed from her shoulder.

"But I do not know that you will keep your word once released. How can I protect my family from you, from your followers, if you are unleashed?"

The crow lifted off and flew at Faustine's face. The lady gasped and ducked, covering her head with her arms. A flurry of feathers ruffled against her limbs, but nothing more.

"I will not damage you," Elle's voice squawking out of the crow's beak. "Not directly. But if you do not release me, I will make your life difficult."

Faustine peeked out from beneath her arms. The mice had disappeared, and Elle stood a bit taller.

"You are forbidden from hurting my family. That was your agreement with my husband, and it is one you have kept these many years. Why are you doing this now?" asked Faustine.

"I have found the way home," Elle informed her. "But you are holding me back. Have you ever tried to keep someone from their home? Someone on the brink of despair, Faustine? Do you know what rage and desperation feel like? They are emotions with which I am unfamiliar, but I have seen them in many forms amongst humans, and I may be able to conjure them in myself. They will be directed against you and your family unless you release me, Faustine."

Elle's voice came out low and flat. Her wide green eyes stared unblinking at her stepmother.

"Give me time to think it over, Elle. Please. Give me time."

Elle glared at Faustine.

"Your time is running out, my lady," she mocked in a singsong. "And, as I said, I will not need to do anything directly to your family.

The prince will help me with that. He is on his way now to ask you for my hand, and *you* have no choice but to give him your blessing. He is a prince after all and *you* are but a woman."

Elle took an unhurried step toward her stepmother. The crow landed on her shoulder and melted into her, returning her to her usual height. She took another step and grew taller and thinner. Another step and the girl's head almost hit the ceiling.

She loomed over Faustine.

"You have so very few choices in this world, Faustine. Make the right one before the prince forces you to do so."

Faustine curled up in a ball, sobbing.

CHAPTER 17

The prince mounted his favorite stallion and left as the morning sun crested the eastern rim of the woods. Normally, he would bring an escort. But after three days of balls and guests and servants, he wanted to be alone.

Leaving the protection of the castle walls, he followed the dirt road cut through surrounding fields, past the far woods, and across pastureland. Farmers sat in wagons, harvested summer fruit, and milked cows.

Charmant looked at his people, sensitive to any signs of illness or disquiet. Everyone he saw seemed normal, performing their everyday duties. He passed through the closest village, nodding to the guard at the gate. The man bowed and let him through.

The morning market hubbub surrounded him as he cantered through the town. He let his horse meander through stalls as he listened to vendors and villagers haggle over summer fruit, eggs, and cloth. He heard children laugh and play, ducking between wheelbarrows and into alleys.

He had the urge to give all he could to these people, to his people. He thought of that word his father's advisor had used.

Immunity

If such a thing as immunity against the plague could be purchased, he would do so.

Lost in thought, he exited the town. Woods grew to his left, more pastureland to his right. He felt secure in the knowledge that the area was frequently traversed by farmers - and occasionally by the castle patrols. His father tried to keep instances of animal attacks to a minimum and worked to stamp out banditry in the area all together.

Approaching the walls of Lady Elle's home, he found the gate guarded by two of her unique-looking servants. He dismounted and gave the reins to one of the frog-like men. His horse whinnied, shying away from the man.

"I am here to see Lady Elle Marchand," he announced.

The man holding his horse nodded to the other guard who brought a horn to his wide lips and blatted a strange combination of sounds. The portcullis lifted and two men walked out. One bowed to the prince and led him forward. The other, who had the same bowlegs and straight back as his fellows, but not the flat face and wide mouth, took his horse. The stallion nuzzled the man, and both entered the walled courtyard, walking toward the stables.

The chalet grounds sprawled before Charmant. The morning sun glanced off gray stone and twinkled on the morning dew. A scattering of ancillary buildings stood around the grand home, with pear and walnut trees planted between the structures.

The silent attendant stopped just in front of the door and bowed. Then, he wrapped his long fingers around a bell pull and yanked. A gonging sound echoed inside.

A rail-thin man with patchy white hair and a sallow, pocked complexion opened the door, blinking in the brilliant light.

"I am here to court Lady Elle Marchand," the prince told him.

"Yes, of course Your Highness," he wheezed. The old man took a step back and bowed so low, it looked as if he would fall face first on the flags of the threshold. The man continued to bow, shaking as he held his position.

"Um," Prince Charmant swallowed in embarrassment, "you may rise."

The elderly man straightened with joint cracking slowness.

"Your Highness, I must warn you, sire. Lady Marchand is not what she seems. You should run from this house, sire," the words flooded out of the man's mouth in a rush. "She has driven all of the other village servants mad. She holds back on the family out of respect for her late caretaker. But she is evil, sire. My wife is in the Marchand asylum, and I know I am not far behind. I have seen too much, know too much."

Before he could determine how best to respond to the man's babble, a crow barreled past Charmant, flying between his shoulder and the doorway, right at the man's face. It banked up at the last moment, nicking his ear with a claw. It swooped around and flew back out the door just as a second crow waddled in through the open doorway. It stopped in front of the man, cocking its head as it looked up at him. The man froze, his face a sheet of white, blood trickling down from his ear. The crow at his feet pecked his boot viciously, making the man jump and screech. He hopped backward as the crow went in for another peck.

The prince kicked at the bird, his heart leaping to his throat as he remembered the stories his eldest brother used to tell him. Bad luck and ill health followed those who harmed a crow.

Lady de Noelles swept in from an adjoining room.

"Perrin, what is going on here? Why have you yet to announce..." she paused, sighting the crow. It looked up from its pecking and stared at her.

"Go," she commanded.

The crow lifted its wings and jumped, hopping toward her.

"Leave," she urged in a trembling voice, "do not torture the poor man. He has been through enough. Go."

The crow gave a shrugging flap of its wings and turned. It stalked past Charmant and his frog-like attendant. At the door, the crow gave a little hop and took flight. The prince stared after it as the lady shut the door, returning the threshold to darkness.

Charmant's mouth hung open and one word floated through his mind.

Witchcraft

"I am sorry about that, Your Highness," she said, curtsying. "Pray have patience for one more moment while I assist my servant."

Charmant watched, wide-eyed as she turned to Perrin. Would she give the poor man a tongue lashing? Would she turn him out for embarrassing her - for exposing her - in front of her prince?

Worry inched across Charmant's skin. The poor man was clearly out of his mind, terrified by this woman's devilry.

Lady de Noelles Marchand put an affectionate hand on the servant's back and whispered in his good ear.

He dropped a stiff-backed bow and limped away, disappearing into the depths of the house.

"Let us adjourn to the sitting room. It is much brighter in there and you can speak with my daughters and Lady Marchand over some refreshments."

Dry mouthed with shock, the prince nodded. Goosebumps prickled his skin, but he did not want to show this woman how frightened she made him. Instead, he straightened his back and flexed his fingers. Licking his lips, he realized she remained, waiting for him.

"Do you have a refreshing room in which I may wash the dust from my journey?"

The lady looked stricken, her hand flying to her mouth.

"Of course, Your Highness, I am sorry I did not think of it," she looked at the frog faced attendant, still at Charmant's side and heaved a sigh. "I suppose you must take him there," she instructed the man.

He bowed and led Charmant down a corridor to a small room. The prince washed his face and hands and drank from a goblet of well-watered wine. The attendant brushed dust off his clothes and took a rag to his boots, rapidly shining them.

When they were done, the man led him to a bright sitting room.

One high window and two wide-open French doors leading to the back garden allowed the brilliant morning sun to track a glimmering path through the room. Positioned in the doorway with the sun shining behind her stood a golden vision. Charmant inhaled a deep breath when he saw Lady Elle, relaxing for the first time since he'd entered the chateau.

Lady Elle smiled as their eyes met. She curtsied and straightened in one flowing motion. Charmant's breath caught in his throat and his body, still tense from the encounter in the foyer, relaxed. He bowed in turn and watched as she took small, deliberate steps toward him. It wasn't until she reached the table at the room's center that the prince noticed the presence of other women. Lady Elle's two stepsisters, Adeline and Enora, stood next to their mother. Presumably they'd curtsied as well, but the prince had not noticed. He only had eyes for Lady Elle.

"Prince Charmant," Elle said in that contralto voice which sent shivers up Charmant's spine. Lit by her voice, his skin flamed with desire. All he wanted was to touch her, hold her, make her his own.

"My lady," his hoarse voice contrasted against her musicality. Bowing quickly, he pulled the silver shoe from his bag. "I believe you left this at my castle. You departed so rapidly that I could not return it to you at the ball."

"Oh yes," her grass-colored eyes flicked to her stepmother, "I was called home."

She accepted his gift, their skin brushing in that instant, sending sparks dancing up the prince's arm.

"Thank you," she smiled at him.

Then, she did something startling. She sat down in one of the chairs and put the inhumanly small shoe on her foot.

He could not see the stocking-covered foot but that brief glimpse revealed a tiny extremity. Prince Charmant's stomach churned, the fire in his heart cooling.

Elle's smile died when she saw his expression.

"I forgot; you do not know my history."

"It is no matter, my lady," the prince tried to be chivalrous, though curiosity burned through his mind.

"No, you deserve to know the truth. Please, sit and have a fortifying glass of wine. I will tell you my story."

A chair appeared behind the prince, as if summoned. Glancing over his shoulder, he saw an attendant behind him, displaying the cushioned object with one hand. Charmant sat.

"Years ago, when I was small, I lived in a shop. The owner was not kind, nor was he particularly cruel. Though he did two things which were peculiar.

"First, he displayed me each day as if I were a doll. I was a tiny child, two or three years old. It was hard to stay still, but the man threatened grave consequences if I moved a muscle while customers were in the shop. So, I obeyed him. He would dress me in doll's clothes and position me in various poses. Some were comfortable, others were not. I had nothing to do but stand or lay or sit and listen to the many languages surrounding me. Though dull, this helped me to learn much about language and it gave me the opportunity to make my escape. But I will get to that in a moment.

"The shopkeeper also bound my feet. I suppose he must have done this from the moment of my birth, because I did not notice that my feet were strangely formed or smaller than any other's until I moved here, to France. In fact, I continued to bind them on my own until my father saw me do it and told me that I could stop. But by then it was too late, and my feet would not grow further. They remained forever stunted."

Charmant stared at Lady Elle, his mind racing. The poor girl had been through so much. She continued to tell her tale.

"One day, my father came into the store and purchased me. The shopkeeper did not reveal I was a real person. Instead, he told my father I was a doll, a good luck charm he kept around the store.

"It was only when we reached my father's rooms that he discovered my true nature. Fortunately, I learned some French during my time in the shop and learned more under Father's tutelage. He always said I had a proclivity for language."

She cast her eyes down to the ground and sighed.

"So, that is the story of how I came to live in France. It is a much better life here than I could have imagined when I lived in that small shop in Constantinople."

The prince stared at Lady Elle, spellbound by her story. She looked up at him, her mouth spreading into a gentle smile.

"I miss my father every day. I wish he could be here to see this, to see you. I am sure he would have been delighted to know that I, once a small child displayed as a doll, am now conversing with a prince."

A thrill ran through Charmant, making him a little light-headed. He sipped his wine, fortifying himself.

"Your father is looking down at us from heaven above, my lady," he told Lady Elle. "And I hope to please him further."

Charmant turned to Lady Elle's stepmother.

"Would you consent to our marriage, Lady de Noelles Marchand?" he asked.

The woman's face lost all color. Charmant's eyes narrowed, watching her.

Elle's stepmother took a slow, deep breath and gulped. He waited.

"As you wish, Your Highness," she finally whispered.

Prince Charmant bowed to the lady, though he had little regard for her in his heart.

He turned to Elle, his focus on her and her alone. He remembered her reaction when he had suggested their joining just three days ago. This was a woman he still had to woo, and he would do so with a flourish.

"My lady," he declared, dropping to one knee in front of Elle and bowing his head dramatically. "Will you consent to marry me?"

Lady Elle's face lit up; her smile glowed from ear to ear.

"Oh, Your Highness, of course I will."

She glanced at her stepmother, her smile dimming, then directing the full force of it at the prince once more.

"Wonderful," grinned Charmant. "My father's counselor will make all of the arrangements."

Lady Elle stood on her tiny feet and walked to the prince. She put out her hands, palms up.

"Would you like to take a stroll through the orchard, my prince?" she asked.

Charmant placed his hands in hers and stood. The gesture felt oddly feminine, and he worried that he should be the one standing and helping her up. He shrugged off the concern. Once married, they would be partners in all things, just as his mother had been to his father.

The two lovers held hands and made for the doors leading to the garden and surrounding orchard. Charmant turned back and bowed to Lady de Noelles Marchand and her daughters.

"We will return shortly," he stated.

As he stepped out of the room, Charmant heard a creaky voice announcing Monsieur Elouan Martin. The prince and his lady turned back to the room. Elouan strode in. He bowed to the ladies and spotted Charmant.

"Your Highness, my lady," he said, bobbing down and up in a rapid bow. "There are arrangements to be made, are there not? I am here with my scribes to make them for you."

"I..." started the prince.

"I see that you are walking to the gardens with your lady. I have been sent to give you this," the man took five efficient steps, covering the distance to the prince and bowing again. He held out a scroll and a small, golden ring inset with emeralds.

Charmant gasped.

"My mother's ring!" he exclaimed. He took the ring out of Elouan's hand and turned to Lady Elle.

"This was once the Queen's ring. Now, it is yours," he told her, sliding the small band over her finger.

Lady Elle winced.

"It is beautiful," she grimaced.

"Is it too small?" asked Prince Charmant, worried he had hurt his princess. He slid the band off her finger, encountering no resistance.

"No, indeed," she sighed. "I have a particular condition. Some metals bother my skin. It is nothing. I shall, of course, wear your mother's ring."

The prince's heart sank. This beautiful woman, duty-bound to make the best of any life provided to her, just told him she would live in pain as long as she could be with him. A curious mix of sadness and pleasure flowed through him, making his shoulder blades twitch, and causing his neck to go stiff.

"No, my lady. I would not have you uncomfortable for the rest of your days. What metal would you prefer?"

"Silver, my lord. Silver or platinum are the two metals that provide the most comfort to my skin."

Charmant glanced down at the dark bracelet encircling her wrist.

"I have never encountered platinum. Is the bracelet you always wear such a metal?"

Lady Elle glanced down at her wrist. Her face set in a hard line. It was an expression Charmant had not yet seen on her visage. Lady Elle flicked her eyes to her stepmother, then back down at the bracelet. Charmant tried to follow the look, only to see Lady de Noelles Marchand's expression twist into one of terror. Her eyes wide and her mouth a horrifying rictus, Lady de Noelles Marchand stared at the bracelet with concentrated fear.

Prince Charmant looked at Lady Elle's wrist again. The thin bracelet wrapped her wrist like a vine. It almost looked drawn onto her fair skin. As he examined it, he spotted faded engravings carved into the metal, their detailed swirls captivating his eye. It almost seemed to move as he followed the lines and details in the circlet.

Lady Elle moved her hand over the bracelet, snapping Charmant's attention back to her.

"Yes, this is platinum. I have worn it since childhood."

"I see. Well, we shall have a silver ring made for you, my lady. Do you have a preference as to the stones we use?"

"I do love diamonds," she blushed.

A gasp escaped her stepmother's mouth. Prince Charmant ignored the woman. He did not know what was going on, but he believed that the sooner he could remove Lady Elle from her stepmother's machinations, the better.

"Silver and diamonds. What a striking combination. Perhaps our wedding could be themed around those two exquisite items."

Lady Elle smiled prettily, looking up at him through her lashes.

"Yes, that sounds wonderful," interrupted Elouan. "However, I must insist that you also review the scroll. It comes directly from the king."

Charmant tore his eyes away from the enchanting lady in front of him and took the scroll from Elouan. Unrolling it, he read the scrawled words, written in his father's shaky hand.

"Come home, my boy. Allow Elouan to do his job. We have much to discuss."

"I must leave your charming company," sighed Charmant as he re-rolled the scroll. He tucked it and his mother's ring into the pouch that once held his lady's slipper.

Lady Elle put a delicate hand on his arm.

"Surely, you can spare a moment for our garden stroll?"

"I am afraid I cannot. The king has summoned me home. I shall leave Elouan and his scribe here to work out the details of our marriage contract with Lady de Noelles Marchand. I will return as soon as possible," Prince Charmant looked down at Lady Elle. Her fair skin glowed with an inner vibrance and the summer sun shining through the open doors lit up her hair in a halo.

The sight of this strong woman who had once rebuffed him stirred his desire, tying his stomach into knots and lengthening his nethers. He dropped a chaste kiss on her hand and promised himself that they would soon have more.

"Soon," she whispered, reading his thoughts. "We will be together again soon."

CHAPTER 18

P rince Charmant burst into his father's room the moment he arrived at the castle.

"You summoned me?" he asked, bowing.

"Yes," scowled his father, "you ran off half-cocked to see your lady this morning, making no arrangements with me."

Charmant straightened and looked at his red-faced father. Sweat soaked through the king's heavy clothes and he looked about ready to burst. The prince's heart softened when he recognized anxiety in his father's countenance.

"I am sorry," his voice filled with contrition. "You are right. My mind was consumed with my own happiness. Though, I did give a thought to the kingdom. Elouan told me of Queen Blanche and how some of her people seem to be immune to the plague. He hinted that Lady Elle's wealth might enable us to purchase such immunity."

"But," the prince continued. "I failed to think of how you would feel, with me gone off alone while you slept. I am sorry."

The king smiled, his red face fading to its usual color. He reached out his hands.

"It is true that I worried about you. I accept your apology."

Charmant took his father's hands and gave them a gentle squeeze.

"Now," declared the king, freeing his hands and turning to two large books open on his desk. "Let us discuss these."

Charmant walked to the desk and looked down. His mother's handwriting filled one of the books. It detailed the intricacies of her wedding to the king, down to which foods were appropriate for the occasion.

"Your mother kept meticulous records of everything that went on in the kingdom. I often told her she could have a scribe make records, but she preferred to write herself. I suppose with so few women able to form letters, she was proud to have the skill," the king smiled fondly, stroking the words with a gentle finger. "You and your lady will need to go over the wedding details. While much of the routines of a royal wedding are prescriptive, this detailed account shares where your lady may make her mark."

"We were just discussing the theme for the wedding, sire," Charmant's face went hot as passion welled up in him. Even the thought of Lady Elle brought his blood up - and made other parts rise as well. "She has sensitive skin and requested a ring of silver and diamonds, if possible. The silver is what is most necessary, however, as gold brings her pain. I mentioned that silver and diamonds could be the theme of our wedding. Perhaps one of your artisans could create an illusion that would fit such a theme?"

The king, who Charmant knew secretly enjoyed creating spectacular parties, brightened up.

"I believe we could!" he exclaimed. "I shall fetch the lead artisan from the Color Ball after our discussion. But, before we get carried away with wedding planning, I need you to look at the second book."

Charmant circled the table and read the open page. It was headed "Marchand Hôpital."

"Old Marchand funded a hospital for those suffering derangement and disfigurement in our community. It is a place for outcasts to find a home and get the care they need from dedicated monks. He also provided a stipend for the monastery as long as they continued to administer his hospital.

"While such a philanthropic act is right and proper for a noble, it was an unusual action for a simple merchant to take. So, he shared the burden with my late cousin, the king. These are the king's notes about the hospital. I admit, I find the whole enterprise odd. But, once he re-established his chateau, the hospital was his first project. After commissioning the hospital, he funded many other improvements in the kingdom.

"In many ways, Marchand had the heart of a noble, if not the blood."

Charmant smiled at that. While he knew Marchand adopted his lady, the fact that she was daughter to such a man only strengthened his faith in her ability to take on her royal role.

"If you wish to consult with your artisans," said the prince. "I will read about the hospital. If that is your wish. I do not know why I would need to know much about it."

"I should have explained," said the king. "There is a note that the man to whom his daughter is married - meaning Lady Elle - must take on the administration of the hospital. Marchand notes that his estate will always provide the funds for the monastery and hospital, in perpetuity. But the hospital is the responsibility of anyone who wishes to take Lady Elle's hand."

"Curious," expressed Charmant.

"Yes," sighed the king. "So, read up on the place while I consult with the artisans."

Charmant lifted the heavy book.

"I shall take it to the terrace while you have your talks," he told his father. The king nodded and escorted his son out of his rooms.

"Get the artisans," the king commanded a servant as Charmant walked away. "We have a wedding to plan."

CHAPTER 19

Charmant lugged the large book down to his favorite summer seat on the terrace. A servant fetched him a cloth and he placed the book on it. Keeping his place with a finger, Charmant checked the first page to understand the book's purpose. The title page said "Accounts, Family Charmant, 1305-1315."

"Strange," muttered the prince. In his experience accounting books occupied slim volumes, filled with numbers and tedious notes. He hoped his father hadn't handed him a list of figures from which he was expected to decipher meaning.

Turning back to the open page, Charmant read.

"Accounting for the Marchand Hôpital, established 1308.

"Established by Loup Marchand to house several of his staff, the Marchand Hôpital opened for public use in 1309. Built on monastery grounds, M. Marchand has pledged to pay for the upkeep of his servants in perpetuity, until the last dies or is rendered sane.

"Prior to opening the hospital for public use, M. Marchand housed the madmen and women of his household in a small home on his chateau grounds. However, as many of his staff have now been replaced by a mysterious clan who return to their homes after three years of service, he has moved the upkeep of his former servants to the Marchand Hôpital.

"Endowing the hospital and neighboring monastery has allowed the hospital to stay open and house ill villagers and the poor. The Crown is pleased with the endowment."

Charmant turned the page, but no additional notes were provided. No sums. No facts and figures. Just this cryptic message about mad servants.

He riffled through the pages and discovered that most of the accounts involved M. Marchand. He paid for two local churches, was the landlord for a local pub, owned a mill and a distillery, as well as oddly named lands in other kingdoms. Some of which were in other countries.

"Rich as Croesus, indeed," muttered the prince.

"Yes," his father's voice came from behind him, startling Charmant from his studies. He jumped up and bowed, knocking his chair over in the process.

"My king," he sputtered.

His father waved a hand.

"Be still, son. I wish to discuss your wedding with you."

Charmant smiled, his heart racing.

"I have determined that we must have it within the week, before all of the nobility travel home. It would be a shame to waste this moment, the goodwill of our court. Many of them have holdings to return to and would be unable to attend the wedding unless it occurred at a much later date. I am assuming, by your evident passion, that you do not wish for a long engagement to Lady Marchand?"

The prince grinned, almost hopping with excitement.

"You assume correctly!" his voice came out loud. He cleared his throat. "You know me well, my king," he said in a quieter voice.

The king clapped his hands.

"Good!" He grinned at his son, "I love a party."

CHAPTER 20

The following days were a whirlwind of wedding planning, marriage paperwork, and more planning. The king never did anything by halves, but he was both hindered and helped by the rushed preparations.

Because the balls had just occurred, the staff and artisans were on hand to put together a glorious, over-the-top royal wedding. The castle chapel dripped with diamond-like crystals and candles. Local merchants worked overtime to source flowers and food for the event, and the king distributed money and food liberally to the townsfolk as he demanded that they work harder than ever before to pull off the gala event.

Charmant often found himself closeted with Elouan and his soon-to-be mother-in-law, sorting out all the paperwork connected with Lady Elle's dowry. Because it had been established before her father's death, and he had died several years before, finding the accounts, ledgers, and deeds included in his fiancé's dowry was quite the task. Normally, Elouan's secretary would be on hand to help, but he was tasked with tracking the vast sums the king spent during wedding planning.

Charmant also had to contend with the decision of which estates included in the dowry ought to be kept, and which should stay with the de Noelles Marchand family. He could not accept most overseas estates without it being seen as a coup by the ruler of those lands. Additionally, neither he nor his father had the resources to protect such lands once they fell into royal hands.

The one foreign land which Lady de Noelles Marchand insisted must be included in the dowry was ill-defined. It was the land of Lady Elle's strange servants, the Noamhites. She explained that these marshlands were located somewhere in Britannia, but that no other Briton would go near the area.

When Charmant and Elouan refused to accept this land as part of the marital contract, Lady de Noelles Marchand threw up her hands and told them, "The Noamhites will follow Elle whether you take ownership of the land or not. They have pledged their lives to her father, and they will follow her to your castle. If you own the land, you will have control of them as well - and believe me, you will want some kind of control of those... people."

Elouan furrowed his brow, "You say they will come to the castle whether we want them to or not?"

"Yes," Lady de Noelles Marchand sighed. "They go anywhere Lady Marchand goes."

"I see, in that case we will take ownership of the land, but we cannot pledge to protect it. The ownership is in name only."

"Believe me, the Britons want nothing to do with that land. The Noamhites can protect themselves."

The rest of the negotiation and paperwork went as one would expect. The only other sticking point was the Marchand Hôpital.

In the codicils, old Marchand stated that anyone who cared for Elle must visit the hospital annually to deliver payment to the monks, and to inspect the hospital and ensure all patients and visitors were properly cared for. No filthy linens or chains for his former staff. The inheritor of the Marchand Hôpital must ensure everyone got good, plain food and were well-tended to, even if they were ill or on death's door. He expected the inheritor to attend to the hospital with a caring heart.

Charmant felt a twinge at this. He had often been insulted by his brothers for being too gentle, too fond of fishing over hunting. Soldiering had given him a hard exterior, but inside he was ill-suited for the violence inherent in such a life. Here was old Marchand, rescuer and adopter of Lady Elle, sharing insight into his own gentle heart.

"The annual inspection is due in two weeks," Lady de Noelles Marchand told them. "Since you will be the new owner of the hospital, this will be an excellent introduction to the place."

"Yes, I have read of it. It seems an odd bequest, but I am happy to fulfill it," stated the prince.

Elouan and Lady de Noelles Marchand exchanged glances. Then, the lady shrugged.

"That takes care of that," she sighed.

CHAPTER 21

The morning of the wedding, Lady Elle left her adopted home and took a carriage to the castle, accompanied by twenty-one Noamhite servants and trunks filled with valuables. Dawn crested the horizon as they set out, lighting the way and drawing villagers and farmers alike to line the King's Road.

Though her fine carriage drew the eyes of every observer, her ominous frog-faced attendants kept the celebrants well out of the way.

Arriving at the castle, Lady Elle was swept into the chaos of final preparations.

"The prince mustn't see you before the wedding, my lady," Octave led Lady Elle into a room prepared just for her.

Lady Elle raised an eyebrow at him. The servant smiled.

"It is Charmant family tradition."

She smiled at the servant politely.

"My attendants will assist me from here," she told him. "I know you are busy."

The servant bowed to her gratefully.

"You are too kind, my lady. Every one of the staff is delighted that you shall rule us."

Lady Elle forced another smile, nodding the man out of her room. When he was gone, she turned to her attendants.

"Busy yourselves. I will check the dig."

Eagerness swelled inside her. She had not been able to monitor the dig's progress for the last several days, but she felt the power growing stronger as her people chipped away at the earth concealing its force.

Leaving her room, she hurried through the castle, dimming her radiance as she went. By the time she reached the cellar door, her form would not have caught the eye of the prince himself. Not that he would be wandering the halls. He was likely dressing, readying himself for their midday ceremony.

Elle pushed through the door and skipped down the steps to the storage room. The pull within her drew her past casks and vegetables, tugging her beyond the blanket at the end of the room, and dragging her down the long passageway.

Smooth dirt beneath her feet sloped down, down into the bowels of the earth. The walls and ceiling were supported with wood, and she could hear banging from farther down the slope. As she approached her Noamhites, she smiled at the buzz of activity.

Ten men worked at a feverish pace. Two at the end of the tunnel dug, two piled dirt into buckets, two packed the crumbling soil walls while another two pushed wooden beams in place, holding the tunnel open. The final two men lifted buckets heavy with dirt and hauled them up the path, toward her.

A grin stretched across Elle's face when they spotted her. All work ceased and the men flattened themselves to the ground, scooting over on their hands and knees to provide her with a clear path.

Sweeping past the Noamhites, Elle pressed her hand against the soft, wet soil at the end of the walkway. She lengthened her limbs, transforming them into javelins. Stretching her body to the extent she could while still restricted by the bracelet, she brushed against the power source.

Energy shot up her fingertips, rushing through her left arm and spreading into her body. The power ended at the wrist of her right arm, stopping at the bracelet. The limb went immobile as it filled with a searing, burning pain.

Elle wanted to scream in frustration, to rattle the walls with her mighty voice, bringing dirt and wood down on them all.

Instead, she pulled back, reshaping her body into the human shape it had occupied for so long. Without glancing at her servants, she marched back up the slope. Icy anger mixed with determination filled her, leaving frost in her wake. She would find a way to remove the bracelet.

The prince is the key, she told herself. Concentrating on a solution warmed her. *Once I marry him, my obligation to Marchand's family will be complete.* The idea warmed her still more. Her mind filled with possibilities, lightening her heart and steps as she made her way back to her rooms.

Chapter 22

Charmant stood at the chapel doors, greeting nobles as they filed in. His stomach fluttered with butterflies and his hands felt clumsy and numb.

A profusion of candles filled the chapel, the firelight glimmering off crystals lined with silver. White roses overflowed silver vases with cleverly placed clear gems reflecting light into their snowy petals.

With pews packed tight, Charmant and his father knew the room would feel close, so they instructed the servants to open the chapel skylights to the summer sky, letting fresh air breeze through, flickering the candlelight and causing the faceted crystals to sparkle like diamonds.

Looking at the beautiful room, Charmant dreamed of the next well-attended gathering that would occur there. A Christening, God willing, of a boy. Followed, he hoped, by the Christening of many other children, male and female, enough to bring his father joy in his final years. Enough to fill the castle with laughter and playful screams. Enough to guarantee his family name lived on for generations.

He had not told Elle, but he and his father were the last of the

Charmants. All of his family and extended family had died in the plague or due to misfortune. The pressure of keeping the Charmant name alive had driven his father to spend an extravagant amount on summer balls, and the joy of a new addition to the small Charmant clan drove his father to another extravagant expenditure on this day.

Charmant's numbed hands clenched and unclenched, causing tingles to run up his arms and pins to prick his palms.

Elle

He could think of nothing else. After all, this was her day. The day she gave herself to him here at the chapel, under the watchful eye of God.

The bells tolled and the nobles in the chapel kneeled.

It was time.

CHAPTER 23

Charmant stood at the chapel door, his back straight, eyes searching. Soon, he would lead Elle to the priest and the two of them would kneel and become man and wife. His legs wobbled as he tried to quiet his jitters.

Then, his breath caught.

Elle stood before him, resplendent in silver and white. A gleaming silver veil covered her face and hair, billowing down to her waist and weighted with diamonds. Her white dress, embroidered with silver thread, covered every inch of her body, yet one could still see the shape of the woman beneath.

Charmant felt the now-familiar burning come over his skin. The itch that he knew only she could scratch. And soon, very soon, she would do so.

Her dainty steps took her to his side and her two squat attendants melted away. Charmant gave Lady Elle his arm and escorted her up the aisle. Together, they kneeled. Together, they prayed. And together they rose as husband and wife.

The congregation stood when they were presented. Charmant beaming and Elle glowing with ethereal beauty. Around them, servants and attendants threw white rose and lilac petals into the air. The church choir broke out in a hymn and husband and wife, prince and princess, walked arm in arm down the aisle.

A piercing scream shattered the joyful celebration. Followed by another. Then, wrenching sobs.

The entire room fell silent, everyone searching for the source of the screaming.

An angry woman's voice interrupted the silence.

"Get off! Get away! Oh, why are you doing this? Get away!"

Lady de Noelles Marchand's voice cried out again. The crowd backed away from her and Charmant now saw her clearly. She and her daughters wore dove gray frocks. Crimson marred the simple loveliness of the girl's dresses.

Two songbirds swooped around their faces, bloodied claws clutching chunks of hair and skin.

Charmant dropped Elle's arm and ran to the women.

"Get the doctor, my father's doctor," he shouted as he ran.

The blood-covered songbirds dove at the two girls' faces, pecking at their eyes. As Charmant approached, both birds fled, silent, dripping, and malevolent.

Prince Charmant grabbed at his tunic, trying to tear the finely woven fabric. It didn't so much as split a seam. He pawed at his side for a knife, but in his finery, only a sash of office draped over a formal kirtle. No bag nor a knife at his hip.

He ripped off the sash and used it to wipe blood off the girls' faces. Their eyelids had been gashed and ripped, their faces scratched, and chunks of hair removed - exposing scalp. Blood poured from the wounds like crimson waterfalls. Their mother, in her panic, tried to use her dress and the weight of her body to stop the bleeding.

The prince was in the middle of wrapping his bloodied sash around the worst of Enora's wounds when the doctor and two attendants gently pushed him to the side.

"Thank you, Your Highness," the doctor told him, his hands rapidly wrapping the sash over Enora's head while his attendants poured liquid over Adeline's face and scalp. Overwhelmed by pain, she fainted in her mother's arms.

Another attendant came over and poured a liquid down Enora's throat, causing the girl to slump.

"A sleeping draft," the doctor addressed the prince, "provided by your lady wife."

Lady de Noelles Marchand's head whipped around, her eyes searching. Charmant guessed she was looking for her stepdaughter.

Octave took Prince Charmant's arm and led him away.

"Though this tragedy has occurred, you and the princess must meet your people as one. It is a vital part of the ceremony. The dressers and I shall clean you up so that you may present a united front with your new princess."

Numbness swept Charmant. He could barely feel the pressure Octave asserted on his arm and waist as the servant led him away. All he could register was his breathing, which became more rapid, more labored, until it came in sobbing gasps. That's when he realized not all the wetness on his face was blood. Tears coated his cheeks, streaking white lines through a red coating.

"This is a terrible omen," he choked out, staring blindly ahead as Octave pushed him into a room with bathers and clothiers. "Those girls. The beginning of our marriage. The bloody birds. Terrible. Witchcraft."

The attendants bustling around him froze.

The prince turned blazing eyes at each servant. The normal castle servants, men with stooped shoulders and brown hair, shrunk back. The attendants Lady Elle brought with her, men with straight backs and frog faces, stared. Their eyes unblinking.

"Out, all of you," yelled Charmant. His stomach gave a quick turn, and he crouched over the washbasin and retched.

CHAPTER 24

Charmant sat in a daze and watched the people swirl around him. They were all celebrants, nobles who had attended his wedding and seen the horrors which came after. However, here they were, dancing and frolicking as if nothing had happened.

He glanced over at his princes. She didn't seem much better than he. Her face, expressionless, her inner light, dimmed.

Rallying courtly manners, he reached over to her and squeezed her hand. She looked at him and forced a smile.

Glancing up, he saw his father watching them with sad eyes. Charmant could only wonder at his father's thoughts, but he imagined they were something like what the prince had said to his attendants. This was all a very bad omen.

Not long into the dancing, Elle excused herself. It likely appeared inappropriate, her leaving. But perhaps she was looking in on her sisters and trying to think of another tincture that could help. His chest tightened and he blinked to keep back the tears.

Not only did he worry about how Elle was taking the attack on her sisters, but he also wondered what the people would say. He knew they would call it an ill omen, but would they believe, as he did, witchcraft caused the birds to attack? If so, they wouldn't suspect Enora and Adeline's mother for committing the atrocity.

To what end? Did she whip the birds up into a frenzy as her fury about Elle's happy union mounted? Did she attack her own kin to perpetrate some kind of curse upon his lady wife?

He did not know and had not a clue who to ask.

Perhaps Elle could tell him of her stepmother's true nature. Once she revealed all, he could help rid them of the awful witch. Surely, they could accuse her of witchcraft together and, once she was safely executed, they would be safe, too.

Or perhaps the spell Lady de Noelles Marchand had just cast would make her other two children do something unspeakable to protect their mother.

There was no way to know. He would have to talk to Elle about it all, lay out his observations, and allow her to share her own experiences with the witchy woman.

"My prince?" asked a familiar contralto voice.

"My princess," he smiled, his mind returning to the present.

"You seemed many miles away."

"Just lost in thought. Awaiting your return. Shall we dance?"

He stood and bowed to Elle, then led her to the dance floor. The familiar motions soothed the tumult in his mind and soul. Perhaps dance was its own kind of spell. One worked by common folks to find themselves. He smiled at the thought.

When the dance ended, they had their wedding feast. Prince Charmant could not eat much. The blood red sauces and rich meats made him think of those flayed faces. Hunks of bone showing through bloodied scalp.

He ate nuts and dried fruit, only taking a token nibble of any new dish laid before him.

After the feast, he and Elle went to their favorite haunt, the back terrace. Both prince and princess stared out into the night, letting the drifting sounds of frivolity melt into the warm summer air.

"Can I tell you something?" asked Elle, abruptly.

"Of course, anything," replied the prince, his mind swirling once again. Was she going to reveal what he suspected about her stepmother?

"It is about Lady de Noelles Marchand."

The prince looked at her, trying to keep his expression neutral.

"I did not tell you everything about my past. There is much to tell. But, let me try to share what is pertinent.

"When my father purchased me in that shop, he also purchased a key and a book. The key goes to this," she pulled her sleeve back to reveal the black bracelet. Charmant looked at the bracelet and again felt pulled toward it, his eyes unable to flicker away. With effort, he dragged them back to his wife's face.

"The book tells how to open it. This bracelet, it is a symbol, a way to tell the person who purchased me that I belong to them. A way to control my loyalty. I am not sure how it works, but it binds me to whomever has the key and the book."

"It is magic, then?" asked the prince.

"I supposed it is. The technology involved would certainly look so to the peoples of this place."

"What?" The confused prince stared at Lady Elle.

"Merely that any way of doing things, that is unusual or beyond this time might look like magic," she shook her head at his perplexed expression. "Magic or not is unimportant. When my father married Lady de Noelles, he willed the key and the book, and my upkeep, to her. He died a few short days later, when they refused to take me along with them on a tour of their estates. I knew in my heart something would go wrong and I begged them to take me. But they refused."

"I am glad they refused," Prince Charmant declared. "You may not have survived."

She paused, looking into his eyes.

"You love me, do you not?"

Charmant's heart jumped to his throat. Had he shown his true feelings so blatantly?

She smiled gently, "I can see in your face that you do, though I know it is considered unmanly to admit to tender feelings. So, we shall leave the words unspoken. Now that you have laid claim of me through marriage, you should have the key and the book. And, if you choose to love me, I would appreciate it if you could give them to me so that I may free myself of this lifelong shackle."

The prince stared at her.

"Are you saying that your stepmother has control over you through that bracelet?"

"She has control of my loyalty. Not my actions. But I do not belong to her any longer. I belong to you. And, if you are the kind man I believe you are, I would like you to return that feeling of belonging to myself. I would like to no longer be enslaved in any way. I would like to have free will."

Prince Charmant nodded, letting words spill from his mouth without thinking.

"None of us, we are taught, have free will. We only have God's will. However, no person ought to be chained to another and witchcraft is illegal. I will speak with your stepmother tomorrow and get that book and key - or she will face the punishment for her witchcraft."

Elle leaned in and hugged him, wrapping her arms around his chest and squeezing the breath out of him.

"I will reward you for all that you have done for me and will do. I promise."

In that moment, Charmant forgot about his melancholy. He forgot about the two young ladies at death's door. He forgot about omens and witchcraft. He could only think of Elle, right there in his arms.

Leaning down, he kissed her, and she kissed back.

Behind him, applause broke out.

The couple turned, arms slipping from each other. Charmant's face flamed red when he caught the eye of his father and a local marquis facing the couple and clapping enthusiastically.

"To the marriage bed with you," commanded his father, shooing them both with enthusiastic hands.

"Make us a princeling!" shouted the marquis, his voice loud with drink.

Charmant grabbed Elle's hand and pulled her through the ball-room. Few people danced, many sat on couches and chairs, talking, drinking, and slumped over in wine-induced oblivion.

"Let us go abed," whispered the prince, face still aflame, but now grinning.

He caught the look on Elle's face and stopped rushing her along.

"What is wrong, my lady?" he asked.

"Nothing," she whispered, her voice so quiet he leaned down to hear her. "It is a wife's duty to produce heirs, is it not?"

She straightened her back and answered her rhetorical question.

"It is."

She looked up at Charmant.

"I am ready."

CHAPTER 25

Flushed with excitement, Charmant fairly pulled his bride through the hall to his room. At the door, she stopped him and asked one of her attendants for a drink.

Sipping the straw-colored liquid, she offered it to him.

"For good luck," she told him.

The prince drank a sip, finding the drink delightful and sweet. His first taste ignited his thirst, but he held back, offering the goblet to Elle.

"Drink the rest," she told him. Putting her hand out to the attendant, they produced another goblet, pouring more of the mixture into it.

After tossing the entire goblet down in one swig, Charmant motioned for more. The attendant poured and, together, Charmant and Elle walked into their marital bedchamber.

The servants had transformed Charmant's room, adding fresh flowers, restuffing the mattress, and anointing the room with scented oils. The smell of musk and roses overwhelmed him, arousing his ardor. He pulled his new wife close and kissed her, tasting the sweetness of their shared drink on her lips.

Elle was compliant as he walked with her to the bed.

"Sit," he instructed her, his voice husky with desire.

He stood and gazed at her as he undressed. Completely naked, he assessed her expression. It was oddly flat. As if she'd seen all this before, many times, and was unimpressed.

Perhaps I have shocked her, and she does not know what to do.

"I shall undress you, now my lady. I will show you what is to be done."

Suiting action to word, Prince Charmant undressed Elle. She did not help him in any way, her arms drooping and body obedient. Her clothes came off easily.

Both naked, Charmant looked at Elle. Her perfect body, her glowing skin, her golden hair, all should arouse him into a frenzy. Instead, he felt tired and a bit worried.

"Why do you say nothing, my lady?" he asked.

Elle looked at him, one eyebrow cocked.

"Is this not what you want? I am but a womb for your seed, am I not?"

The prince felt himself shrivel. He did not want her lassitude. He desired passion on the first night. But she was right. They needed to create an heir as soon as possible, whether she felt passionate or resigned.

"I see that it does not please you," murmured Elle, looking pointedly at his manhood.

Shock coursed down his spine.

"Your knowledge of the male body surprises me."

"I have seen animals in the field and my father used to breed horses. There is not much difference between the human body and equine anatomy."

That struck the prince.

"Our lovemaking should not be like that of horses. If you have seen animals rutting, you may have seen screaming, distressed creatures forcefully seeded. That is not the way of it."

"Isn't it? I have heard of, been warned against, men who wish to do to me as those stallions did to the mares."

The prince flushed, embarrassed for his sex. Suddenly, he saw himself through her female eyes. His naked flesh represented everything she had protected herself against for her entire life; a man about to push his way into her whether she wanted it or not. He sank to his knees.

"My love, my wife," he said. "It is tradition that we complete the marriage with a physical union tonight. But, if you are not ready, if my nudity makes you afraid, then I can wait." The last three words choked in his throat. He had been anticipating this night the moment he laid eyes on Elle. Yet, here he was, saying them.

Elle smiled and reached out a hand, stroking his cheek.

"You are unusual," she observed. "Not many men are so kind or would be so patient. I have heard stories that make men sound worse than beasts. I would like to grant you a gift for your kindness."

She stood, her skin glowing in the candlelight. Sparkling dust motes surrounded her with effervescence.

"Lay down in bed," she instructed. "I will make myself ready for you."

The prince did as she asked. He found he was stiff once again, waiting for his princess. She walked to the basin, that ethereal light following her as she washed her face and hands.

He felt his eyes go heavy, the light doubling and tripling, blurring into prismatic color. His princess seemed to change in that light, but he could not be sure as he dropped off to sleep.

Charmant woke to an unmistakable feeling. A feeling of envelopment, covering his manhood with heat and wetness. Straining his eyes in the dark room, he saw a female outline sitting on him, riding him.

He groaned in pleasure, grabbing at the lady on top of him and joining her in lovemaking.

As Charmant neared completion, gray light seeped through the shuttered windows, illuminating his partner's face with curious clarity.

The light revealed pallid, frog-like features surrounded by stringy hair. Her eyes were a brilliant green with elongated pupils and eyelids that slid across them, like the eyes of a hawk. Her wide, almost lip-less mouth stretched from cheekbone to cheekbone. Charmant tried to stop moving, stop his body from releasing into the monstrous creature, but the woman-thing would not stop rocking and he couldn't restrain himself. He spent his seed, then turned, vomiting over the side of the bed.

She pushed him back, tucking him in and stroking his brow with long fingers. Blackness rolled over him.

CHAPTER 26

Charmant woke up to birdsong. Kicking off his blanket and leaping out of bed, he expected to land in a puddle of sick.

His bedside was clean and scrubbed, just as it was the previous day. Heart hammering, he whipped his head around, looking for signs that his dream had been real. The room startled him with its normalcy.

Elle sat up, her naked body gleaming in the morning sun.

"Good morning," she yawned.

Charmant stared. Then, light-headed, he sat down on his mattress and put his head between his legs. Soft hands touched his back and he flinched away.

"What is it?" Elle asked.

"I had a horrible dream, a nightmare."

"Shh..." Elle soothed. "You are awake now." Her musical voice was still muzzy with sleep. Her naked body pressed against him, arousing him. But he couldn't imagine trying anything now. The dream was too fresh, too disgusting. He felt unclean.

At that moment, he wished he hadn't had the terrifying experience in the lake. He could use a cold dip. So, instead of grabbing his new wife and making love to her, he stood up, slipping out of her grasp. Walking to the water basin, he immersed head, plunging his face in the cold water and gasping as he pulled himself out.

Dripping over the basin, he stared. The marble water receptacle glowed in the early morning light. Surrounding the pristine basin spread a dark, plague-like stain of black mold.

Charmant stepped back in horror.

Elle tiptoed over to him. She had put on a dressing gown and handed him a clean, dry towel.

"What is that?" Charmant asked. "Tell me I am seeing it."

Elle stared at the stain, her mouth dropping into an "O." Then she sighed and ran her fingers through her long, honey-brown hair. Morning light danced and glittered on the strands, making Charmant want to run his own hands through it.

"It is her mark," she stated, dropping her eyes to the floor. One crystal tear dripped down her face.

"Whose?" asked Charmant.

"My stepmother's. She is using her will to remind me of her power. She will not rest until she knows she has me under control once again." Elle stretched out her arm, letting the sleeve of the gown drop back and revealing the black, writhing bracelet.

Charmant stared at it. Since he'd last seen the bracelet, it had changed. The markings were different, and thorns grew from the sides, dimpling Elle's skin.

"Is it painful?" he asked, reaching for her arm.

She clutched it to her breast.

"Very," she told him.

Elle turned and heaved a huge sigh. Walking to the barred windows, she peered out at the day through the slats.

Charmant waited, wondering if she would say more.

"I am sorry I lied to you about the bracelet, Your Highness," she murmured. "I told you it was platinum, that it provided me with comfort. But she was in the room when we spoke about it, and I didn't dare tell you the truth.

"This bracelet, as I said on the terrace, binds me to whomever has the key and the book. My stepmother possesses those items. So, though I am married to you, I am still bound to her. I do not know what that means for you, if she can affect you and invade your dreams like she has done to so many."

Cold fear prickled Charmant's skin. He nodded vigorously.

"I have experienced dreams in which Lady de Noelles Marchand appears. They often begin pleasantly, but end in a nightmare. Last night she did not appear, but instead it was a monstrous beast."

Elle glanced over to him.

"I am sorry, Your Highness," she sighed. "I should never have married you."

Charmant walked to her and put his hand under her pert little chin.

"Do not say that," he said. "There must be some way to stop her. I can have her arrested for witchcraft."

Elle stiffened.

"No, please my lord, do not have her arrested. The key and book will be lost forever if she is arrested and I will never be free of this," she lifted her wrist.

"Of course," the prince dropped her chin and impatiently yanked on the shutters, flooding the room with golden light.

"I am sure she is in the castle now," suggested Elle. "I doubt my poor sisters could me moved after yesterday's injuries. Perhaps you can speak with her and convince her to give you what you seek."

Charmant nodded.

"It shall be done."

He strode to the door and opened it, his naked body on display for all to see.

"Send for my dressers. I must talk with Lady de Noelles Marchand as soon as possible," he commanded the bowlegged, frog-faced man standing outside of his door.

CHAPTER 27

C harmant strode down the hall, guided by one of Elle's servants. He had been informed that Lady de Noelles Marchand still resided in the castle, tending to her injured daughters, as Elle predicted.

While Elle seemed protective of the girls, Charmant wondered if they knew about their mother's witchcraft and her ill treatment of Elle. He knew he did not have the entire story. For example, why would the woman want to bind Elle to her and her family? Was she subjecting his bride to horrors from which she could not run? Sending the girl to collect witchy herbs in the wood? Forcing her to commit sacrifices? Would not the younger girls know of these wicked goings on?

The servant opened a door to an adjoining hall with guest rooms and there stood Lady de Noelles Marchand, quietly closing one of the bedroom doors.

Charmant stopped for a moment, observing the woman as she glanced up. She looked sad, old, and worried. She did not for one moment appear to be a witch disguised as a noblewoman. But wouldn't a witch want to seem harmless?

He straightened his back and walked up to her, refusing to bow as she gave him a brief curtsy.

"I would talk with you, my lady," he growled.

She looked up in surprise.

"Of course, Your Highness. What is it?"

"I demand the key and the book. I demand you free my wife of whatever curse you have laid upon her."

Lady de Noelles Marchand stiffened; her eyes blazed into his.

"I see," she said. "I do not know what she told you, but I shall give you the items you requested. You are entitled to them as her husband."

"And you must get out of my dreams."

The Lady's angry eyes lost their fervor. Her mouth dropped into a gaping hole of shock. She pressed both hands to her lips and looked at him again, this time with fear.

"You didn't think I noticed that you were invading my dreams, turning them to nightmares?" he pressed.

She shook her head vigorously, hands still pressed to her mouth.

"You thought I would not see you looming over me like some malevolent crone? I know what you are, witch."

Lady de Noelles Marchand's back stiffened again. She dropped her hands to her sides and stared at Charmant, her eyes searching his face. Heaving a deep sigh, she looked at the ground.

"So, that's what she meant," she whispered, "when she said she would make my life difficult."

"You do not deny it?" demanded Charmant. His blood was high, his hands gripped into fists.

This is what it is like to confront true evil, he thought, glaring at the woman in front of him. She slumped.

"Of course, I deny it, but would there be a point? Why should you believe me?"

Blood rushed to Charmant's ears. The woman seemed to be saying that he was being unfair. That his accusations were unjust. How dare she?

He changed his stance, looming over the woman. She shrank back.

"I will give you the key and the book. Please, just leave my family alone."

Charmant's brow furrowed. Again, he wondered why this woman accused him of being the frightening aggressor. Had she not trapped Elle, bound his wife, and bewitched her?

"Give them to me and then we shall see. If your daughters were not involved in this, I promise I will not harm them. But for you, witch, it will be the gallows."

Lady de Noelles Marchand put her hands up as if to bat his words away.

"I am no witch. I do not even know how to use the key and book. They were given to me by my husband, and he obtained them when he adopted Elle. Please, before you decide, read the book and visit the Hôpital Marchand. You will find answers there. Though, they are not the ones you seek."

She turned her back on him, heading down the hall.

"Wait one moment, woman."

She turned back, glaring at him. "I am still nobility, Your Highness. Please address me as 'my lady.' Now, do you want the book and key or not? I carry them with me wherever I go. They are on my person now. Though, to get to them, I must remove some clothing. Did you want me to strip naked in front of you so you can watch?"

Charmant blushed, shame prickling his scalp. He bowed, his body remembering his manners before his mind could tell him to stop. The lady disappeared into a room down the hall.

Left alone in the dark passage, Charmant paced.

Was Lady de Noelles Marchand a witch? He wondered now. While his dreams had been disturbing, nothing had occurred in the waking world beyond birds acting unnaturally. Why would she use the creatures to harm anyone? Why would she hurt her own natural born daughters? She clearly despised Elle. Why didn't she send birds to attack his wife instead of her own flesh and blood?

Perhaps she knew that, as a princess, Elle could claim royal protection and he could, at a word, have her arrested and executed as a witch.

But now that she had planted questions in his mind, he wondered. *Was she a witch?* He did not want to falsely accuse anyone.

A door slammed.

Charmant looked up as Lady de Noelles Marchand marched toward him, her expression set. She thrust a book bound in red leather and a thick, sealed parchment into one hand and an elaborately wrought key in the other.

"Here. Take these. But, before you give them to Elle, visit the Hôpital Marchand. You may find reason to question your blind faith in the woman you married. A woman, I might add, whom you have known for less than a fortnight. Good day, Your Highness." She dropped into a brief curtsy, straightened, and then opened the door next to Charmant.

He peered in, catching sight of her bandaged daughter before the lady slammed the door in his face.

CHAPTER 28

Tucking the key into his belt pouch, Charmant fiddled with the parchment and book. They were too large to tuck into a pouch, but too precious to entrust to a servant. Pushing the parchment into the belt at his waist, he peered down at the book. Strange patterns swirled in the soft leather cover, turning his stomach. Lifting the book to his nose, he sniffed. The thing smelled strongly of Lady de Noelles Marchand's perfume, along with something gamey. It did not have the fresh, chemical scent of leather or hide that denoted a recently bound book.

"What am I to do with you?" he wondered aloud, staring at the book.

The cover gave him no answer. For a moment, the desire to step into one of the rooms and toss the book into the fire swept over him. Gripping the thing tighter, the prince took a deep breath of that strange, gamey odor and wondered if he had done the right thing.

"Of course, you've done the right thing," he told himself. "This book is clearly filled with strange magics and must be used for..." His mind stopped there, unable to determine what the book would be used for. Why did Elle need it again?

He shook his head. "I've removed it from the witch," he muttered, forcing his legs to move.

Putting one foot in front of the other, the prince managed to exit the hall, walking straight into one of Elle's strange-looking attendants.

"Pardon me, Your Majesty," the man croaked, his eyes focused on the book.

The man's stare made the prince nervous. Should he hide the book and key on his person, just as Lady de Noelles Marchand had done? Should he give them to Elle?

He wanted to hang onto them until he could follow Lady de Noelles Marchand's advice and go to the hospital. Perhaps he would find answers there. Or perhaps the mad former servants would tell him what he suspected, that Lady de Noelles Marchand cursed them with madness.

His step faltered as he thought about it. Wasn't the hospital established well before Old Marchand married his wife? Either way, a visit would be illuminating.

Instead of returning to his bed chamber, Charmant sought out Octave and a scribe, making arrangements to visit the hospital the following day.

He sent a message to the monks, informing them of his visit and telling them that their payment would come one week after the inspection. By providing such short notice, he hoped to surprise them and assure himself that they were taking the care laid out in Marchand's agreement.

Preparations made, Charmant felt antsy. He did not want to return to his waiting wife. Instead, his itchy skin and aching legs begged to be enveloped in smooth, cool water.

Perhaps a visit to the lake would be alright. He could stay on the shore and rinse his skin in the clean water. He did not need to swim or even fully submerge himself, though his arms and legs ached to pull his body through cold, clear water.

Once again, he made his way outdoors. Trotting through the orchard, he noticed men harvesting fruit from the trees. Their strange gait and amphibious faces told him that they were his wife's attendants.

While he knew that the odd-looking servants would join the castle staff, his heart gave a nervous leap when he saw how many men filled the royal orchards.

Have I seen any of my staff today? Charmant wondered to himself. He couldn't recall seeing any of the usual men guarding doors, walking the halls, or bustling about. He'd only seen Octave and the castle scribe for a few moments when he was getting off his messages. The castle steward appeared gaunt and exhausted, haggard after weeks of balls and preparations.

Perhaps Elle has given some of the castle servants a break by replacing them with her staff. The thought made him uneasy.

Glancing at the quiet, frog-like men, Charmant quickened his pace, arriving at the lake as if pursued.

The lake stretched out before him, its blue waters promising an end to the crawling sensation that plagued his skin. Sitting, Charmant removed his boots and rolled up his hose. Glancing around, he saw no one occupied the shore.

Perhaps just a quick dip? he wondered to himself. Glancing out at the water, he shook his head. It was impossible to see what lurked below in the lake's depths. But he could walk in ankle deep and splash about a bit. Surely that large thing could not reach the shore.

I probably imagined it, he told himself. *I likely got tangled in a plant and then saw a fish or some debris and mistook it for a monster as I thrashed about.*

Charmant snorted at himself, glad he hadn't told anyone of the "lake monster."

Still, it is not wise to venture out into the depths, he decided. *I shall walk along the shoreline, get clean, and dress.*

Quickly, he stripped off his hose and removed his belt. The scroll fell out and a chord of nervousness struck him. What if the key, scroll, and book were not safe left alone on the bank? What if someone stole his things while he frolicked in the water?

The prince paused, casting his eye about. He could see no one, which meant both his servants and his wife's were not in his immediate vicinity. But that didn't mean none could come upon his clothes while he bathed.

Carefully, the prince wrapped the book and the scroll in his sash. Then, he piled his hose and boots on top of it. He fished the key out of his pouch and walked to a nearby boulder. Feeling vaguely ridiculous, he dug in the soft sand at rock's base, lodged the key into the sand, marked the rock with a charred bit of wood, then covered the spot again. He stuck the charred wood in the ground as a makeshift marker.

Like a burial plot, he mused, stepping back and nodding at his work. Charmant walked back to his clothes and removed his tunic. Naked, he walked to the shoreline and splashed cool water over his hot skin.

CHAPTER 29

The power source dragged at Elle, thrumming through her
every fiber.

She swayed at the end of the tunnel, watching her
people dig with a newfound vigor. They would reach the source in a
day, maybe two. With the prince under her thrall, doing her bidding,
she would soon be able to return home and leave this sorry place
behind.

A smile crept over her normally blank visage. The power yanked
at her fiber, filling her with giddiness.

*I will leave something for the prince and that wicked stepmother
of mine,* she told herself. *Just as a little treat.*

She gazed fondly at her followers, her people. Their entire
lives, generations of their tribe, had waited and suffered for her
return home. It was their life's work, their task. They were her
servants - her slaves, suffering on her whims. The power filled her
up to bursting. Sparks of joy shot out from her, striking the dirt
walls.

A croaking cough came from behind her, interrupting her
thoughts. She whirled and found a sweating attendant, one of the

least Changed. When her flaming eyes rested upon him, he dropped to his knees, burying his face in the dirt.

"What is it?" she snapped, her burning joy turning to freezing anger in an instant. This worm dared interrupt her contemplation? Frost sizzled out from her feet.

The man scooted back from the ice, mumbling into the ground.

I must calm myself, she admonished. Stamping her feet, she shook out the anger.

"Stand," she ordered, straightening to her full height. "Deliver your message."

The man got to his knees, unable to stand. Unable to look at her emerald eyes.

"I saw the book, oh gracious goddess. The prince has it, but he will not leave it. He has been carrying it with him since the morning. But our people saw him running to the lake. He cannot bring it there, unless he means to drown it."

Elle stiffened. The man she thought in her thrall had disobeyed. He had retrieved the book and then failed to bring it to her.

The prince is truly an odd human, less prone to animal urges than others. How annoying.

She stamped her foot again, attempting to keep the annoyance from flaring into frigid anger.

"Indeed. Tell the others and find a way to retrieve it. Leave the prince unharmed for now but get that book."

The servant bowed again, crawling backward up the path on arms and knees.

"Run!" she yelled, her rage crystallizing the damp air around her, shooting flecks of ice toward the man.

As if kicked by a horse, he flung himself to his feet and sprinted away.

It would look strange for one of her servants, covered in filth, to be found running through the castle. But she had given Octave and all of the other servants the day off. Most had left the castle for one of the surrounding villages, though she believed Octave skulked around somewhere. If he commented about her servant, she would deal with it.

I need that book; she raged as she turned back to the dig. She stared at the dirt wall, boring through it with her eyes as if glaring could reveal the power source faster. Another thought struck her as she seethed. *Where is the key?*

One of the digging men shouted.

"There is something here!"

Elle rushed to him, shoving him aside and yanking a pick out of the wall. She pushed her hand through the dirt. Her extremity encountered a massive rock. Rubbing her fingertips along it, she closed her eyes, feeling the rock's texture.

"It's chalcedony," she muttered. "Perfect."

A wall of quartz blocked their way, protecting the power source beneath.

Elle turned to her people in the tunnel.

"Go through the castle and find all of the diamonds. Gather them up. They will be your tools as we work to cut through this rock."

The man with the pick, now flat on the ground in a groveling bow, lifted his head for a moment.

"We?" he asked before planting his face into the mud.

"Yes," she told him, leaning down to lift his chin and looking into his eyes. "We. I must help you with this part."

CHAPTER 30

U p to his knees in lake water, Charmant splashed around, his cares floating away along with the dirt and itchiness that had plagued him for days.

Why do we not live on the water? He asked himself, dreaming idly of a floating castle. The answer came to him when he imagined the amount of stone necessary for his own small castle. It could only exist in his dreams.

Sitting in the shallows, he looked up at the brilliant blue sky and tried to think of more urgent matters. Tried to shape all his questions into a cohesive list.

He needed to know:

Was his mother-in-law a witch?

Was something wrong with Elle, as his mother-in-law implied?

And how could he rid himself of the terrible dreams that had begun haunting him?

From there he could determine the answers to other quandaries, like:

How could he approach the slighted Queen Blanche and ask for access to her secret of immunity?

What could be done to improve the chances that he and Elle would create an heir and many others, reinvigorating his family line?

Could he get rid of these strange attendants, without offending Elle?

At that last, he smiled a bit. The servants were odd, but they did seem to be helping his exhausted staff. He stood and turned around, letting water slough off him as he took a step toward the nearby shore.

As he moved, he spotted some of Elle's odd attendants on the shore. They were picking up his clothes, shaking them as they went.

"Hey!" he shouted, taking another step. "Those are mine."

The attendants pretended not to hear him. They quickened their search, however, shaking out his sash and letting the scroll and book fall to the sand. Charmant tried to run but the slippery lakebed made him slow. He shouted and waved his arms.

Beneath the shallow water's surface, something wrapped itself around his ankle, cutting into his skin as he stepped forward. Mud slipped from beneath his left foot, and he toppled.

The slap of the cold water in Charmant's face surprised him and he gasped, pulling liquid and lake mud into his lungs. Struggling in the ankle-deep shallows, he tried to push himself up. Scrabbling through the silty mud, he pushed his face above the water for a moment, attempting to gasp in air. Instead, Charmant retched, coughing up lake water. Sucking in one short gasp of sweet air, the thing around his ankle yanked, dunking the prince.

Charmant dug his hands into the mud as the thing dragged him deeper. Pushing his hands into silt, he tried to find leverage so that he could free his ankle. The sediment slipped around him, clouding the water and making it impossible to see.

I must keep my head, thought Charmant. He took a moment, lungs screaming, and assessed the situation as best he could. The underwater creature held him firmly by the ankle, but he was a good swimmer. Perhaps, instead of pulling forward, he could push back and the thing around his ankle would relax, giving him the opportunity to free himself.

He tried it, pushing backward toward the encircling tendril.

I hope I am not feeding my foot into the maw of some horrible beast, he thought.

The grip on his ankle loosened slightly but remained strong. The prince's vision began fading, his mind getting muzzy. His hands scrabbled along the lake bottom like little crabs burrowing into the muck. They latched onto a rock and with the last of his strength, he pulled it out of the ground and twisted, lashing out.

His rock-laden fist punched something cartilaginous and springy. The thing let go of his ankle and pushed him up to the light, just as his vision went dark.

CHAPTER 31

Prince Charmant found himself gripping a tree branch, retching up lake water. Something slithered around his chest and squeezed, sending the last of the water shooting from his lips. He could breathe again, though his chest burned horribly. Looking down, he saw a long, green tentacle. It ended in five spindly fingers that pressed against his chest.

Forcing air into his lungs, Charmant screamed. He lost his grip on the branch and thrashed in the water. The fingers pealed themselves off his chest, revealing suction cups where the pads of a finger should be. The arm unwrapped itself from his body. He tried to swim away, but this time two tentacle hands grabbed him, one taking hold of his ankle, the other of his back. They hurled him toward the shore.

From there, the prince crawled to the sandy bank. His mud-covered body ached from head to foot, and he continued to cough and wheeze. But he crawled to his defiled clothes, pulled on his tunic, grabbed his hose, belt, boots, and the scroll, and stumbled into the orchard.

Glancing back, he remembered the key. Before he could consider running back to the beach to retrieve it, a domed head slid out of the lake, revealing a flat face. Saucer-sized eyes glowed white in the sunlight.

The prince turned toward the castle and ran.

CHAPTER 32

The castle halls bustled with frog-faced servants at every turn. Prince Charmant tried to walk among them with aplomb, even as he shook internally. He wanted to find somewhere undisturbed to hole up and cry.

Instead, he walked on shaking legs through halls filled with strange, flat faces, all eerily similar to that of the lake creature.

What are they? he asked himself, shivering at the memory of the tentacle-like fingers pressing against his chest. The prince stared at the servant's hands, noticing their length and irregularity of skin coloring for the first time. Normally, he tried not to observe servants when they could see him staring, but today he could not help it. His eyes fixed on long, thin fingers, wide, pale eyes, and flat faces. Some men stood bowlegged, but now Charmant observed many had bandy legs, some bending in an awkward direction. Others took hopping steps, as if some deformity prevented them from walking. The hopping servants wore large, comically wide shoes.

Charmant dripped his ways through halls, ignoring croaked offers to help.

He shut himself in his room, glancing about and checking his wardrobe for anyone hiding within. Placing the damp scroll on the bed, he went to the black-ringed washbasin. There, he scrubbed his body raw. The water within the basin soon turned black with filth and his washcloth befouled. The prince had to resort to scraping the mud from his person by rubbing a clean tunic against gritty skin. He worked to get every piece of lake debris off of him.

Finally clean, he dropped the lake-befouled clothes on the floor. The pile of dirt and muck turned his stomach, and he placed an unused tunic over the mess.

Wrapping his goose-pimpled skin in fur-lined blanket, he sat on his marital bed, and picked up the thick scroll. Unsealing it, he found a note from Loup Marchand, Elle's adoptive father along with a thick bundle of thin paper. Pulling a candle close, Prince Charmant began to read.

CHAPTER 33

MARCHAND'S LETTER

Dear Reader,

I have much to account to you about my adoptive daughter, Elle Marchand. I will admit now that everything I have written here is akin to acknowledging an association with the devil, with witchcraft, with all that is profane.

But you must understand that, at the time the child came into my life, I was but a poor merchant, a trader trying to bring honor, prestige, and money to my family and community. With her help, I have done this, leaving a legacy wherein the good, hopefully, outweighs the bad.

Reader, if your eyes are following these words, you likely have had strange encounters with me and my child. It means that, whether you wanted to or not, you have participated in something profane by association. For that, I am sorry. I hope it does not drive you mad, as it has so many others.

This brief letter was followed by a mass of closely written papers. Feeling their heft, Charmant smoothed the pages out on his bed into a small stack.

Flipping through the pile, Charmant saw that they were not laid out like a letter, but instead in a way with which he was only tangentially familiar. He had learned Latin from ledgers and records of legal proceedings. However, his father was a prodigious collector of the written word, insisting that one day everything important would be stored in books. Long ago, Charmant joined his eldest brother as their father toured them around the substantial castle library. The king had shown his boys one of the gems of his collection; a battered old book filled with stories. Some were histories and others imaginative tales.

A "manuscript" his father called it, though it was not illustrated or holy as were manuscripts from the monastery.

This pile of papers had the look and feel of such a manuscript.

Carefully, Prince Charmant picked up the first page and read the title.

Elle: Adoption and the strange days that followed

Raising an eyebrow, the prince read on:

I met Elle when I was a young man. At this writing, I am thirty-seven years old. I met her in a market in Constantinople at the age of twenty-three. That may shock you, as she appears childlike and young, very young. It may further shock you to discover that, when I found Elle, she was sold to me as a doll, a good luck charm.

The shopkeeper had her positioned upon a tiny doll's bed, surrounded by mice and birds. Nothing moved in the sweet display.

Having not yet established myself in the spice trade, I was dealing with the merchant, hoping to buy several fine rugs. I did not want a strange doll and her animal companions. But the man told me that she had brought years of luck to his shop and now that he was old and ready to sell the shop, he wanted a young man to have her. He implored me to buy her and gain my own luck.

Later, I was able to purchase the contents of the man's shop for a pittance, for he had not sold his business, but instead died soon after our trade.

At the time, I took Elle and her companions as the price of doing business. The man loaded her and all of her accoutrements into a crate. Later, I found the book which accompanied this note, along with a key, which I have enclosed here.

Arriving at my rented rooms, I stored the rugs and the crate in a corner. Then, I pulled out my accounting books and tried to determine if I had enough money and goods to set sail for France. I believed that, with some shrewd haggling and an agreement to work on the boat, I could make it home with both my cargo and my life intact.

Then, I heard a thump.

The crate in the corner gave another thump, shaking the rugs leaning upon it.

Thinking there might be a snake or other animal trapped in the box, I sidled up to it, unsure of what to do.

A sweet, soft voice called out in French.

"Help, monsieur, please I am trapped!"

I panicked, believing a demon or some other monster resided in the box. Then, as more soothing, sweet words came through the wooden slats, I found myself drawn closer. Surely, no demon would speak to me in my native tongue. They would not have that calming voice.

I found a bar and pried open the lid. Inside, a quantity of straw cushioned the doll and her companions. But now no doll or companions occupied the box. Instead, there lay a small girl, curled into a ball with her head between her knees. She looked up at me and smiled.

"Thank you, monsieur," she gasped, her face tear-streaked and her emerald eyes glistening.

I helped her out.

"What in the world are you doing in that box?" I asked.

"Oh, monsieur, it is a long, sad story," she told me. "I was cursed at birth by an evil witch. She turned me into the doll set you saw. The tiny doll and her little birds and bed, those were all formed from my own body and skin. She imparted the ability to change back only if that evil man sold me and I served my master as his lifelong slave. The witch wrapped my wrist in this."

She thrust out her arm.

An obsidian bracelet writhed around her wrist. The thin, sharp ornament dimpled the girl's skin, its leaves pushing in but not quite cutting. Black and blue bruises surrounded the jewelry as it seemed the girl had tried to move her bracelet to a more comfortable position without success.

"What is that?" I asked.

She hung her head.

"It is some kind of cursed object. The merchant who sold me should have given you a book and a key. They come with me wherever I go and, one day, someone with enough power will be able to release me from this curse."

I reached into the box, pulling out straw and piling it on the floor. The bottom of the box seemed to be a piece of wood, but upon further inspection, I found it was a false bottom and easily pried it open.

Therein I discovered a book and a key. A brief note accompanied the book. It explained that Elle was a good luck charm and had magical powers. However, the shop owner's child found her presence upsetting, and he had to rid himself of this strange, living charm. There was no explanation given about the book and the key.

I held the two objects up to her. She backed up a step.

"What am I to do with you? With these?" I asked.

"I have been able to provide those who own me with luck and fortune, and I hope I can do the same for you, monsieur," she murmured, eyes downcast. "The book and key are essential to my release, but they are painful for me to touch. If you would be kind enough to preserve them, I shall be in your debt. Perhaps, when you are rich, you will find it in your heart to discover someone powerful enough to release me from my curse. Until then, I would be pleased to travel with you and impart all the luck that I can."

This is what we did for many years. I returned to France often, but rarely stayed longer than a few months before setting sail again to another strange land. Always, my adopted daughter remained at my side.

She was an odd thing, appearing to be different ages each time we landed. It did not seem to discomfit any of my associates. Indeed, I am unsure if they even noticed my "daughter."

Elle caused no problems until we returned to France for permanent residence.

After traveling for so many years, I found it pleasant to take an estate inland, within the kingdom of my birth. I was proud to build a home near the castle and gain the ear of my king. I shared my wealth with the people of the surrounding villages, and I was lauded within the towns surrounding my chateau.

Hiring servants was a simple matter at first.

However, Elle caused a complication. Her presence in the French countryside did not pass unnoticed the way it had during our travels. In our chateau, my associates expected her to grow up as a young lady of means and wealth, as my daughter. She had difficulty doing this. Daily, she changed her size. On Monday, she would be doll-sized once again, sending her little mice friends or a few birds off to do her bidding. Tuesday, she would stand as tall as a debutante. Wednesday, she would shrink to the size of a four-year-old.

These changes drove our first two servants mad.

I scolded her, explaining that there would be talk, that she would be run out of town.

"You must grow like a normal child," I commanded her.

"I will try, father," she replied. "There is something strange about this land. Perhaps the magic needed to lift my curse is near."

Though Elle was odd, I also found her endearing and her plight tragic.

"I hope that is the case," I told her. I truly did hope with all of my heart. Elle had been nothing but helpful to me during our travels, and I wished her a happy, normal life. I wondered what she would look like once we discovered a way to lift the curse. She was unsure of her age, but I had traveled with her for over a decade at that point, so I knew she was older than she appeared.

Elle tried to keep her size consistent, and she succeeded most of the *time. She was as diligent and helpful as ever, but servants kept going mad.*

It would begin with dreams. I overheard talk amongst the servants. They never told me directly what happened, but whenever they whispered of their growing madness, it began with dreams.

One servant described them as pleasant, even enjoyable, until the moment when they turned into nightmares. When attempting to articulate what occurred in the nightmare, he gibbered and wept, and mentioned Elle's name.

It became clear that, no matter how much Elle restrained herself, no one but myself was immune to the dreams and the subsequent madness.

I asked her what we should do. Surely, we could not send a series of servants howling and raving to the small neighboring monastery. The monks cared for a few sick, mad, or elderly villagers. They were not prepared to take on a household of mad servants. Not only did we have nowhere to place our existing servants, but we would soon run out of people from the local area willing to work in the chateau.

Elle stared at me blankly for a long time.

"Perhaps we can send for servants from abroad?" she asked.

I had to explain to her that, even if we did, those servants might also go insane.

"I know of one place where none will go mad at my presence," she revealed. She told me of her birthplace, some moors in Brittania. The people living there had a strange mutation and they had lived with her for a time without going mad. Instead, they thrived in her presence.

I did not wish to travel again. I was settled, wealthy, and ready to enjoy my fortune. But I kept the idea in mind as I watched the servants in our home dwindle to three. I had to search farther and farther afield to find people willing to work in our chateau. Many who came were warned away by locals and never crossed our threshold. Those who did, went mad.

I paid for the Hôpital Marchand and the monks broke ground while Elle and I packed our bags for Brittania.

The blasted heath and its occupants

We traveled lightly, as we had done so often when I was an aspiring merchant and she, a tiny doll-like child. Our trip went smoothly, though we left the last town behind many miles before our destination.

Being a merchant, I always tried to travel in the company of other people. After all, people have money and can trade. Traveling with Elle's company alone through the heather and bog-covered lands she claimed as her home terrified me. Something, some miasma soaked into my bones, tainting them with the wretchedness of the place.

Setting out across the moors, I was initially enchanted by waves of green, speckled by white-headed cottongrass and the occasional June flower. I did not know the names of many of the plants, but the small stars of color broke up the tedious monochromatic gray sky stretching above us. No one populated the desolate land. Instead, abandoned and crumbling stone homes covered in a powdery gray lichen peppered the moors.

Once, I suggested sheltering in one of these structures during a surprise cloudburst. But Elle told me the lichen spreads to skin, infecting it like a disease. After that, I steered my horse clear of the evil hovels.

That first day on the moorland was quite pleasant. Our horses did not mind the exertion as they plodded across the rolling hills of the high country. It wasn't until the second day, when we encountered the blasted heath, that the dampness and oppression of the place affected me and our equine companions.

On that second day, our horses crested a rise and then stopped, refusing to go on. Looking out at the view ahead of us, I could not blame them.

Below lay a tangle of slopes and glens, each bereft of greenery. The chalky soil lay barren and gray on cracked, dry earth. As we watched, a rabbit traversing a nearby slope slipped, skidding into the gray soil. It righted itself, pink nose twitching and ears swiveling. Then, it started *sinking into that ominous ground. The animal struggled, trying to pull itself free of the strange sticking soil. Instead, it sank more rapidly with each frantic movement.*

I looked to Elle, my good luck charm and my adoptive daughter, hoping for direction away from this blasphemous land. Instead, she pointed across the hillsides, sketching out a precarious path for us to follow.

I trailed her assiduously as we traversed that malevolent land. Where her horse stepped, mine did likewise. It took two days to leave that atrocious heath behind, only for us to journey into noisome wetlands. The hateful miasma of this place even now lingers in my nose.

Rotting things lurked beneath the marshes, and each step stirred up the fetid stink of death. Below the film of water lay pitfalls just as dangerous as the sinking dust that spread across unwholesome glens to our rear. Again, I followed Elle step for step, trusting her to lead me through the brooding land of her forebears just as she'd lead me through many trades during my career.

At last, we arrived at a small stretch of dry land, a barrier between the wetlands behind us and the shallow lake ahead. A crude dock held two boats and a small shack. Emerging from the brittle building, a strange man wrapped from head to toe in rags shielded his eyes and blinked at us.

Elle smiled at him, and he fell to his knees, pressing his rag-covered face to the ground.

I was baffled by the reaction, but Elle took it in stride, so I did as well.

She jumped down from her horse, tying it to the swollen wood of the man's shack. Doing likewise, I watched as she stepped onto one of the flat-bottomed boats. Again, I followed the woman and watched in astonishment as the man stood, remaining half-folded in a bow. He released the boat from its moorings and stepped onto the damp planks. With a pole, he ferried us to an island located in the middle of the lake. Rotting mud and thatch houses dotted the damp earth, but no people appeared upon our arrival. This is not the norm. I have visited small hamlets many times. When a stranger comes within the midst of a secluded village, people often swarm them, seeking new goods.

In the case of this lonely island, nothing and no one stirred.

The ferryman leapt off the boat and dragged it ashore, moving more surely in the muck than he had on dry land. Once he moored the boat, he ran to a small shelter built beside the landing spot. Standing just inside, he reached up and pushed, then jumped back. The loud clanging of a bell broke the hush of this abandoned-looking place.

Gray-green heads peeked out from doorways. Strange, pale eyes scanned the boat. Then, a cry went up and the inhabitants flooded out of the shanties. There were more people than I could imagine occupying this scattering of twenty or so shacks.

Some wore ragged clothing; others wore nothing as they loped down to the waterfront. When they arrived at the bell house, they fell to the ground and bowed, faces pressed into the mud.

I watched as Elle scanned the odd people. I saw her face darken in annoyance and I witnessed her transformation. Specks of light floated around the girl, coalescing around her head and stretching her body toward the heavens. Her feet remained on the ground, but her body stretched up and up, growing knife thin. Her clothing, always impeccable even in this muck, absorbed into her and she stood, towering and naked, her white skin gleaming with an inner light. Her voice grew deep and guttural as she shouted strange words at the people.

They covered their heads and buried their faces deeper into the muck. I cowered away from the woman who I'd once called daughter. In that moment, in the place of her birth, she turned inhuman. If she'd grown wings, I would have called her an angel, of Heaven or Hell, I do not know. Instead, she towered over all and yelled like some pagan goddess.

Turning to the swamp we'd just traversed, she roared into the cold, damp air.

Something moved just under the liquid surface. Then something else.

Suddenly, dozens of man-like things burst from the water, reaching five-tentacled hands out to Elle as she raised her own arms and called them forth in a language unknown to me.

The things in the water lifted their white-eyed, frog-like heads and gazed at her, nodding eagerly to the rhythm of her strange words.

Elle turned back to the people crowded on the shore. Looking at them with fresh eyes, I could see the frog-like, tentacle monstrosities into which these people were transforming.

Five younger men, all with a strange gait and popping, frog-like eyes, stood and cowered.

Elle shrank back to herself, to the girl I had known for over a decade. Her clothes grew around her, sloughing water and mud. Once again, she appeared as a child. My mind tried to hold on to her as a tall, goddess-like being commanding armies of monsters in the boggy depths. But the blasphemous image slipped away. Even now, as I write this, the memory slides from my mind whenever I try to recall her strange, chromatic luminosity. It is crowded out by a false memory, one in which the people of that island open their arms and embrace Elle. One in which my adoptive daughter tells them how I rescued her, and they vow to send seven sons every five years to serve in our house.

That is why I wrote this letter, here in a mist-shrouded, seaside town. We have booked passage back to France and I cannot help but be filled with fear. What am I bringing to my homeland? Are those monsters confined to the moors of Brittania, or do they swim beneath the sea, surviving in the sweet lakes and rivers of my beloved France?

I do not know and the memory fades. But the terror remains.

I must rest now. Do not give Elle the power to remove that bracelet. I do not know what she is, or what she would do to this world, to France, if she were free. But I do know that she will seek the power to release herself forevermore.

Do not set her free.

CHAPTER 34

The letter shook in Charmant's shivering fingers. On his bed, wrapped in a blanket, the prince could not stop shaking. The fading light sent long shadows stretching across his room, like long, tentacled fingers.

A servant knocked, then entered and began lighting candles around the room. Charmant gazed into the frog-like face of the man calmly lighting each wick as if he were a normal member of the staff, not some strange cult filled with people turning into a monstrosity from Hell. As if the man did not worship the new princess, a woman - no, a demon - who had bewitched the prince and come to this place, his seat of power, his family home.

They have overrun the castle without one drop of spilled blood, thought the prince. He could not take his eyes off the servant, who noticed Charmant's stare and smiled faintly, licking his lips with a long tongue.

A gong sounded from the dining room.

In spite of all that Marchand's letter had told him, how much had changed in his heart and mind, the prince must still appear at dinner.

It struck him then that Marchand may have, like his staff, gone mad. Perhaps this letter was a record of his lunatic ravings. It certainly seemed as if a disturbed mind had written it.

He would have to read it again and discern the truth of it. For now, though, he had to go to dinner, keep up appearances, and assure himself that his father, the last family he had in the world, was alright.

I do not know what she is, he thought, *but I can protect my last remaining family member from any danger she might pose.*

With that resolve in his heart, Charmant rolled up the letter and sealed it with a bit of wax.

He looked around to see if the frog-faced servant still scurried about his large room, but the man had gone. Before his dressers could enter, Charmant tucked the letter into a leather pouch he'd carried during his time as a soldier. Inside lay the tinctures and bandages, needles and thread they'd all carried to tend their wounds.

The musty smell of the tincture-filled bladders met his nostrils as he stuffed the letter inside the pouch. For a moment, his mind wandered to the last battle he'd fought. The one after which a messenger shared the bad news that his entire family, save his father, had perished in the plague. The world smelled of copper and his friend, Alain, cried out. Charmant struggled and fought his way to his friend's voice, but he was too late. The man lay dead, an arrow pinning his heart.

In his castle room, clutching one of the remnants of his life as the youngest son of many, resolve stole over Charmant.

I will protect my family. I must find out if my wife is a monster and keep my father safe while doing so. No more deaths. No more deaths.

He tucked the pouch into the back of his wardrobe, emerging to see two servants bustle in with clean tunics and hose, ready to dress him.

Dinner that evening was a test of nerves and wit for the prince. He managed to eat, though his stomach churned, and his mind spun with questions and quandaries. How could he best protect his father?

Perhaps send him away? Sending him away would be the most effective method, but how? He was the son and his father, the king. He could no more order his father away than an ant could lift his castle.

Finally, after Charmant took an obligatory bite of the last course, he told his father he'd like to retire early.

His stomach sank and guilt pricked his throat as his father's face turned from annoyed to afraid.

"Are you quite well, my son?" he asked.

"Yes, of course, Your Majesty. I simply wish to rest."

"Of course, you must gather your strength for the ride to the monastery tomorrow. How many days will you stay there before your return home?"

Charmant started. His visit to the monastery had slipped his mind. Had he made travel arrangements just that day? It seemed a lifetime ago.

"I believe two or three days, Your Majesty, no more."

His father frowned, "I leave the judgment to you, but if you wish to stay longer and make a more thorough inspection of the hospital, send word so that I may know you are safe, but delayed."

Charmant looked at his father whose gentle eyes were filled with concern. Love and gratitude made his heart ache.

"I shall give you no reason for concern, Your Majesty," smiled the prince, stepping to his father's side and kneeling. "Goodnight, father," he whispered, kissing a wrinkled hand.

The king looked at him with surprise, a smile turning up his lips.

"Goodnight my son. Safe travels and blessing be upon you."

Leaving the great hall, Charmant paced to his room. His brows furrowed at each frog-faced man he spotted. Hadn't the letter said something about no more than seven men coming to serve at a time?

I will have to read it again, he thought. Stomach twisting at the prospect, Charmant walked through his bedroom door to find two frog-faced men ransacking his room.

CHAPTER 35

O ne man, lank black hair obscuring his features, was pushing the bed back into place, while the other stood on a stool, examining the top of the wardrobe.

"What are you doing?" demanded Charmant.

The man on the stool whipped around, startled. He wobbled for a moment, then his hands gripped the wardrobe door and stuck, the stool toppling beneath him. Holding onto the piece of furniture for a moment, he leapt from his perch as the door creaked out, landing safely on all fours.

The black-haired man gently put Charmant's mattress down. He bowed; every movement filled with sarcasm.

"Your Highness," he croaked, smirking as he straightened. "I do apologize. We seem to have lost our key and were hoping to recover it." The man's eyebrows quirked meaningfully.

Charmant's stomach dropped. Even though he knew what the man was referring to, he kept up the charade.

Thinking fast, he said, "I am sure that there is a spare key. Go ask M. Girard for a new one."

The black-haired man, shook his head regretfully.

"Sadly, there are no duplicates for this key."

Balling his shaking hands, Charmant tried a new tack.

"I would be alone. If I see a key, I will return it to the hall guard. I am sure they will get it back to you."

"Oh, you are too kind, Your Highness," the man bowed again, adding a flourish to his gesture. "But you see, you do not know my name."

"What is it?" sighed the prince, projecting irritation at the man's attempts to be clever. The other man stood, bowed briefly, and walked to his companion, tugging his arm.

"Cormac, Your Majesty."

"Indeed. I shall tell the guards to pass the key on to you. Now, leave."

Cormac glared at Charmant as his companion all but dragged him out of the room. Cormac reached back and slammed the door shut behind them.

Hands shaking and brow covered in cold sweat, Charmant dragged the fallen stool to the door, blocking it from any other unexpected entrants. He then opened his wardrobe and removed all of his soldiering tools.

Setting aside the clothing, he piled his hardened leather and wood shield, battle sword, a few knives, and several pouches. His armor loomed in the corner, mounted when he returned from battle. But the rest of his things he'd shoved to the back of the wardrobe, burying his tools as well as his memories of his soldiering days.

Now, as he touched each object, he recalled the long marches, the bloody melees and battles. Most of all, he remembered his friends. While his closest companion and staunchest supporter, Alain, had died, others remained loyal to him.

He wondered if now was the time to call his friends. But how could he, when the person taking over his castle was his wife and her people? When not a drop of blood had been shed in the process?

Perhaps the monastery visit is providential, thought Charmant. *I can ask the abbot about demons and glean information about Elle from the madmen.*

He looked down at his things. Even though they'd avoided bloodshed by passively allowing Elle's people full run of the castle, he'd keep his battle implements close by. One never knew when a good sword or sharp knife might come in handy.

Returning the clothes to the wardrobe, Charmant placed a knife at his bedside. He placed the sword and other weaponry beneath his bed, where he could easily access it. Next, he examined each pouch. One was a kit for cleaning his blades. This he placed next to the swords and knives. Another contained his personal seal and some papers. The last was his medical kit, the one in which he'd stuffed the letter from Marchand.

Conflicting feelings warred within him. His hands itched to pull out the letter, to trace each word until he could uncover the truth or madness behind every line. Another feeling kept his hands still, causing his mind to fog and entire body to slump. It was exhaustion.

In one day, he had discovered that he'd made a terrible choice of wife. He found that the woman his body yearned for, that he thought he'd breathed for, might be a monster. But then, she might not, and this could all be a mistake. The one thing he did know was that her servants had overrun his castle and stolen the book from him. Now, they sought the key to her bracelet. A bracelet that trapped her somehow. A bracelet he now thought should not be removed from her person.

Charmant flopped down in bed. His body vibrated with nerves. He was both completely exhausted and eager to go to the monastery and find out more about Elle.

Maybe I should just ask her, he thought, then dismissed the idea. How could he ask a woman, his wife, if she was a monster?

Hand wrapped around his dagger's hilt, he closed his eyes and tried to relax.

Voices stirred him from a doze. Someone speaking outside his door. Springing up, he strode to the door on quiet feet. The contralto voice of his new wife drifted through.

"The door is blocked, I cannot open it," she said.

Charmant looked down at the chair. It hadn't budged. He didn't think it would actually block someone trying to get in, just slow them. Fuzzily, he put a hand on the chairback, intending to move it. Then he remembered his wife could be a monster.

Elle's voice continued to drift in from the other side of the hall, as well as the murmurings of a male voice. Charmant stopped paying attention. He stealthily moved the chair and, when the conversation lulled, he flung the door open.

"Your Highness?" whispered a startled Elle. Her wide eyes flickered down to the dagger in his hand.

"My Lady. I would request that you sleep in your own quarters this evening."

"Of course," she curtsied and gave the hall guard a raised eyebrow.

The guard bowed to her and the prince.

"I shall escort the princess, sire," he mumbled.

The two walked away, the guard showing Elle to another room down the passageway. It once belonged to Charmant's sister, Charlotte. He gulped, remembering the young woman who had resided inside only a year previous. She, determined to be a spinster, had resisted her parent's attempts to marry her off. Now, as Charmant watched another enter her room, he wished she had been forced out of the castle, isolated from the dread disease that killed her.

Visions of his sister haunted him. Her auburn hair always clouding around her face in unruly fluffs, she closely resembled their mother, which meant she looked little like the rest of her siblings. Yet, she was the strangest and most invigorating of his clan. Always reading and writing, she enjoyed dressing plainly and sneaking into the village. Charmant's eyes pricked with tears. If she had been allowed to travel, as she'd begged. If she was born a man and had moved to the monastery, perhaps she would be alive today. Perhaps he could consult her wisdom and share the burdens he now bore.

But she lay dead, buried in the family graveyard. And now his strange wife, a woman who was perhaps a monster, lay in Charlotte's room.

After closing and blocking the door, Charmant tucked himself into bed. He banished thoughts of his siblings, instead, focusing on tomorrow's journey. He eyed the small window, contemplating opening one shutter to ensure the morning light woke him, but he determined it was not worth the risk. Though the window was narrow, it would not be safe to leave it wide and inviting.

Sighing, Charmant tucked his weaponry about him and closed his eyes, praying for a light, but dreamless sleep.

CHAPTER 36

Down the hall, Elle opened her door. She had put on a show for the prince, but it was clear he suspected her.

She gestured to the guard.

"I must begin my work," she told him. "Keep up the charade for now. The prince and king must not know."

The man kneeled before her, face touching the ground.

Elle stamped her foot and stuck out her hand.

"Do you have them?"

The man fumbled at the pouch at his belt. Untying it, he handed her the leather bag. She peered inside. Diamonds only half-filled the bag.

"This is everything?" she demanded, her voice rising.

The man trembled and lay flat, smashing his face into the cold stone.

Elle walked on and over him with impatient feet, each frosty step burned into his back as her anger poured ice through her skin.

Sobbing softly, the man did not move.

Her steps warmed as they took her to the cellar door, where she descended rapidly. Inside, a flurry of activity greeted her. The men had gathered everything she'd requested. She'd hoped for more diamonds, but the king had used crystal for most of his wedding decorations.

Pointing, she said, "You, you, and you, carry these items to the blacksmith's foundry. I will keep him sleeping while we work."

With that, she left the cellar, followed by three men lugging all that they had gathered.

She and her men stopped at the door of the blacksmith's workshop. A light glowed within.

"Did you send him an extra wineskin as I ordered?" asked Elle.

One of the men nodded, his protuberant eyes wide and fearful.

Sighing, she opened one of her own pouches and pinched out a powder. Then she motioned for one of her men to knock.

The door swung open, revealing a small man with huge arms and a slightly hunched back. His eyes widened in surprise when he saw the princess and he stumbled into a drunken bow. Elle smiled.

She motioned for the most human of her minions to speak.

"Good evening. My Lady hopes to consult with you. One of her jewels has come loose. The chateau blacksmith fixed such things, and you are reputed to be the best in the land. Would you take a look?"

The blacksmith's eyes widened. He licked his lips.

"I am not the one to deal with jewels," he slurred. "Swords and plows are more my line."

He swayed, eyes flicking between the man who had spoken and the princess on his doorstep.

"If it pleases Your Highness, I will take a look at it. If I cannot fix it, the royal jeweler certainly can."

Leaving the door open, he turned and stumbled inside.

The smithy stank of wine, hot metal, and fire. Elle saw the wineskin on the floor, some of the golden liquid dripping out.

One of her men rushed to pick it up. He presented the open top to Elle, and she sprinkled the powder inside. The man shook the container gently, mixing wine and powder to create a sweet slurry.

The locksmith lumbered to a long, low table. He stared at the mess upon it, as if wondering how it got there. The Noamhite with the wineskin offered it to the blacksmith with a froggy smile.

"You dropped this," he croaked.

The blacksmith wrenched it from the man's hand, reaching his other hand back to strike the servant.

"Shall we share a drink before you begin work?" asked Elle in a light tone.

The blacksmith stayed his hand, looked at the princess and blinked.

"Yes, of course," he slurred, weighing the wineskin in his hand. There did not appear to be much left.

Elle smiled as another of her minions pulled out a new wineskin, handing it to her.

"To your good health," she declared, raising the bladder of wine.

"And yours," mumbled the blacksmith, pouring the rest of the wine down his throat.

Elle waited, watching the man as he swallowed.

Smacking his lips, he smiled.

"Now, what can I do for you, my..." he stopped, his eyes droop-ing. All at once, he fell back, crashing down upon his bench and falling into a deep sleep.

"Get him to his room," she told two of her men. "You, bring the rest of the metal in."

The servants lugged the huge man back to his sleeping alcove. The other brought the various metal bits Elle had requested.

When all three men returned, Elle instructed one man to stoke the fire. The other two heeded her instructions as she showed them how to weld their meager store of diamonds to three wheels. From there, she showed them how to craft the various parts necessary to allow the wheel to rotate as they applied pressure to a short handle. Finally, she showed them how to attach the remaining small store of diamonds to the end of a scraper.

"This will have to do," declared Elle as dawn brightened the blacksmith's smithy. She eyed the sunlight impatiently. "We must begin grinding that stone. We must break through. And we must find that key."

CHAPTER 37

Falling into dizzying blackness, Charmant's dreaming mind grappled at the world around him, trying to locate a handhold to stop his descent. Nothing filled the surrounding void.

Moments later, dots of light in every hue pricked the darkness. The lights did not show him where he was going or where he had been, they simply appeared as he dropped. The sensation was both frightening and inevitable. The pit of his stomach twisted, alternatively pushing bile up to his throat and dropping like a stone to his feet. Chill air bit him, frosting his clothes and exposed skin as he fell. Any moment he would hit the ground and be struck senseless. His body told him to prepare for the landing and, at each new light or change in air pressure, he braced for the fatal landing.

Dropping, dropping into the never-ending pit, Charmant struggled to comprehend what was happening.

Am I falling through a hole in the world? Am I flying through the stars?

Reaching out a hand, he felt nothing but icy air whizzing by. Instead, he focused on the points of light. Each gleamed in a different hue. While one shone bright white, another turned azure, and another darkened to emerald.

The lights entranced him, their display calming his mind while his body continued to grasp at the nothingness around him, seeking a nonexistent handhold. The prince watched as the lights cycled, bright white, gold, azure, emerald, viridian, scarlet, violet, silver, then back to bright white.

"Interesting," he whispered.

At his word, the lights blinked off, then on. Off, then on.

Fear clotted his throat, stopping a scream before it could begin. The lights grew larger, closer. They blinked off, then on.

In a final blink, all of the lights remained off but for two bulbous white, two smaller emerald, and four tiny silver lights. These eight lights stared at him, glared at him, blinking asynchronously.

Eyes. They are eyes and they are watching me.

Charmant tried to breathe, tried to scream. Instead, the eyes pressed down on him, choking him, freezing his every muscle as he continued to fall.

A new sensation hit him, something gripping his forearm, halting his fall. The abrupt end to his descent wrenched his shoulder and pain radiated up into his neck and down to his wrist. The pain of the arrested fall almost obscured the pain of the grip itself. He looked at the dark, slithering thing that held him in place. Its blackness distinct against his frosted skin. Red blood trickled from where the snaking tentacle bit into his flesh.

Charmant could not hold his terror back any longer.

He filled his lungs with freezing air and screamed.

A loud thump woke Charmant, pulling him back from the sharpness and the cold. He lay sweating in his large bed, blankets tangled about him as he gasped at the close summer air. Pale morning light seeped between the shutters.

Sitting up and looking around, Charmant blinked to bring the room into focus. He sat in his room, on his bed.

Scraping sound reached his ear, along with a man swearing softly to himself. The common accent calmed the prince's beating heart. One of his countrymen pushed at the door, not one of the princess' lackeys.

Charmant groaned and flopped back onto his bed. He looked around for his dagger and found it on the floor where he must have pushed it while dreaming. It remained in its sheath, but he decided that a dagger near the bed would look strange to the servants.

A scraping sound screeched across the flags as the servant outside pushed against the door.

The prince reached down and tossed the dagger on top of his discarded clothing from the previous evening. Pain ran up his arm, radiating from two places. One was his forearm, which appeared red in the dim light. The other was his shoulder.

He sat up again and stared at his wounded left forearm. His sleeve was ripped into tatters and blood seeped from a thin gash. The world narrowed around him until blood filled his vision.

"What?" he began.

"Your Highness," a male voice interrupted his thoughts.

Charmant's heart banged into the top of his rib cage as he whipped his head up. The young, brown-haired man who normally served him bowed and reached out.

"May I help to bind that wound, sire? Or shall I call the doctor?"

"Have you knowledge of how to bind a wound?" demanded Charmant, his voice coming out high and fast. He cleared his throat and took a deep breath, trying to calm the terror still shooting through his veins.

This is not a dream. I am safe.

Charmant tried to convince his body of what his mind knew to be true. Refocusing on the young man, he realized he'd missed every word the servant had spoken.

"I am sorry," the prince forced out slowly. "I did not hear what you said."

The servant bowed and repeated himself, his face calm, as if he saw sweating, bleeding princes tangled up in bedding and screeching imperious questions every day.

"Before I came to service in the castle, I apprenticed under an apothecary. I believe I can bind your wound so that it heals cleanly. It is not so deep."

The prince looked at the wound and winced.

"I would be grateful for your assistance. My medical pouch from my campaigns is right there," he pointed. "Take what you need."

The young man bowed and scurried over to the bag, removing a salve and some bandages. He left the needle and thread and other items. With sure hands he dipped a cloth into the cold wash basin and wiped the blood away. Then, he poured wine into a goblet, mixed the salve, and applied it to the prince's skin.

Charmant hissed through his teeth at the stabbing pain but said nothing. The young man then wrapped the wound tightly, but not so tight as to deaden the extremity.

"Strange," he muttered.

"What is it?" asked Charmant.

"Your wound perfectly encircles your forearm, as if you were caught in a snare. It is not something one often sees."

Charmant blinked at the young man, trying to decide if he should glare at him for his impertinence, or take in the information and appreciate the observation. He kept his mouth shut.

The young man looked at him and saw Charmant's mouth set in a thin, hard line. He dropped his eyes in a way that reminded Charmant disturbingly of Elle's servants.

"I am sorry, Highness," he murmured.

Charmant felt a twinge in his heart. He'd seen how those strange people groveled. It was odd and disturbing. He could not expect the same worship from his people, people from whom he was only separated by circumstance.

He smiled at the young man.

"Thank you for your help. I shall remember this day and reward you and your family. What is your name?" asked Charmant, embar-

rassed he didn't know it already. He realized he hadn't bothered to
learn any of the new servant's names. Perhaps he was protecting his
heart against the loss of more companions, after the plague had killed
off so many of the men and woman who had been there throughout
his childhood. Perhaps he was more like Elle than he wished,
expecting obedience as a birthright.

"My name is Yves Joly, Your Highness."

"Thank you, Yves. Could you tell me, are all of the usual castle
servants back to their posts today?"

"Yes, Your Highness. The Princess Elle's men were on duty last
night, and I was told that they discovered a flood in one of the cellars
and spent the night rescuing the stores. So, the castle attendants have
returned to their posts." Yves stopped talking and flicked his gaze up
to Charmant, then back to the floor. It was as if the man didn't know
where to look.

"Thank you, Yves. I am always concerned about my people and
my castle. Please, do not hesitate to tell me what you see and hear,
particularly if it is strange."

Yves returned his gaze to the prince's face, his expression relaxing
as he saw Charmant's kind smile. The servant dipped his head in an
awkward bow, as he still knelt in front of the prince.

"I will be dressing for a ride to the monastery today. Will you and
the dressers attend me?"

"Of course, Your Highness. I shall fetch them," Yves stood, bowed
again and scampered out the door.

Charmant looked after the man. He had been ignorant of the
castle's goings on for too long. He needed to get involved in the business of ruling. It struck him that he now had access to great wealth.
Perhaps he could use it not just to hold his power and place in the
world, but to help his people directly.

Musing about the many needs of the villages he and his father
ruled, the horror of his dream slipped away.

CHAPTER 38

Men swarmed the prince, cleaning and dressing him. Some looked at the bandage askance, but none tried to remove it.

To everyone's surprise, Charmant thanked his dressers and Yves, wishing them all a pleasant day. He ordered Yves to tell the cook to prepare a meal fit to eat on horseback, for he was off to the monastery today. The man, looking pleased at having been selected by the prince for this task, bowed his way out of the room.

Charmant took the moment alone to affix his many weapons and pouches from his soldiering days, including the pouch which held Marchand's letter. He wished to be off as quickly as possible so that he could return armed with knowledge and, perhaps, a plan.

Dressed for his ride, Charmant strode out of his room and into the hall. He walked to his father's door, nodding at the guards and poking his head through the entrance. The rise and fall of his father's dim form reassured him that the one family member he had left in this world was sleeping peacefully.

"No dreams, Father," whispered Charmant. "In the lord God's name, I pray you have no dreams."

If the guards thought his words were strange, Charmant could not say. They bowed as he left and stood quietly until he left the hall.

Yves met Charmant at the stables with a frown. The prince's stallion was prepared with the meal, along with other necessities of travel, tied to the saddle.

"Will you come, Yves?" he asked.

Yve's stubbled cheeks flushed as he stammered, "Your Highness, I would be honored to join you, but I will slow you down. I have never ridden a fast horse. Only the carthorse my father keeps for plowing."

"The monastery is but a half-day's ride from here. Your slow horse will do just fine. Summon a guard to join us and we shall be off."

Yves scampered away, returning quickly with a guard. The prince vaguely recognized the man by his light hair. Many of the guards had the same brown hair, but this guard's head shone bright and blonde. Searching for the man's name, the prince mounted up and set his horse walking.

The party soon left the castle walls and headed toward the monastery. And the prince, determined to enjoy the ride, decided the guard's name would come to him in its own time.

The day was fine and so was the ride. It took them through the nearest village, across a field, and to the Abbey Road. They passed farms and vineyards, enjoying the warming air and golden sun as they trotted down the well-traveled dirt path.

Arriving at the far side of the monastery's outer wall, they listened as the bells struck None.

"Let us take our meal here, outside of the wall," declared the prince, dismounting. "The monks will be at their praying, and I do not wish to interrupt their holy work."

The men fell to the baskets and bladders of food and wine, digging into meat pies, almonds, walnuts, dried fruit, and a few early plums.

Charmant relished moments like this. He recalled many a meal with his men. Awaiting a battle, traveling between villages, or simply pulling guard duty along the border of his land. Travel food was the best food, and it was always eaten with zeal and equanimity, with little regard to station or class.

After completing their meal, the men mounted their horses and cantered to the portcullis set into the outer bailey. Allowing his guard to announce him, the prince watched as four monks managed the gate and the greeting, allowing his small party through. Once inside, a monk led them through the dirt passage which encircled the monastery, showing them to the gate which provided access to the abbey proper.

Charmant expected the monks to be indoors, worshipping and performing their various duties. He thought he would be greeted by the abbot and his prior. Instead, an entire monastery's worth of monks stood just beyond the entrance, with the abbot at the congregation's head.

Dismounting, Charmant and his companions bowed to the man of God. The abbot smiled, laugh lines deepening on his round face. He sketched a rapid bow, springing up and down with the energy of a much younger man.

"Greetings, Your Highness. Welcome to our humble abbey. I am Abbot Jacques Laurent It has been a long while since you were last here. I believe, during your last visit, you were but a boy. Now you are a man, wed to Lady Marchand. How pleased we are to see you. Come, pray with us, join us for a meal, spend the night, and in the morning, you shall meet the unfortunates housed in our hospital."

The abbot turned and motioned to the twenty or so monks arrayed behind him. They filed back inside, Charmant, the abbot, and his two men following.

After prayers and an excellent meal, the abbot asked Charmant if he'd like to accompany him to his offices.

The prince followed the abbot and his prior to the man's inner sanctum. The office consisted of a long room, lined with books and scrolls. Two desks sat at the end of the hall-like room, one large and commanding. The other smaller, and positioned behind the first. The abbot sat at the larger desk and the prior, the smaller.

Charmant took a seat in front of them both, ready to listen.

The abbot began.

"Many decades ago, M. Marchand endowed our humble abbey and commissioned us with caring for his servants, all of whom were struck by a mysterious madness. From your missive, I gather you know about M. Marchand's endowment, and you may even have some understanding of the illness from which his servants suffer.

"I am doubtful, Your Highness, if you understand the results of this illness, but I shall warn you now. Those poor madmen believe many strange things. They tell stories of devilry in the chateau. I have, myself, visited Chateau Marchand many times and can share that I have never seen any demons or devils within.

"M. Marchand showed kindness to these people. In spite of the accusations they alleged against him and his daughter, he built a hospital to house them and provided us with a generous stipend to keep them in comfort for the rest of their days. Additionally, when each was admitted to the Hôpital Marchand, he provided their families with money so that they would not go without. Quite a generous person.

"I hope that, when you see the great care we take in attending to the bodies and souls of these unfortunates, you will see fit to continue the legacy begun by M. Marchand and carried on by the Marchand de Noelles family.

"As you visit them, please remember that these unfortunates are mad. They will say and do things which shall disturb you. God knows they have been tested and, with our help, they may yet receive God's grace and find sanity in heaven."

Charmant tried not to gape at this little speech. His mind raced as he put together the information the abbot shared. None of it was completely unknown, except that these mad people accuse both Marchand and Elle of something.

I wonder what.

Standing, the prince bowed to the abbot.

"Thank you for your warning, Father. May God keep you."

The abbot, his face lighting with pleasure, stood himself and bowed in return.

"My prior shall take you to your rooms, Highness. We will tour the hospital in the morning after prayers. Good night to you and God bless you."

CHAPTER 39

Elle attended dinner with the king, keeping up her charming facade. With the prince out of the castle and the key still missing, she was more determined than ever to remain in the king's good graces until the moment of her departure.

When dinner came to an end, she retired to her room. She still needed to find the key and check on her people's progress with the primitive grinders they'd built. She'd taken an advanced technology and tried to pair it with the crude materials of this planet. Who knew how well the grinders would work, though they were better than metal picks and shovels.

First, though, the key.

Sitting on her bed, she shut her eyes and melted her mass. Shrinking her human form, she emitted as much unformed ooze as the bracelet would allow. The pooled substance flashed with inner chromatic light. Now doll-sized, Elle shaped small animals of all types, amassing a veritable menagerie of beetles, mice, flies, rats, and other creatures.

The small animals scuttled away, squirming under doors and

scrambling through mouseholes; they made their way into the prince's rooms and began to search.

A long while later, Elle gathered her mass to her, reabsorbing the animals until her body returned to its full size. Cold anger poured out of her, sending shocks of ice and frost across the summer-warm bed beneath her. The key was not in his room. It was not anywhere she could imagine a human would hide it.

She pushed the fury down, locking it into a cage of resolve. The prince would return in a day or two, and she would be ready for him. She would force him to tell her where he had hidden the key.

Stomping to her favorite trunk, she flung it open, taking inventory of the herbs and powders within. Her truth serum sat in its pouch, ready to loosen princely lips. She just needed a pinch of the stuff mixed into a small glass of wine and he would tell her all.

Returning the serum to the trunk, a glimmer of silver caught her eye. Summoning the object, she watched as one of her shoes made its way out of a tangle of silks.

"You are always hiding from me, aren't you?" she asked the tiny shoe. She had resorbed its companion, but this shoe managed to allude her. An idea struck and she smiled.

Closing the trunk, Elle checked her physical form. All looked as one would expect. Pretty, human, clothed. That accounted for, she and the shoe paced out of her room, down the hall, and into her husband's bedchamber.

A large wardrobe sat in the corner.

"Go on," she instructed the shoe. "Find a hiding place."

The silver shoe squirmed across the ground, hopping up and hitting the wardrobe door. Sighing, Elle pulled the door open and allowed the trinket to jump into the large wooden box.

Objects massed inside, leaving little room for her silver slipper to remain undiscovered. Elle helped the shoe by tugging an old dusty shirt from the bottom of the wardrobe. She caught the little shoe, feeling its resistance as she wrapped it.

Damn thing, I have imbued it with my essence for far too long.

Her lips drew up into a smile.

It is the perfect trinket to scare the hell out of that annoying prince.

Jamming the wrapped shoe into an old boot, she slammed the wardrobe shut.

Exuding a bit of water, she cleaned the wardrobe's greasy dust off her hands. Then, smiling to herself, she danced out of the room, through the great hall, and into the cellar. The large storage space no longer held food and wine. Her men had lied to the steward, telling him it had flooded with muck from the latrine. They'd removed all of the foodstuffs and lugged out buckets of mud, bringing in more tools and planks to shore up the tunnel.

Walking through the shaft now, Elle redistributed her mass, putting more musculature into her arms. A Noamhite carrying a bucket of mud up the slope dropped it at the sight of her and let out a croaking gasp. He immediately pressed his face to the ground.

Elle stepped past him, ignoring the man and marching toward the sounds of scraping and chiseling at the end of the tunnel. Her fury dulled as she listened. It sounded promising.

She turned the corner and watched the men; all had their backs to her and all worked hard to grind the stone before them.

One man stepped back, wiping his brow. He spotted Elle out of the corner of his eye and gasped, nudging his companions. They all turned and bowed to the ground.

Elle saw the progress they'd made and frowned. It looked as if they had barely scratched the surface of the quartz. She pulled a tool from one man's hands and grunted. The diamond was worn, but it still held.

"Stand. I will demonstrate a better way."

The men stood and made way for her. She walked to the stone, placing her hand on the obstruction. Power thrummed just beyond. The power she needed to return home lay so close, contained in the stone's interior.

"Your attempts are too small. You must cut an entrance," she explained, mapping out a rectangular door with her finger. "We must all be able to fit through, including the Changed One in the lake."

That caused a murmur, as she knew it would. The elder in the lake was an old companion, one of her first turned, and she intended to take him with her. His size was double that of an ordinary man, but he could squeeze through tight spaces, as he had when she ordered him to France months ago, as soon as she heard of the summer balls.

"He will come with us," she snapped, turning to the men and stretching her shape so that she towered above them, her head touching the tunnel ceiling.

The Noamhites cowered, then bowed, faces flat in the mud.

"Observe," she told the bowing men, pulling her shape down to strengthen her arms once again. "I will show you how."

The men kneeled and watched. Elle ground stone with her makeshift device, showing them how to use each implement to cut out a door. Stepping back, she gestured to them. Standing, the men picked up their tools and began their work along the lines she had mapped for them.

Lady Elle nodded as she watched small shards of quartz fall from beneath the diamond-tipped instruments. It was but a matter of time now.

CHAPTER 40

Charmant woke at dawn the next morning after a completely dreamless sleep. Refreshed for the first time in weeks, he completed his morning ablutions swiftly, prayed with the abbot, enjoyed a brief breakfast of rolls filled with dried fruit and almonds, then walked with the abbot, Yves, and his guard to the Hôpital Marchand.

The Hôpital Marchand perched on the North side of the abbey complex, completely separate from the traditional cross-shaped collection of buildings that comprised the holy estate. Walking past the tip of the cross, the men traversed a path through fruiting vineyards and lush kitchen gardens. Just beyond the vegetables growing in neat rows, they came upon a heavy wooden door embedded in a tall stone wall. Two monks stood on either side of the barred door.

The abbot smiled at these holy men as they bowed and removed the bar. When the abbot, prince, and his servants passed, the men closed the door. Behind them, the loud clunk of metal on metal told the group that the door had been barred once more.

Charmant raised an eyebrow at the abbot.

"M. Marchand did not wish those inside his hospital to be restrained," the abbot explained. "He felt their madness was due to no fault of their own and wished that we treat them gently, with kindness and prayer. As you know, he and his family have inspected the hospital year after year to ensure his instructions are carried out. In exchange for following these instructions, we receive our stipend.

"While we do not chain the poor creatures in the hospital to walls or even prevent them from going out-of-doors, we cannot allow them to wander the abbey. They would disturb our holy men and interrupt their Godly work. So, we keep them behind this wall, and we keep the door well-guarded.

"None may leave unless they are in the company of a holy man, as you are in my company now."

Charmant nodded and looked around.

They stood at the head of a winding path cut into a hillside. A low wall at the top of the hill obscured their view.

"Is the hospital in a valley?" asked the prince.

"Yes, this particular valley is rather desolate, with only a small scraping of soil layered over rock. We built the hospital into the rock on the far side of the valley, allowing the inhabitants to enjoy flowers and grass, small streams and ponds, without the structure flooding. It is rather an ingenious structure. I often feel it is a shame to hide away such an architectural marvel. One of the king's artisans designed it."

They walked past a wide field undulating with dew covered grass. When they topped the hill, they found a simple door latched shut and set into a crumbling stone wall built along the hill's crest.

The abbot opened the door and let the party through. Latching it behind them, he gestured to the view beyond. While they could not yet see the valley or the hospital, a riot of flowers, fruits, and vegetables obstructed their view. The terraced garden beyond burst with plant life, greenery growing in barely controlled abundance. Two monks toiled among the plant life, along with two other men not dressed in monastic garb.

"Those two men are Guillaume and Antoine, hospital inhabitants. They were once M. Marchand's gardeners, and the place they seem to enjoy most is the garden."

"May I speak with them?" asked Charmant.

"It is, of course, your right to speak with any of the hospital inhabitants, but I do not believe you will learn much from those two. According to M. Marchand, they were taciturn when he hired them, and since their madness became apparent, they stopped speaking all together.

"If you wish to speak to some of the insane, I am happy to locate those least afflicted so you may interview them. Though, even those who only suffer occasionally will share nonsensical stories. And, unfortunately, anyone you speak with will accuse your wife and her father of terrible devilry. If we were not under such a restriction from M. Marchand, we would flog each madman to beat the devil out of them. But we cannot, so we do not."

Coldness dripped down Charmant's spine, pricking his skin with goosebumps.

"Do they all tell of similar devilry? And they all claim that M. Marchand and my Princess Elle are the source of such sinful works?"

"Yes," sighed the abbot, leading the group away from the silent men toiling in the garden. "I would have to check the records, but I believe almost every one of our inhabitants came with stories of your lady committing some sort of terrifying act. As time moves forward, the stories expand. They claim she takes the form of a demon and plagues their sleep. Some continue to see their nightmares in the waking world. Others will simply refrain from sleep until they cannot keep their eyes open. That is how we went from twenty-seven inhabitants to eighteen. So many try to keep themselves from sleep, they will do anything to stay awake. Sometimes, gruesome things."

Charmant's mouth formed an "O." He was not sure what kind of gruesome acts would keep one from sleep, but he could guess.

The group of men continued walking down the path until they

caught sight of the Hôpital Marchand. The sight froze them in their tracks.

The hospital was a long, low structure, built into a recess halfway up the stepped quarry wall. Constructed of the fawn and yellow limestone comprising the quarried valley, it looked as if it had grown from the local limestone. Small slits peppered the structure, as if it were built not just to house the insane, but to protect itself against attack.

While the building itself was unremarkable in design, its odd perch and surrounding desolation made it appear like something out of a dream. Goosebumps prickled the prince's skin as the sight recalled his nightmare in which he fell into a never-ending chasm filled with incandescent eyes.

Though the long slope to the quarry bottom was quite gentle, the prince felt off balance, like he would fall down the precipice and be required to climb up to the building on hands and knees. A vision of his body, broken and trapped in the strange building flashed across his eyes, causing him to sway.

Yves laid a hand on his shoulder, steadying him.

"What do you think of the Hôpital, Your Highness? The architect was a genius, was he not?" declared the abbot, his eyes on the building.

"A mad genius, I believe, Father."

"You are correct, of course. The architect now resides within the last structure he built. He was, in fact, among the first admitted."

Charmant turned to the abbot, his eyebrows raised in surprise.

"You mean..." he started.

"Yes, yes, the architect, M. Gagnon, lives here. Once a grand artisan, employed by M. Marchand his designs grew macabre. Still marvelous, you understand, but leaning toward nightmarish. He stopped speaking and simply drew designs, day and night. This structure is one of his."

"It is both beautiful and frightening," murmured Charmant,

pulling his eyes from the structure and refocusing them on the path ahead.

"Shall we enter, Your Highness?"

Charmant gestured forward. "Lead the way, Father."

CHAPTER 41

Inside the structure, Charmant was relieved to see that the interior did not echo the strangeness of the exterior. The group entered a sparsely populated hall filled with a long communal table and several comfortable side tables and cushioned nooks. Four or five men and women sat or paced, all ignoring their visitors.

"Shall I take you on a tour of the facility before you speak with the inhabitants?" asked the abbot in a hushed voice.

Charmant nodded.

The men walked through the large hall and into a door-lined passageway. An open square carved in each door allowed the group to peek into the nondescript rooms beyond. Most residents lay inside, sleeping or dressing, though it was now well into morning.

"Many of our unfortunates just fell asleep, Your Highness, and will not be awake yet," whispered the abbot. "Most of those sleeping cannot talk with you, anyway. They are too mad. After our tour, I will situate you and your companions in a room for refreshment and conversation with the madmen of your choice."

The prince nodded and followed the abbot.

Each sleeping figure looked comfortable. None were chained and all had rooms decorated with small items like flowers, woven trinkets, and fragrant herbs.

"Did the inhabitants collect those items, or did the monks place them to lighten hearts and minds?"

The abbot shrugged, nodding to a monk at the end of the passage as they approached.

"These people must do something with their days. Some collect flowers or pebbles. Others do a little weaving or mending. Still others sit and rock."

Charmant gazed into the last room in the row. The door to this room stood open. He stepped to the doorway and looked around. Two slits cut into the exterior wall lit the small room. Each aperture sat high up in the room, far too small and elevated for a person to reach and squeeze through, but large enough to act as skylights. The sleeping mat was positioned as far away from the windows as possible.

He stepped out of the spare room and peered into the porthole cut in the door across the hall. The man inside sprawled on his back, his eyes closed, hands clenched, and mouth set in a grimace.

"They all suffer from nightmares," the abbot explained from behind the prince, "devils haunt their dreams."

Charmant rubbed his left forearm automatically.

The abbot caught the motion and frowned. He led the group through the door at the end of the passage. They entered a small antechamber, then stepped through to the chapel. Inside, six people knelt or sat, praying or staring off into space. A smiling monk sat with one of the supplicants, singing a soft prayer as the person rocked. The cool dark of the chapel turned each person into shadowed shapes, rather than individuals. Looking around, he noticed that only two rushlights were lit at the far end of the room, positioned away from the flammable wooden pews.

The abbot led the group past the madmen and into a small, private chamber with three chairs, a low table and an unlit candle. A fireplace crackled with warmth, but no one occupied the room.

The abbot gestured to one of the chairs, indicating that the prince should sit.

"I would speak with you privately for a moment, before you interview some of our more coherent residents."

"Certainly," said the prince. He turned to his men, "Please wait outside. We seem to be perfectly safe here. None of the unfortunates are violent, I believe."

The abbot nodded and the two men bowed and left the room, closing the door behind them. They would still be able to look in through the small porthole carved into the door, and might hear a portion of the conversation, but that did not bother Charmant.

That is, until he saw the look in the abbot's eye.

"My son," murmured the abbot. "There is something you have concealed from me."

Charmant shifted in his chair.

"What do you mean, Father?"

The abbot indicated his left forearm.

"May I see it?" he asked.

Baffled, Charmant rolled up his sleeve to reveal the bandage. The abbot unwrapped the wound, hissing a breath between his teeth as he saw the sliced skin.

"You have been marked," he whispered, "just as they have."

"Father, please tell me what this is about? What do you mean I have been marked?" Charmant's voice rose with each word.

The abbot motioned downward, trying to placate the prince.

"Please, we do not want the poor unfortunates living here to hear you. They will become agitated. Now, my son, will you answer some questions?"

The prince nodded, pressing his lips together to contain the bile rising from his roiling stomach.

"When did you receive this wound?"

"The evening before I came to see you," replied the prince.

The abbot raised an eyebrow. "How did it happen?"

"In a dream," the prince shared. He told the abbot of the dream, opening up and telling the man about all of his recent strange dreams.

"I thought they were caused by Lady de Noelles Marchand, Princess Elle's stepmother. She appeared in so many of them. I believed her to be a witch," he concluded.

The abbot reached out and touched Charmant's hand.

"It is true that some of Lady de Noelles Marchand's servants are here, along with those of her daughters. However, unless there is something wrong with that chateau, it is unlikely that the Lady is the cause of their madness. She employed many of them long before her marriage to M. Marchand, and they only grew mad after they took residence in the Chateau Marchand."

With a sinking heart, Charmant nodded.

"Would you still like to interview those who are sane enough to talk with you?" asked the abbot.

"Yes, please," nodded the prince.

CHAPTER 42

The first interviewee was a stout, gray-haired woman. Though elderly, her cheeks looked as if they ought to be rosy and full. Instead, her cloudy skin shone bone white in the candlelight.

She shook and cowered as the abbot directed her to the room.

"There is no need to be afraid, Huguette," the abbot soothed.

"My lord," curtsied the shaking woman, unable to make eye contact with the prince.

Charmant stood and offered her his seat.

"I believe this is the most comfortable chair, Madam," he smiled. "Please do take a seat and feel welcome."

Continuing to shake, the woman sat. Charmant chewed his lip as he watched the abbot trying to soothe her. Clearly, she was terrified.

"Excuse me one moment," Charmant said.

He went into the hall where Yves and the guard stood.

"Yves, I need your help," he said. Then he turned to the guard. "Guard, what is your name?"

The man stiffened, "Pierre Gautier, sire."

"M. Gautier, could you please go to the kitchen and find our guest some morsel upon which to nibble? She is frightened and needs some soothing. Treat her as you would an elderly grandmother. Bring her something comforting."

The guard's mouth opened in shock.

"I need information from her and, perhaps, several others. Our purposes will be made easier if we treat her with kindness," snapped the prince.

Pierre's teeth gave an audible click as he shut his mouth and nodded. Turning, he marched through the chapel and out of sight.

Charmant turned back to Yves, "Will you accompany me and help me put the woman at ease? I have soldiered, but I have never interrogated. Surely, you understand how to talk with a fellow servant better than I. And, surely, you will not take anything she says seriously. She is mad."

Yves bowed, "Of course, Your Highness."

Charmant walked back into the room and bowed to the abbot.

"Thank you, Father," he said. "Could I have some privacy in which to talk with Madam Huguette?"

The abbot looked uncertain, and the woman clutched at his hand.

"Father, father," she whined. Her gray eyes filled with tears.

"My lord only wishes to speak with you, nurse," soothed Yves.

Charmant turned in surprise. He watched as Yves' face broke into a smile and the woman's eyes narrowed, then widened. Her distress gone, she stood and walked slowly over to Yves on arthritic joints.

"Why, if it isn't Yves Joly! The apothecary's son. Many was the time I visited your father's shop for a tincture or two. My love, what are you doing here? She has not taken you, as well?"

Yves bowed over the woman, kissing her knobby knuckles.

"No, nurse, but we wondered how you faired. And now, my lord wishes to discover more about what ails you. He is trying to help."

"No one can help, my boy," sighed the nurse. "Only God himself will soothe my fevered brow. Here on earth, no one, not even the kind abbot and his monks, can end the dreaming."

Yves glanced at Charmant, who stood astonished. The prince nodded and smiled.

The young servant kneeled before the nurse.

"What dreams?" he asked.

She sighed, glancing at Charmant and then back at Yves.

"Oh, my boy. The madness may be spreading. Do you wish to hear of my dreams, truly? They are terrifying and maddening. They started this cursed illness."

Yves nodded.

"Well, then we will need to sit, for we shall be here a while," declared the nurse. She made her way back to the chair. Yves stood and leaned against the wall.

The abbot cleared his throat.

"If you are comfortable with these two men, M. Yves and his lord, then I shall take my leave," he stated. "I wish to check on a few of the sleepers."

The nurse nodded and kissed the abbot's hand.

As the abbot left, the guard, Pierre came in, accompanied by a monk. The two men laid out bread and cheese, a pitcher of watery wine, and a few dried figs and almonds. All were silent as they worked. When they bowed out, Charmant indicated the food, but the nurse shook her head.

"Thank you, my lord," she quavered. "Perhaps I will feast after we speak."

Then, she began her tale.

CHAPTER 43

"Where should I begin?" she wondered aloud.

"You were going to tell us of your dreams," prompted Yves.

She waved him away.

"Yes, yes, my boy. But there is more to tell than simple dreams," she looked at the prince, squinting. "I do not know you, my lord. Are you from here?"

"I am, nurse," he told her. "But my family was large and I, the youngest. Many of them died in the plague."

She nodded, "That was a bad winter, and a bad spring, my lord. I am sorry for those you lost."

The prince smiled. No one who knew his title treated him with such kindness, such fellow human feeling. Tears pricked the backs of his eyes as he marveled at this simple woman.

"Yves says you are a nurse, who was your mistress?"

"Lady de Noelles, my lord. I cared for her son until he died and her two daughters until the day I came here. I found them nurse-maids with good, strong milk. I tucked them into bed at night and soothed their crying eyes. I helped them up when they fell and showed them how to mend so their mother wouldn't hear of them ruining any of their fine things.

"Those girls and their infant brother were my joys. Until they were taken away from me.

"It began with the dreams. All of us dream here at Hôpital Marchand. We dream of devils and devilry, of darkness filled with eyes."

Charmant's skin pricked with cold, goosebumps running up his arms. He shivered and the nurse gave him a knowing look. She carried on with her story.

"My first dream occurred almost immediately upon our move to Chateau Marchand. My lady arrived, established house there among Marchand's strange servants and his odd daughter, then they left to tour his estates, leaving us all behind. The evening they left..."

Her face twisted into a grimace at the memory. She reached out for the goblet and Yves jumped up from his place against the wall, pouring the nurse a gobletful of watered wine. She downed it with one gulp, grimacing at the medicinal taste.

"Everyone in the chateau dreamed that night, even the girls."

"Lady de Noelles Marchand's daughters?" asked Charmant. His body had grown uncomfortably cold, and his left forearm burned as the woman told the story. The room which had once seemed cozy now felt vast and freezing.

"Yes, them and even Marchand's child, though I am not entirely sure I believe her. That girl was strange and tricky, prone to lying.

"Yves, for goodness' sake, stoke the fire. Your master is shivering," the nurse interrupted herself.

Yves rushed to the fire and added wood, heating Charmant's back. The prince smiled and nodded at his servant, but the blaze did not stop his shivering.

"We all dreamed of M. Marchand's death. Together. Every one of us participated in the dream, and we all woke knowing that somehow, we'd killed him. When Lady de Noelles Marchand came home, distraught and telling us of her husband's brutal murder, we all knew how it'd happened already. Our hands held the knives. Our thrusts stabbed him.

"The girl, Ms. Elle, she told us that her father was dead well before our lady came home with the terrible news. Our lady was distraught, and we all grieved alongside her. But we also wondered what devilry could have caused us to dream such a thing. Did we participate in the murder, or was our shared dream a coincidence?

"The dreams continued after that. They were darker, though not as deadly. My nights were filled with terrifying visions of eyes, watching me, waiting for something. Then, one evening, I was marked. A long, thin rope made of skin and knives cut into my left forearm, forming a perfect circle around it.

"Shall I show you, my lord?"

"C...c...certainly, nurse," shivered Charmant. His lips felt blued, as if he and this woman were standing in an ice storm rather than a small, hot room in the midst of summer. Around his left arm, his wound burned.

What is happening to me? he wondered. *Am I going mad?*

The lady smiled absently at his use of her title, rather than her name. Then, her face returned to its usual flat expression. She pulled up her sleeve and revealed a fresh wound, only recently scabbed over.

"But, madam, this occurred recently."

"Yes, my lord, it happens night after night. The moment it heals, it is re-inflicted upon my person."

Charmant unconsciously clutched his own arm.

"My lord, you have personal reasons for this interview, do you not?"

He nodded, his eyes flicking to hers. Panic clutched at his throat, closing it and making speech impossible.

"I see, well I should tell you of the other things I observed about little Lady Elle while in that wretched house," she sighed and plucked an almond from the platter. "We may be here a while, please break bread with me, my lord, young Yves."

Charmant nodded again, still unable to speak. He took a token nibble of plain bread, washing it down with a tiny sip of watered wine. Yves and the nurse ate for a while. Then, she wet her lips with another sip before beginning her story.

"Have you seen Lady Elle's little animals yet, my lord?" asked the nurse.

Charmant clenched his hands into fists, tensing his entire body so that his throat might open once again. It was a trick he'd learned as a small boy, when his own nurse grew impatient at his long silences and his brothers began to tease. His beloved sister Charlotte taught him to tense everything so that his throat could relax.

"No," he choked out.

"At first, I thought the nursery and house particularly mouse ridden. It was disgusting, little mice running this way and that day and night. I set traps to kill the wretched creatures, but most were far too clever. It was not until the end of my stay in that place that Elle allowed me to trap one of her mice, to see its true nature."

The prince leaned forward, his mouth opening, but no sound came out.

"What was it?" the nurse asked for him, eyeing him sadly.

Charmant nodded.

"It was the final thing that threw me over the edge. I heard a thump as one of my traps snared something. I had fairly given up on the things, and the sound startled me.

"Leaping from my chair, I scurried to the spot. The mouse lay there. I suppose I set the tension too tight, for it had been beheaded by the snare. The body, still trapped by a bit of skin, squirmed, and writhed. The head, having rolled free, was not bleeding as one would suppose. Instead, it moved, using its jaws to move itself closer to the body.

"I stood, mouth agape, trying to comprehend what my eyes beheld.

"Then, the body stopped moving and the jaws grasped the edge of a blanket, turning itself and catching my eyes with its beady, black orbs. The jaws spit out the blanket and opened again. The dead mouse said, in Elle's voice, 'please put me back together so I may be on my way.'

"I screamed and ran. I know not what happened to that mouse for, by the time I returned, it was gone."

A swirl of disbelief left Charmant numb. He had read about Elle as a tiny doll surrounded by mice and birds, had read Marchand's account of her. But such an explicit story of devilry still could not match his thoughts and feelings about Elle. The only hint of such demon's work had been the attack on her sisters. And the attack of those two ravens at her home.

"I can see you do not believe me. And why should you? I am but a madwoman in a hospital. I pray every night for release from my dreams, from my memories. I pray to see the truth. Yet, every night my dreams return, this mark returns, and I wonder what I may do in penance, so the lord forgives me."

Charmant shook himself. He liked this woman. She reminded him much of his nursemaid, long dead of old age.

"Nurse," he paused, "Madam Blanchard. I appreciate all that you have told me. It must have been difficult for you to recount your torment to a stranger. I cannot tell you how grateful I am. What can I do to improve your days here?"

"Please include me in your prayers, my lord. And stay away from that girl. You seem a nice young man. A very kind and gracious lord. My Lord Marchand seemed troubled, yet kind. You may be a greater man than he, but if you are reviewing his estates, you are now connected with his family. You are connected with Lady Elle. Find a way to keep her far from those you love.

"And please, keep my ladies Adeline and Enora safe. They ostracized their stepsister upon her father's death. I believe their behavior, cruel and childish, infuriated Lady Elle. I believe that one day, she will harm them. Please keep my girls safe."

Charmant's stomach filled with stones as he recalled the songbirds' attack upon the two girls. The pecking and the blood. He had failed to check on them before he left - failed to give them even a thought. Now he worried that his two sisters by marriage may be in danger.

"I will do what I can, nurse," he stood and bowed. "You will be in my prayers."

Eyeing him shrewdly, the nurse stood and curtsied. "You see that you keep yourself safe, my lord. I pray you have a long life untroubled by devils."

She left the room.

Charmant slumped in the nurse's vacated seat, the stories the woman had shared swirling in his mind.

Yves cleared his throat behind him.

Yearning to be alone above all else, the prince plastered a smile across his face and turned to the man.

"Yves, thank you for comforting the old nurse. Could you clear away this food and bring me a pie or soup? I find myself in need of solitude and nourishment."

The young man stood and bowed, removing the tray.

When the door shut behind him, the prince sighed and put his head in his hands. Perhaps it he needed prayer and reflection. Perhaps, instead of these stories from mad people, what he truly required was guidance from the lord above. He needed to confess to the abbot.

Chapter 44

After a simple meal of fish pie, bread, cheese, grapes, and watery wine, the prince stood.

"I do not believe we will benefit from hearing more stories, Yves," he said. "I need the abbot's guidance. Please go find him."

Yves, whose long face had not regained color since the nurse told her tales, smiled at last. He bowed and murmured, "Yes, Your Highness."

Yves returned with the abbot who asked, "My lord, did you wish to continue with the interviews?"

"No, thank you," said Charmant politely. "I believe I have learned what I came here to learn. But I do not understand. And for that, I seek your counsel."

"I am pleased that you ended your query with Huguette. She is the sanest here, yet she is plagued by demons, as are the rest. I do hope she shared her kind treatment and her life of continual prayer with you?"

The prince nodded to the abbot.

"She asked that I include her in my prayers, which I shall. I would like to leave, Abbot. I would pray with you and talk to you about what I've learned. I must make sense of it all."

The abbot nodded and the group turned toward the hall. A bloodied, naked man blocked their path. Charmant's wide eyes took in the body covered in a webbing of scars, scabs, and dripping gashes. A makeshift scourge hung from the man's right hand and around his left wrist dripped a bloody, circular laceration.

"Pascal," declared the abbot in a calm, clear voice. "What are you doing?"

"Her will is to force me to remember, Father. I must scourge myself. I must remove her marks upon me."

He pointed to a long, thin scar, knotted and painful, running from his left shoulder to his forearm. It ended in in the bloody circlet surrounding his wrist.

"This is where she burned me with fire and ice, over and over again. For her pleasure. And this," he pointed to the circle, "is where she marks me still."

As the abbot calmly walked to the man and removed the scourge, placing it in a hidden pocket beneath his robe.

"Let us pray, my son," the abbot whispered, stroking Pascal's hair. As soft words tumbled from both men's mouths, Charmant's eyes searched the man's body, sketching over all of the scars. Surely, Lady Elle could not have inflicted that latticework of pain. But the prince's mind betrayed him, recalling how he'd pressed himself against Elle on the terrace, giving her unwanted attention. His hands had burned and blistered where he touched her.

Mind snapping back to the present, he watched the bleeding man sob prayers as the abbot, now joined by another monk, prayed with him. The man prayed for protection against the unnamed demon tormenting him and it took all of Charmant's restraint to keep his mouth clamped shut as he watched and listened. The prince wanted to shout at this beleaguered man "Who still plagues you?" but he could not drag this madman into a deeper hell. Instead, he watched as two monks replaced the abbot and coaxed poor Pascal away, presumably to bathe his wounds and dress his body.

"Poor man," murmured the abbot, shaking out his blood and tear-streaked robes. He gestured to the prince and his retinue. "Come, let us go."

They walked through the rest of the building with no incident. When they finally reached the fresh air outdoors, Charmant took a deep, cleansing breath.

"Who or what plagues that man back there?" he asked, his mind burning for the answer.

The abbot looked at him sadly.

"He believes one of the de Noelles family has scourged him with fire and ice, and that she continues to do so in his dreams. He is not clear on which lady. It may be your princess, her stepmother, or one of her stepsisters. They all haunt his dreams."

Charmant went cold and his mind reeled. He wished he had not visited this madhouse. The more he heard, the more uncertainty clouded his judgment.

"Let us leave, Your Highness," smiled the abbot. "We do our best to make this place seem normal, but truly, madness lies here like a miasma. It will affect you if you stay too long."

Charmant nodded, allowing himself to be guided down the sloping switchbacks, across the rocky valley, up the terraced gardens, and through inner and outer walls. It wasn't until they had closed and barred the final door that he noticed Yves concerned eyes upon him. It had been ages since anyone had looked at him with genuine concern. The look reminded Charmant of his dead friend and fellow soldier, Alain.

While his heart warmed to the young servant, it also shuddered at the thought of one more friendship, one more disappointment, one more death. If he became friends with this man, if he allowed himself to care, and then Yves died... Charmant wasn't sure his heart could bear another loss.

He clapped Yves on the back, mustering a reassuring smile.

"Why don't you visit the chapel for prayer, then enjoy a hearty meal and pack? We will depart in the morrow at sunup. I wish to speak with the abbot."

Yves bowed and walked away.

"You, too, Pierre," Charmant told his guard. "I am safe enough in the company of the abbot."

Pierre looked from the abbot to Charmant, then bowed and followed Yves.

Alone at last, Charmant looked at the abbot. He allowed his eyes to fill with the confusion he felt in his soul.

"What do I do, Father? Who do I believe?"

CHAPTER 45

"Your Highness," began the abbot. He stared into the prince's confused face and his eyes drooped with sadness and exhaustion. "My son do not believe the ravings of the mad. You prayed and chose a wife, a princess, to bear your sons and continue your family line. She is not some raging beast who haunts dreams. She is a woman."

"I have not shared all with you, Father," Charmant told him. He stopped and pulled the letter from Marchand out of his pouch. "Lady Elle accused her stepmother of evil. She said Lady de Noelles Marchand holds her captive with magic, but then I found and this letter from old Marchand. He cites story after story of Elle being something... inhuman. And her servants? They are part of some pagan sect in Brittania. They worship my wife. That is why they do her bidding."

Charmant watched the abbot as his face went slack in disbelief.

"Father, please read the letter. I do not know what to think. It all seems like madness, but if it is, that means Lady Elle's stepmother, Lady de Noelles Marchand, is a witch. If it is not, then Lady Elle is a demon. What do I do? How do I decipher the truth?"

Hands shaking and heart galloping, Charmant pushed the letter into the abbot's unwilling hands.

"Will you read it? I would like to join my men in the chapel and pray a while."

The abbot took the pages in his hands, leafing through the thick paper and the spidery handwriting.

"Yes, my son, if it is your wish, I shall read this. By giving me this letter and revealing all you have, I am now burdened with a distasteful task. I must accuse one of the nobility of witchcraft."

Charmant nodded, his entire body shaking and tears stinging the back of his eyes.

"I know, father. But is it not better to discover and root out evil than to allow it to fester? Perhaps this is the scourge which brought plague among us."

The abbot nodded. "Go pray, my son. I shall read this letter and pray myself. We will determine what to do."

CHAPTER 46

That evening, after a light dinner, the prior asked Charmant to join the abbot in his office. An afternoon of prayer and contemplation had done much to restore the prince's nerves. He knew that, despite everything, God was on his side.

Entering the long candlelit office, Charmant was both surprised and relieved to see the abbot kneeling in prayer. The prior at his side indicated an empty space next to the abbot. Charmant kneeled and bent his head, letting his mind go blank as he focused on the redness in the back of his eyelids. While he'd spent his afternoon reciting prayers, he had tried to empty his mind, hoping to receive a message from God himself. He kneeled in stillness and quiet for what seemed like an eternity, hoping for a message.

"My son," the abbot murmured, pulling the prince out of his reverie.

"Amen," whispered Charmant, suddenly feeling guilty. He had not asked for anything or even whispered words of worship - nor had he heard a word from on high.

"Yes, Father," asked Charmant, struggling to his feet and turning to face the abbot. The man's face was flushed, his skin glowing. He looked as if he had spent the day out in the garden, the sun and exercise brightening his visage, when instead he'd spent his time fervently praying. "Do you know the truth?" asked the prince, heart filling with hope.

"I believe I do," the abbot told him. "Marchand was mad."

Charmant felt the world spinning around him.

"So, my wife, Princess Elle, she is innocent? It is in fact Lady de Noelles Marchand who is evil?"

"The only proof you have that a prominent noblewoman is evil is the word of your wife, sire," cautioned the abbot. "I have spent many years working with men of honor, and, in my experience, the accusations of women are better left between them. If you retrieved the items your wife asked for, and her stepmother gave them willingly, then you can consider the matter settled. Women do not require the complex honor systems of man to be satisfied. Get your wife pregnant as quickly as possible, and she will become preoccupied with her natural place in life. Perhaps you can try to assist Lady de Noelles Marchand in marrying her other daughters off, so she can experience the joys and duties associated with being a grandmother. Keep the women busy, and they will cease to trouble you."

"Oh, thank you Father," gushed Charmant, the joy and clarity making him lightheaded. He knew the abbot was right. All the complexity and oddness surrounding the de Noelles Marchand family were caused by them being a family of childless women. They merely needed to find their role with husbands and children, and all would be settled.

Quiet questions intruded on his peace. What of the strange attack by songbirds? What of the key, the book, and the bracelet? Who were Elle's strange servants?

The abbot clapped a hand on Charmant's shoulder, pulling him down slightly so the older man could meet the prince's eyes.

"I see you are still concerned. Trust in God and all will turn out right."

The calm gray of the abbot's eyes slowed Charmant's rapid heartbeat. The prince smiled, his shoulders relaxing for the first time since his new sisters-in-law were attacked at his wedding.

"Thank you, Father. Your guidance has soothed me greatly. I can see why old Marchand asked you to oversee his hospital. It is unfortunate he could not join his mad staff and experience your grace and kindness himself."

The abbot smiled and took his hand from the princes' shoulder.

"Thank you, my son. Now, it is time for you to rest. You leave at sunup, do you not?"

Charmant nodded. His questions about Elle and the strangeness that surrounded her tried to push themselves to the top of his mind, but he resolved to think of other matters. Perhaps he would visit the church and listen as the monks prayed the final hour of the day before going to sleep.

The abbot walked him to the door, and the prince set off to the church.

CHAPTER 47

A deep, rumbling cry erupted from deep below the castle. In the flickering firelight provided by torches and rushlights, the Noamhites danced and hopped, chanting "Tha am maighstir a' feitheamh! Tha am maighstir a' feitheamh!" as one of them lifted a small shred of stone above the group's heads. The party stilled, every servant lying flat on the ground as Elle appeared around a corner of the tunnel.

"What...?" she started to ask. Then, she stopped, eyes catching the chunk of rock missing from the almost impenetrable quartz. Rushing to the wall, she didn't bother to step over her subjects. Pushing her finger through the crack, she felt hard, sharp crystals that lined the other side. Even more than the crystals, she felt the power thrum into her from deep below.

"You've broken through," she whispered. Her skin boiled with the heat of joy. She carefully pushed the heat through her finger, allowing it to sizzle harmlessly against the rock.

Lady Elle turned and stared at her subjects.

"This is no time to celebrate," she snapped. "Keep working. And remember, the opening will need to be large enough for everyone to pass through. Even the Changed One in the lake."

Her people nodded their heads, further burying their faces in the ground.

Lady Elle smiled. It would not be long now. She just needed that key, and she could go home.

CHAPTER 48

As the group rode back to the castle, Charmant found he did not want to arrive home just yet. He was still feeling thoughtful, turning over all he had learned, along with the abbot's advice, in his mind. Though the return trip was not a long ride, he found himself wondering if he could stop along the way, explore one of the towns and drink their inferior wine, bolt a bit of pottage, and gnaw on some acorn bread. Something about being on the road, with potential conflict ahead, made him long for the rough life he'd experienced when soldiering.

Perhaps simplicity will clear my head, he thought, though he knew he was just delaying his inevitable return home.

"Yves," he asked his servant, "Is there somewhere we can stop and refresh ourselves? Perhaps at your parents' house or a farm? I feel as though I must visit my people, rather than simply riding through the land."

Yves turned to the prince in surprise.

"While I am sure my mother would be glad to have you in our home, it is but a simple place with many foul-smelling substances. You would likely be more comfortable at the Chateau, or perhaps, if you truly want to mix with the locals, at the tavern? It will be bustling as today is a market day."

"Let us adjourn to the tavern, then," declared Charmant.

"Yes, Your Highness," the men intoned.

The three men entered a large wooden structure, situated at the entrance of the market square. Above the door, a rough-hewn sign depicting a bunch of grapes and a stalk of grain showed the world what they sold inside.

As the prince entered, the chatter in the tavern died down, then halted.

Damn, thought the prince, remembering that he was cleaner and wearing finer clothes than any one person here could possibly afford. He was hoping he would go mostly unnoticed, like he had when he and his fellow soldiers traversed the kingdom.

Thinking quickly, he shouted, "Today's meal will be paid for by the castle, enjoy your food and drink, and be merry."

With that, applause burst forth, followed by shouting and general merriment. Someone brought out a flute and several villagers danced and sang along.

The prince sent Yves to get food and drink for their party, and to find out how much money the man's stores of food, wine, and ale, would cost. Charmant assumed that the people would eat and drink heartily, and likely deplete the man's stores.

Satisfied, Charmant took a seat against the far wall, watching his people enjoy themselves.

"Your Highness?" asked his guard, standing beside him.

"For goodness sakes man, sit. You will eat with me, as will Yves."

The man's face flamed red and he sputtered a protest.

"I was once a soldier, and now I am a prince," said Charmant. "Let us return to the time when I soldiered, and all sat and ate at the same table. Come, sit."

The guard sat at the edge of the bench, eyes sweeping the room as if searching for threats among the merrymakers.

"Tell me your question," commanded the prince.

"Why did you do what you just did?" asked the guard. He hastily added, "Your Highness."

"I suppose I have had a lot on my mind. Being among the people makes me feel better. It reminds me that my concerns may be of great importance to me, but their concerns will also affect me. No one of us is alone in this world, and one decision will affect countless others."

The guard sat silently at this answer.

Yves returned with a maiden. They both bore food and drinks, filling up the table with the meal.

Charmant sipped his wine from the communal pitcher and sighed. It was light, like drinking liquid sunshine. A new flavor hit him as he swallowed, that of the oaken barrel in which this wine aged. The beauty and toil of his kingdom; all was contained in a simple mouthful.

He raised the pitcher to his lips and paused as he heard a loud conversation break through the overall gaiety.

"The beast has stolen chickens, pigs, and even children," boomed a man's voice. "It is said that the reason none have been able to kill it is that it disguises itself as a human being. The beast wears the clothing of a man and walks on two legs, appearing as a huntsman or woodcutter. But when the moon grows full, it transforms into a wolf from moonrise to moonrise, giving it a full day and night to kill and satiate its terrible appetite."

Another, younger voice piped up. "I heard that none know its den and it is rumored that it cannot be killed unless silver has entered its heart."

Prince Charmant looked around, catching the speaker's eye. The peasant, dressed in rough and dirty wool, immediately lowered his gaze to his shaking hands.

"When was the last wolf attack?" asked the prince, almost shouting to be heard over the din.

The man glanced up at the prince with wide, brown eyes. Charmant beckoned him over and indicated he take a seat.

The man looked at the party, trying to determine what he should do. Yves smiled and nodded encouragingly.

"What is your name?" asked Charmant, smiling.

"Alois, Your Highness," said the man.

"Well, Alois, tell us your story."

Alois blushed furiously, red brightening his wrinkled face and highlighting the gray that topped his head.

"I am but a serf, a villein, Your Highness. Forgive an old man for spinning yarns. A wolf has attacked children, chickens, sheep, and pigs, but I do not know precisely when the last attack occurred. I believe it was at the last full moon, sire."

"Where could I find out more? I would have a huntsman find and kill the wolf, to keep my people safe."

The man bowed his head, stammering, "I believe a small boy at the Duval Farm was carried away, sire."

"Thank you," said the prince, seeing that the man was now completely overwrought. He drank the last of his wine and stood.

"We must leave. Thank you for your tale. I shall have the castle huntsman investigate it."

"Thank you, Your Highness," said the man, bowing again and again. "Thank you."

As they continued their slow way home, Charmant thought of the wolf, his wife, and her family. Perhaps, as the abbot had said, all problems could be solved by men and women knowing their place. The huntsman would hunt. Lady Elle would bear children. Lady de Noelles Marchand would marry off her daughters. All would be right in the world.

With renewed certainty and peace, the party arrived at the castle.

CHAPTER 49

"Where is my wife?" asked Charmant upon arrival.

"She has been closeted with her mother and sisters since you left."

"Of course," nodded Charmant. "How are her sisters? I owe them a visit."

Octave hesitated. Then he murmured, "Your Highness, if it is not too forward, I would wait until Lady de Noelles Marchand requests a visit. The poor woman is unwell herself; she has been working so diligently to help her ailing children, both of whom are still very injured. One of the young ladies, it seems, has dropped into a sleep which the doctors have been unable to disturb. The king has sent for additional healers and apothecaries. But, well, the last healer who visited did not seem hopeful."

Charmant's stomach sank, and guilt nipped at the edges of his thoughts. He'd just spent two days accusing this woman and her family of practicing witchcraft and causing devilry. Now, it seemed the girls were on the brink of death.

"What of my lady?" he asked.

"She took over her sisters' care once her stepmother collapsed."

"Of course," Charmant repeated. "I will not disturb them today. Please have someone report their condition to me on the morrow."

Octave bowed.

The king's counselor, Elouan, strode up behind them and bowed perfunctorily.

"When you have recovered from your travels, the king has requested you join him for the evening meal. You shall sit at his right hand."

Charmant straightened up. While his father had granted him power and position since his brothers died, he still had not been placed at his father's right hand. Instead, the king left his rightmost seat empty as a symbol, a remembrance of those lost. This status symbol meant his father trusted him.

With the peace granted by his visit to the monastery, Prince Charmant felt confident that he could take on anything his father tasked him with.

"Oh, before I forget," Charmant mentioned, already walking toward his rooms to bathe and change. Elouan walked beside him, and Yves followed them both. "There is a wolf roaming the woods. One man said it has killed a boy at the Duvall farm. I wish to suggest that we send the castle huntsman to deal with the problem. Or perhaps create a reward for the capture of this fiendish wolf. It would be a great show of the Charmant power and make our people feel safe."

Elouan nodded. "A noble and wise notion, Your Highness. You are thinking like your father. I shall agree with your suggestion when you share your idea with the king."

At that, they separated to prepare for dinner.

CHAPTER 50

"Leaving?" asked Charmant, incredulous.

"Yes, my boy," his father replied, tearing into a pork shoulder with gusto. "I will visit Queen Blanche, as she was gracious enough to visit us. I wish to establish that we are partner kingdoms in trade and no malice is held by your rebuffing her as a potential spouse."

"But you suggested the match between me and Princess Elle!"

"Exactly, and I stand by my suggestion. I believe you two will have many sons and will make great rulers one day. But Queen Blanche holds the power of the ports. She also has a cure or prevention measure against plague, and I would like to induce her to share that knowledge. So, I shall visit the Queen and take a rest cure in her kingdom, as she invited me to do, and you will stay here and rule with your lovely princess. When I return, I expect her to be pregnant with my first grandchild."

Charmant nodded. He did not want his father to leave, because he wanted him here, safe, in the castle. But this diplomatic trip could be good both for their relations with the Blanche kingdom and for their people - if the Queen could be induced to share her cure or immunity with his father.

"You are wise, my king. I have much to learn from you."

The king clapped his son on the back just as Charmant bit into a joint of meat. The piece shot out of his mouth and Charmant tried to cover his gaff by telling the king of the wolf.

"But of course, we should send the huntsman to kill the wolf! And I like the idea of offering a reward for the beast's pelt. It will not only show we are just and wise, but that we care for our people. Well done, my boy," the king smiled broadly.

Charmant smiled back. His father was in fine form tonight, and he was clearly pleased with the progress they had made.

"When do you leave?" asked Charmant.

"In two days' time. It never does to keep a queen waiting, and I have already sent my acceptance of her invitation, along with a lovely gift, in advance of my arrival. She shall be pleased, indeed, to see me I think."

The king leaned in and whispered, "I would have waited a fortnight or so, but I believe one of your lady's sisters may die soon, and I would like to be gone before she does. It sounds callous, but I don't want to be delayed by mourning her. And," he paused, his voice growing thick. Charmant looked at his father's face and saw eyes sparkling with unshed tears. "I am unsure if I can attend another funeral."

Charmant nodded, clapping his father on the back. He said in a loud voice, "You are wise, Your Majesty. Keeping a Queen waiting would be gauche, indeed."

Father and son parted after dinner. Charmant made his way back to his bedroom, hoping his wife would be available so that he could follow the abbot's advice and give his father what he wished. The hallway and his bedroom were empty.

He sent a servant to check on his lady wife and her family and provide him with a report. The man returned after Charmant had been undressed for bed.

"The princess is walking in the garden after attending her family all day. She is expected back shortly. The young ladies are still ill, though Lady Adeline has fallen into an unwakeable slumber and appears worse than Lady Enora. Their lady mother suffers from fever and exhaustion, and the castle doctor is attending her."

"Thank you," murmured Charmant. He tucked himself into bed and closed his eyes, exhaustion overtaking him.

Thump

The prince's eyes flew open at the sound. Though it seemed like but a moment had passed, the black room told him it was quite late.

"Hello?" his groggy voice echoed into the silent space. His heartbeat thumped in his ears, making it difficult to hear the room around him.

I hope this is not another dream, he thought.

"Hello, my love," Elle's voice floated out of the darkness.

Charmant tensed at the sound of her contralto voice. He thought about the abbot's words and tried to relax. It was time for them to do their duty to the kingdom and produce an heir.

"Hello, my lady," he replied, working to keep his voice steady.

If I could only see her, I would feel better, he thought.

He felt the blankets shift on the bed as Elle sat next to him.

"I have been thinking, my lord husband, that we have yet to do our duty and produce an heir. Would tonight be convenient?"

Charmant reached for her, his arms brushing her slim frame before she placed a goblet in his hand.

"That is my most fervent wish," he told her.

"Of course it is," she said. "Have a sip of wine to wake yourself and a few almonds to freshen your breath, then we shall begin."

Sitting up awkwardly, he sipped at the wine in his hand. Instantly, he felt more alert. He took another large gulp and, before he knew it, realized he'd drunk the entire glass. Warmth ran through his veins, both energizing his mind and numbing his limbs.

"Lay him back," came his wife's cold voice.

"Wait! Help!" cried Charmant. A strange, sticky, long-fingered hand muffled his cries as more hands pushed him roughly into the bed. Struggling against the arms that held him, he found his movements weakening until he could barely twitch his extremities.

"That is much better," cooed Elle. Flint struck stone and one of her attendants lit a rushlight in the wall. The soft, flickering glow flitted across Elle's face. She appeared as both the beautiful girl he had married - and not her. Rock dust grayed her skin and her shadowed eyes appeared slime green. Once perfect, her hands on his skin felt rough and overlong.

She stroked the prince's face.

"Now, you will tell me where to find my key."

CHAPTER 51

Elle could not stand this charade. She had spent ages with a prince who, despite being a human male filled with truth serum, refused to tell her the key's location.

Instead, he told her everything about the key, describing its appearance in detail, down to the smallest ridge. Talking through every step he'd taken to the lake and telling her that he had buried it, but leaving out where it was buried. The prince droned on about why he'd been unable to recover it after his encounter with the Changed One.

The one thing he managed to keep from her was the one thing she wanted to know: the exact location of the key.

Infuriated, Elle glared at the prince as he continued to dodge her questions with lengthy descriptions about the letter her father had written, sharing where the key had been in his story, and talking of tentacles, flat faces, and bulging eyes.

He even had the gall to ask her questions. Once, when she asked him where to locate the key, he asked her if there were more of her people living here in France. He wanted to know if the Changed only came from Britannia or if she changed people with a mysterious, devilish power.

She rolled her eyes as he obsessed over the illness that had ravaged his family. The prince even had the gall to ask if she had caused it.

Rage built up within Elle's body. She knew the truth potion would wear off over time. Gripping his left forearm, her hand turned sharp, cutting into the wound that already encircled it. A trickle of blood dripped onto the bed.

"Tell me where the key is, or I remove your hand."

Charmant glared up at her, then his eyes went wide with shock. Her anger had caused her to lose control over her form and her features were melting. Elle let go of the man and stood, composing her visage and reconfiguring her hands to those of the soft and gentle princess. She still needed him. She could not put his life in danger yet.

In the sweetest voice she could muster, she asked, "What do you want? What can I give you in exchange for the key's location?"

"You can leave and never return. You can promise to take your people with you and you can give me your word that you will not harm my family."

"That is what I am trying to do!" growled Elle. Her rage built in her again and she tamped it down, sending shocks of cold into the floor instead of into this infuriating human.

"I swear that I will leave within a week of obtaining the key. I will not harm your family and I will take every follower currently occupying your estate and the estate of my adoptive father with me."

"Swear it on your life," demanded the drugged prince.

Despite herself, Elle admired the man's will. She had used the potion against many men, and it had often caused the truth to gush forth like a geyser. Instead, this young man, this weakling, this youngest of his father's sons, defied his own chemistry to extract a promise from her.

"I swear it," she ground out.

Charmant struggled to find the use of his limbs, pushing past the sedative effects of her medicine. Rage and admiration struggled against each other in Elle's hearts. She smiled and reached out a helping hand.

Grasping the offered hand, the prince told her, "I will show you where it is."

CHAPTER 52

Charmant took a shaky step down from the terrace, Elle supporting his weight. Head pounding and eyes drooping, he made his way along the garden path.

"I can give you something to help you awaken, if you wish," offered his wife.

"No," he slurred. He wished he could shove her away and stride through the trees with easy grace. But his entire body felt as if it were made of liquid. His vision cut in and out as his eyes tracked each motion his feet made. They walked along the path through the orchard, lights dancing at the corners of his eyes.

When they were a few trees from the lakeside, Charmant's headache released its hold. He lifted his eyes from his feet, squinting in the flickering torchlight. Elle's followers pressed in on all sides, watching them.

He turned to Elle.

"Once more, before all of your followers, I will extract your solemn oath that you will remove yourself from the castle within a week of recovering the key, that you will not harm my family, and that these...people will go with you and leave us in peace."

Elle glared up at him.

"I have already sworn thus," she snapped.

"If you are indeed a demon or a fairy or a witch, you must swear three times. That is the only way."

Charmant watched as Elle looked at her followers. They cowered, many falling to their knees at her glance. He saw a smile flick across her face as she enjoyed their terror.

"I swear it before my followers," her voice rang out. She turned to the prince and stretched a smile over her grim visage. "Now, please, proceed."

Charmant straightened his spine and glared down at her.

"Swear once more."

Elle stamped her foot in the sand. Ice glinted in the moonlight as it frosted the land below her feet.

"I. Swear. It."

The prince nodded and stumbled unassisted onto the shore. Eyes firmly fixed on the sand - he avoided looking at the lake.

Walking carefully on the rock and stick strewn ground, he found the boulder he'd used as a landmark. Standing in front of it, he hesitated. Even though she'd sworn three times, he did not trust Elle to keep her word.

Glancing over his shoulder at the twenty or so followers pouring out of the orchard, Charmant realized he didn't have a choice. They would pursue him to the ends of the earth if he betrayed her now. And, as Marchand had said in his letter, the lord only knew how many monstrous beasts worshiped her.

The prince sighed and crouched down, finding the stick with which he'd marked the spot where he'd hidden the key. He dug in the damp ground, using the stick as a spade. A few scrapes revealed the key.

"Here," he pulled the key from the ground and stood, palm out.

Elle glanced at one of her men. He snatched the key from the prince's hand with long fingers. Lifting it above his head, a cheer went up. Her supplicants whooped and danced, shouting a strange set of words that sounded like "Tha am maighstir a' feitheamh."

Charmant leaned on the boulder, his head in his hands. The uncertain firelight hurt his eyes, which channeled pain straight to his head. A soft hand lifted his chin and he looked into emerald eyes.

"If you would like me to leave in the agreed upon time, you must keep your father and your servants out of the cellar," Elle told him. "We told them it is flooded and have removed the stores, but you must confirm my words and keep everyone out."

"The cellar?" asked Charmant.

"There is a power source beneath your castle, one strong enough to send me home. It is deep underground, and we will reach it soon, but my people must work with diligence to cut through rock and access it."

Charmant put his head back into his hands. His eyes were swimming and pain radiated down his head to his neck.

"You ought to go indoors and rest. The pain will be gone in the morning," Elle said in a flat, uncaring voice.

He looked up again as she walked away with her people, leaving him in the dark next to a monster-filled lake.

Charmant pushed away from the boulder and stumbled into the orchard, trying to follow the dancing lights of Elle's servants. The flickering torches doubled and tripled in his blurring vision. He felt ahead for trees, using them to pull himself forward.

As he fumbled, he tripped, smacking his knee on a tree root on the way down. Charmant rolled onto his back and clutched his knee. Above, the stars swam through the stygian sky. He could no longer control his eyelids as they shut over his blurred vision.

The prince slept on the cold, damp ground.

CHAPTER 53

Elle walked through the orchard, her fierce, hot triumph leaving patches of burning grass for her servants to stifle with stamps of their wide, booted feet.

The time is upon me, thought Elle. Her body recalled the feeling of her true form. It ached to stretch in ways this woman shape could never do. It longed for additional limbs, for long, cartilaginous tentacles, for a different gravity, for a million things that had been lost to her when she got trapped here on Earth, only able to form into land-locked animals.

She looked at the frog-faced men surrounding her, using their own bodies to stamp out the flames of her joy.

These people, once her captors, were now her slaves.

Their lore forgot that their people once trapped her here. She had traveled across stars and space to the Noamhite homeland centuries ago with the intention of instilling awe and forcing their people to do her bidding. Instead, the clan's druidic ancestors destroyed her way back to her dimension, trapping her in this form, on this planet. They used her to protect their clan from others, not realizing that mere association with her kind would fundamentally change the Noamhites.

How the clan matriarchs would moan if they could see their sons, fouled by long association with Elle, transformed into something completely new. How they would gnash their teeth and bind Elle more tightly, reduce her power so she could never get home at all

Elle reached the edge of the orchard and turned to her people, summoning the will to reduce the heat within her. She instead used her pent-up energy and emotion to stretch herself as tall and thin as the bracelet would allow, sending some of her matter into the air in the form of two songbirds. They flapped on either side of her face.

The men gathered in front of her, many of their torches no longer aflame due to their wild waving and frolicking.

She opened her mouth to speak. The songbirds opened their mouths, too, hovering silently.

"We have everything we need to go on our final journey," she announced. The songbirds above each shoulder echoed her words in a simulacrum of her speech.

Elle and her birds continued.

"This is the journey to which your ancestors in the sea and lakes have aspired for many thousands of years. I shall dig with you now, help you to grind away at the stone below this castle, and together, we will find the power source which will bring us home."

Many of the men cheered, waving their torches wildly. Some collapsed, bowing with tear-streaked faces. A few fell to their knees and stared, opened mouthed, at Elle and her companions. She let the two birds, who were part of her own matter, fly into a nearby tree.

"Let us go to the tunnels tonight. The stonework is difficult, but we shall complete it within the week, as I promised the prince. I will leave my spies in this orchard to ensure he keeps his word."

Elle turned, shrinking back to her usual form. As she strode into the castle, the songbirds watched her men file in behind her.

CHAPTER 54

Stars swirled above Charmant, dizzying him with their varying hues. He felt his body shift into something strange, tall, and inhuman. Standing, a crown of stars circled his pate. Looking down, clouds blocked his feet from view. Lifting a hand in front of his eyes, he twisted massive, tree-size fingers sticking out of lake-size palms.

I could lift my entire castle with these hands, he marveled.

Wiggling his toes, he vaguely felt his feet. Stepping forward, he almost slipped as something thick and liquid popped beneath him.

Squatting as far down as he could, his head descended past whisper-white clouds, the world below growing clear in gruesome detail. He'd stepped on something large, fat, and blood-filled. Intact head and feet lay above and below the thing's pulped body. Narrowing his eyes, Charmant managed to focus on the creature's face.

Alain's twisted visage stared up at him. It was the expression his best friend and fellow soldier had worn when Charmant found him on the battlefield, stabbed through by a fatal arrow. Inwardly, the prince's heart filled with dread and grief, the same emotions he'd experienced on the battlefield when Alain died, over a year ago.

Yet, physically, the giant prince could only watch. His crouched form sat motionless; his giant eyes fixed on the body. The heaviness of his heart transformed his hands and arms into solid things. He felt completely unable to move until Yves appeared carrying a spade. The servant bowed to Charmant and then plowed the implement into the pulped mess of Alain's flattened body. Gray and purple offal sprayed its fetid contents across the bloody mass and Charmant felt something inside his mind snap.

The giant prince stood, raising a foot to crush his faithful servant. As he rushed upward toward the chromatic stars, Charmant shrieked at his own, out of control body.

He tried to shout "no," to force his enormous foot backward and keep Yves safe. Instead, a high-pitched, screaming laugh bubbled up his throat and burst past his lips.

CHAPTER 55

Light jabbed Charmant's eyelids. Gasping, he squinted for a moment, immediately closing his eyes again as the dawn pierced his vision. Taking stock of himself, he stretched his arms. Normal-size fists hit a dew-slimed tree trunk. Sitting up, he opened his eyes and looked around. Dark trees, barely lit with gray, early morning light surrounded him. Below him lay crushed ferns and rotting fruit.

Shifting became a chore as each joint shouted at him. A shiver ran up his clammy back, making his entire body tremble.

"How long have I been in the orchard?" the prince wondered to himself in a thick, dry voice.

Staggering to his feet, Charmant took a shuffling step toward a break in the trees ahead. His stride tiny, so small as to barely move his body forward. Feeling lightheaded, he examined his feet. They were the usual size, not the enormous extremities from his dream.

Bracing himself against a tree, the prince patted his body, touching clammy, goosebump-prickled skin with frigid fingers. Cold ran up his arms and legs in long, drawn out shivers. He reached down to touch the damp leather of his slippers. He was himself. The unreality of his dream faded as his hands felt the solidity of his body.

Cold and achy with a scratchy throat, Charmant dragged himself hand over hand, gripping slick trees as he pulled himself out of the orchard. The castle loomed dark in the gray dawn, eliciting a relieved sigh that devolved into a coughing fit. Gasping, Charmant managed to shamble across the damp garden path and up the stairs. Grasping the nearest column, he scanned the porch for the castle guard. At night, with no celebrations on the schedule, this entrance should be well protected.

Instead, the terrace doors burst open and two of Elle's henchmen loped out.

Charmant straightened, trying to look imposing in his haggard state.

"What are you doing?" Charmant demanded in a raspy voice.

One of the men kept walking while the other looked at him, his bug-eyes narrowing as much as they could.

"We are preparing to leave," he snapped, not pausing to bow.

Charmant watched the two hurrying backs until they disappeared on the leftmost path, the one leading to the family graveyard. He wanted to follow them, to find out what they were up to. God help him if they were robbing his family graves or otherwise disturbing the dead. His shaking intensified and his stiff neck protested as he turned his head to track the men's progress down the path. There was no way he could follow them in his current state.

Moving forward on wobbly legs, he crashed into the terrace doors and stumbled inside. The spacious ballroom sat empty, awaiting dancing feet and laughing voices. Dirt crunched beneath his boots, marring the appearance of a clean, empty room.

Those men must be tracking it back and forth, he thought, kneeling to touch the damp soil. As he crouched, his left knee locked up and he fell to his side, gasping at the sharp pain lancing up his leg to the small of his back. The prince writhed, trying to loosen the painful cramp's hold. Finally, the agony abated to an ache and Charmant pulled himself to his feet once more, not caring about the dank soil now clinging to him.

"Bed," he croaked in a dry voice. The room echoed back to him, "bed, bed, bed" as he limped away.

Staggering through the empty castle, Charmant used all his strength to take one step after the next. With each exhausted footfall, he wondered where all the guards and servants were. This was the exact scenario in which they would be useful, yet the entire place sat empty. No servants dozed in front of his father's room; no servant paced the flagstones to scent the stale air with sweet herbs.

After what seemed an eternity of empty rooms and passageways, his door emerged from the darkness. Charmant swung the door open and stumbled into the darkened room. Soft shafts of dawn light filtered in, providing gray, hazy illumination for him to view the empty bed. The prince sighed in relief, hacking out a cough as he did. Elle was not in his room, nor were her strange minions.

Staggering to a chair, Charmant sat and stripped, removing dirt-smeared and damp clothes. Skin prickling in goosebumps, he remembered the cut on his arm.

"God's bones," he swore softly. He'd have to care for the wound before collapsing into bed.

Elle had cut through his shirt and the bandage he'd placed over the wound, so the dirt and damp from a night spent in the orchard now clung to the scabby, sticky mess. Standing creakily, he stepped to the cold washbasin. Dipping a nearby cloth into the water, he soaked the bandage until it loosened, then peeled it back to expose the wound. Immediately, blood dribbled from the cut.

Charmant gritted his teeth and lurched to his wardrobe. Rummaging around, he found the bags he'd taken to the abbey. The old battle kit he'd carried lay ready, still filled with needle, thread, bandages, and salve.

Looking around, he spotted the carafe of watered wine sitting next to an empty goblet on his nightstand. Pouring a cup, he took a long gulp, then mixed the powdered salve with wine until it thickened into a paste. Using his pinky, he hissed through his teeth as he applied the stinging mix.

Agonizing fire ran up his arm to the shoulder, telling him the salve was doing its work. Biting back a cry, he wrapped a cloth around the laceration, trusting the damp salve to keep the bandage in place.

That done, the prince put on a simple tunic and lay in his bed. He closed his eyes and prayed for a dreamless sleep.

CHAPTER 56

Ghostly, unformed images trailing gray shrouds plagued Charmant's dark dreams until Yves shook him awake. The sun slanting through his narrow bedroom window showed him the day was almost done.

"Sire, Your Highness," whispered the servant. "You look ill. Shall I call a healer?"

Sweat-soaked and coughing, Charmant shook his head.

"Do you not, Yves, have a curative brew you can provide me? Something your apothecary father would recommend, perhaps?" he croaked.

Yves filled a goblet with well-watered wine and handed it to the prince. The one in which Charmant had mixed his salve was gone.

I wonder how long he worried over me before waking me, thought the prince as he sipped. It felt nice to be fussed over, especially when all of his bones ached, and he could barely see through a throbbing headache.

"Yes, I do have such a brew, my lord. When I saw you coughing, I took the liberty of making a tea my mother prepared whenever I caught a chill. Would you like some? I must warn you, it's foul-tasting stuff. But it always worked for me."

"Yves," croaked the prince, his throat still dry. "I would take anything to feel better. I am sore all over. I feel as if my brothers had put me in a sack and beat me with sticks."

Yves raised an eyebrow but didn't comment. Charmant was reminded that his brothers were dead, along with his mother, sister, and all his childhood servants as well as the cousins his siblings were slated to marry - or had they already been married? His mind grew foggy, and he began to slip back into sleep.

Returning to his side, Yves supported the prince's drooping head and poured a foul, dung-tasting brew down his master's throat.

The prince gave a yelp and a cough as he choked it down.

"Oh," he groaned. "I hope your mother knows what she's about. That stuff tastes wretched."

"It has always worked for me, Your Highness," Yves replied. "Rest for a bit and allow it to heal what ails you. I shall return to dress you for dinner."

Charmant's stomach gave a lurch at the thought of his father's usual evening feast filled with meat-heavy courses. He didn't think he could choke down an almond in his current condition.

In spite of himself, he let out a whimper and curled into a ball on his sweat-soaked bed.

Yves placed a cool cloth on his head and rolled him from side to side, deftly layering a dry blanket below him and one above him, then tucking him in tightly.

"Sleep, Your Highness. If the brew works for you the way it does for me, your appetite will be roaring back in no time."

A while later, Charmant woke. It felt as if Yves had given him the wretched medicine only moments ago, but when he opened his eyes, he saw candlelight flickering in his eastern-facing room as the sun had traveled to the west side of the castle.

Yves stood beside him once again, smiling.

"How do you feel, Your Highness?" he asked.

Charmant took stock of his body. The aches had left him and he felt refreshed. Rubbing his eyes, he noticed tiredness, but no pain.

"What is in that stuff?" he asked, sitting up. His head swam for a moment, but then his vision steadied. "It is miraculous."

"Drink this, Your Highness," Yves handed him a glass of watered wine, which Charmant downed eagerly. Yves refilled it with a warm, golden liquid. Charmant looked at him, suspicious.

"It is honey mead, Your Highness."

He sipped and the thick fruity flavor struck him.

"This is the strangest mead I have ever tasted," he remarked, peering into his glass.

"It is my mother's blend. I keep it and the concoction you drank earlier today to maintain my health and that of my fellow servants. I will have to tell her it revived royalty. She will be thrilled."

A memory struck the prince. He'd had fevers and illnesses in childhood and, though he'd been sick more times than he could count, he recalled one crystal moment. His mother and childhood nursemaid stood over him in a bright room. They'd tucked him into warm blankets and took the shutters down so a light summer breeze rustled the dry, fragrant herbs hanging from the ceiling. He'd just woken to find them talking in soft voices, smiling at one another over their needlework. His mother, seeing his wakeful face, walked over to him and placed a cool, delicate hand over his sweating forehead. He shut his eyes and enjoyed the sensation of her coolness against his hot, aching skin. Above him, her musical voice whispered a lullaby as he fell back into sleep.

Charmant smiled at his servant, heart aching with longing for the mother he'd lost and a hint of jealousy.

"Your mother sounds lovely, Yves."

"She is truly wise, Your Highness. My father doesn't admit it often, but he learned quite a bit from her."

Drinking the rest of his mead, Charmant put down the glass and stood. Yves lit the room's rushlights and ushered in the dressers, helping to bathe and dress the prince alongside the experts.

As he dressed, Charmant felt his stomach tighten, hunger creeping up on him. By the time they were finished with him, his stomach growled loud enough for everyone to hear. Yves smiled, but all of the other servants remained downcast until Charmant himself chuckled.

"I suppose it is time for dinner," he exclaimed. "Let us be done and we shall all have our meal."

His dressers looked at him, a tentative smile crossing their faces. They hurried their work with skilled hands and bowed as he left.

CHAPTER 57

The evening's meal was uneventful. The king told him that he would be leaving in the morning, which meant that Charmant would have to take on the day-to-day running of the kingdom.

"It is not much work, son. Just listen to the people. You have a good heart, and you will do what is right. Oh, and do not forget to send that huntsman to kill the wolf," the king told him.

Charmant nodded. A rush of relief washed over him, and he sent up a silent prayer of thanks.

Thank you for sending my father away from the castle. Thank you for keeping him safe from the hell spawn that I married.

"I will do all that you say and more, father," he declared. "I will not let my kingdom down."

The uneventful evening rolled into a bustling morning. Charmant woke early after another restless night filled with unearthly dreams. His visions of falling through a great chasm filled with eerie singing faded as he wished his father a pleasant journey and sent him on his way.

When the doors shut behind the king, Charmant heaved a great sigh. He did not trust his wife to keep her word and protect his family. Looking around, he was pleased to see that Elle made herself scarce during his father's departure. The evening before he had given his father the excuse that she was tending to her sisters and stepmother, but Charmant knew that she spent her time commanding her servants in the tunnels, seeking a way back to her home.

The thought struck him that she would be opening a passage to another place. Maybe even to Hell.

Should I tell the abbot? he wondered. He shook his head, lost in thought. The abbot would think him as mad as those he housed in the hospital.

"Your Highness?" asked a familiar voice. It was Yves.

The prince stood straight and smiled at his favorite servant.

"Yes, Yves?"

"There are people here to see you, people seeking the advice of the king?"

"Of course," nodded Charmant. He mounted the dais and sat to the right of his father's empty throne. He would deal with Elle after he cared for his people.

"Oh, Yves," said the prince before he allowed the first supplicant into the great hall.

"Yes, Your Highness?"

"See that no one - not even you - disturbs my lady's servants. They are repairing the cellar and she told me it is delicate work. I do not want my castle staff put into danger. Apparently, the ceilings down there are quite waterlogged and unstable."

"Of course, Your Highness. Thank you for considering our safety," bowed Yves.

Charmant nodded. "You may allow the first person to come in now."

After listening to legal matters, complaints, and requests for much of the day, Charmant took a break. The shiny newness of attending his people had worn into a dull sheen. He was glad to help but felt dizzied by the number of people who wished to talk with him.

"I must end after the next person," he told Yves. "The rest will need to come tomorrow."

"There is just one supplicant left, Your Highness," Yves replied.

Charmant heaved an enormous sigh of relief.

"Let them in." He sat up, trying to portray regality as the two men walked in with bowed heads.

"How may I help?" asked the prince.

The men looked up. Both were dressed plainly, though they had clearly tried to clean themselves before approaching the castle. As Charmant assessed them, he noticed that they looked alike, though one was young - almost a boy - and the other an older man. Father and son, he surmised.

"Oh, Your Majesty," the older of the two began. "Our shepherd boy has been murdered. His mutilated body left in the field and two sheep were carried off as his body grew cold."

"Do you believe it was the wolf I have heard so much talk of?"

The men paused, looking at him with wide mouths.

"You have heard of the wolf, Your Majesty?" the younger blurted.

"Indeed. When did you say this happened?"

"Just this morning, Your Highness. We came as soon as we could."

"Call the huntsman," Charmant commanded Yves. Excitement zipped through his veins. The capture of this wolf would mark the beginning of his reign and would deliver him the love and adoration of his people.

The huntsman came presently.

"You must put an end to these wolf attacks, huntsman. These men will show you were to begin. In fact," he raised his voice, "let it be known throughout the land that any wolf killed and brought to the castle will result in a reward of one gold coin per head."

A buzz went around the room and a herald asked, "Shall we tell the news to the town criers, Your Highness?"

"Yes," said the prince. "I will not have my people attacked by wild animals. We live in a civilized land and must put these beasts in their place."

The men bowed and the huntsman left with them. Charmant stretched and smiled to himself. This would bring the adoration of his people; he just knew it.

"I must have a meal, and then visit my sisters and mother-in-law," he told Yves, standing.

"Yes, Your Highness," bowed his servant.

Charmant walked to his room, feeling as if he'd put in a good day's work. Though only midday, he had already tackled many issues plaguing his land.

As he opened the door, something rumbled below his feet, causing him to grab onto the door frame. Around him, masonry shifted, and dust fell.

"What on earth was that?" he asked the empty room.

CHAPTER 58

We are in! thought Elle. *After centuries of waiting and searching, we are here, in my place of power, and we are in.*

Around her, men worked furiously, carting away crystal-studded rocks. The purple geodes sparkled in the candlelight, dazzling the eye and bringing a smile to Elle's face.

The men carefully removed each rock, passing it up the tunnel. As Elle stared at the gaping rift, one large piece of crystal cracked off, falling inside the enormous cavern within.

"Brace yourselves!" Elle called. She pushed against a wall, strengthening the tunnel with her own body. The men did the same.

The crystal hit the bottom of the cave with a loud crash and the entire structure shook violently. Mud and timber fell inward, partially burying the frantically dug tunnel.

As soon as the shaking stopped, Elle shouted orders.

"Shore up that wall, fix that beam," she yelled, pointing with one arm. "Make sure the entrance is still open. Keep digging!"

Her internal time sense told her they had only a short period before the cavern healed itself for good, burying her and her men in the process.

CHAPTER 59

In the castle above, Charmant found himself examining every inch of the structure, assessing the damage. Turning a corner, he found Octave doing the same thing.

"It appears that the castle is sound, Your Highness," the servant told him.

Charmant nodded his thanks, but continued walking. Visually scanning the stone and the ground, he occasionally poked or prodded a block, trying to dig into the mortar that joined them. After a tour of almost every stone in the entire castle, he had to admit that the solidly built structure held despite the strange rumbling from below.

There is one place yet to examine, he thought, standing in front of the looming cellar door. With great effort, he dragged a hand to the banded wood door. While every room and turret in the castle belonged to him, the thought of walking into the cellar filled his stomach with acid dread.

It is my castle, he thought.

As though someone else read his mind, a voice whispered in his mind, *but it is her domain.*

Heart lurching into his throat, Charmant glanced around. The unpopulated hall stretched out behind him. No one whispered in his ear. He shook his head, trying to dislodge the frightening voice, so different from his own.

Gritting his teeth, he pushed.

The moment the door cracked open, wings brushed his face and little claws dug into each shoulder.

Charmant turned his head awkwardly and stared into two beady eyes.

The songbird on his right shoulder glared at him, then deliberately shook its head three times. He turned to the other direction to bring himself face to face with a second songbird. It caught his eye and shook its head three time as well.

He removed his hand from the door and took a step back.

Both songbirds lifted their wings and launched themselves from his shoulders, gliding up to the top of a decorative tapestry that adorned the hallway. From there, they stared at him until he left the hall completely, returning to the great hall. There, he crouched, hands on knees, sucking in great lungfuls of warm summer air.

Octave almost walked into him; the servant's eyes still busy assessing the castle walls.

"Your Highness," he bowed. "I did not see you there."

Pausing, Octave looked at the prince with curious eyes. Charmant could not help but contrast this man's eyes with the small bird's eyes. Those had been black and angry while these soft hazel eyes crinkled in concern.

"Are you well? Ought I to call a doctor?"

"Thank you, no," the prince forced himself to straighten. "I am bracing myself for a visit to my sisters and mother-in-law. I fear their condition may be difficult to see."

Octave nodded gravely.

"Ah, yes. I shall fetch you a bracing draft of wine. That will help lift your spirits."

Charmant pushed a smile onto his lips as the servant hurried off.

Though dread filled his heart, a corner of it now glowed in gratitude. Good people filled this castle.

I must keep them safe, somehow, he thought. A vision flashed across his mind. In it, Elle used the key to open a fiery portal to Hell, laughing as the castle crashed around her, consigning those within to a horrible death.

Octave broke into his apprehension, handing the prince a goblet. "Drink this, Your Highness. And may God smile down upon your visit to the afflicted."

Tossing the entire goblet back in one large gulp, Charmant's stomach roiled. He craved the disgusting tinctures and sweet mead that Yves gave him when he was ill, not this harsh brew. But he gave his faithful servant a smile and started his trek to the de Noelles Marchand sick chambers.

A thought struck him, and he turned back to Octave. The servant was touching a rock, digging into the mortar, probing the castle's stability.

"Octave?" asked the prince.

The man turned and bowed.

"Yes, Your Highness?"

"I do not know what that tremor was."

The servant sighed, his shoulders slumped, and his cheerful veneer vanished.

"I am hoping to ascertain the cause myself," he stated.

"I think," Charmant paused while his steward looked at him expectantly. "I think perhaps the castle staff ought to visit their families over the next two or three days. I am unsure if it is safe here. I believe I will try to convince the ill ladies to move back home."

Octave's face went white in the darkening hall.

"Your Highness, that is most irregular. Are you certain? What of the princess? What of you?"

"I believe we can all make a tour of the chateau de Noelles Marchand for two or three days. And, of course, any servants who do not have family nearby can stay in the outer buildings and come with us.

I... I do not want any more deaths on my conscience. Please, humor me, Octave."

The servant straightened his spine and bowed low.

"Of course, Your Highness, as you wish. The evenings have turned pleasant and I believe many of our servants who do not have family nearby can stay out of doors until your party leaves for the chateau. We can set up a camp and, perhaps create a bit of a festival atmosphere."

The man's eyes were lighting up as he mulled over the idea. Charmant's strained smile turned genuine as he listened to his servant's musings. Just like the king, the castle steward clearly loved a party.

"That will include you, Octave," the prince pointed out. "We cannot have you coming to harm in this place. And please send messengers to the nearest stone masons. They must look at the castle."

"You employ a stone mason and two assistants," Octave informed him gently.

"Excellent. While I visit my sick family, tell the stone masons that they must stay behind as the rest of the staff evacuate. I wish them to inspect our castle's solidity."

Charmant licked his lips. In his heart, he knew the cause. But he had to do something. He couldn't let Elle tear down his home.

"Tonight, Your Highness?" asked Octave.

"Yes, tonight. They must ascertain it is safe before everyone returns."

The man's eyes went wide.

"You wish the evacuation to occur tonight?"

"Yes, and make sure as many people as possible have a roof over their heads and dry ground beneath their feet. I do not want to see anyone camping out in the orchards or by the lake. It is too cold and damp there. They will catch a chill," Charmant said, thinking fast.

Octave bowed again, shaking his head a little.

"As you say, Your Highness."

Charmant nodded and turned back to the west wing. He hoped convincing his mother-in-law and her daughters to leave the castle would be as easy as ordering the castle steward. Somehow, though he was the prince, and this was his castle, he knew Lady de Noelles Marchand would not be easy to convince.

CHAPTER 60

"We cannot leave," rasped Lady de Noelles Marchand. "You are cruel indeed to evict us from your castle."

"It is for your safety and that of your daughters, my lady," urged Charmant. The importance of the situation filled his heart and pushed him to insist. "I believe you and your children are in particular danger."

The bedraggled noblewoman looked up at him from her bed. Visibly shaking, she tried to speak, her voice coming out in a dry, hacking cough. Licking her lips, she tried again.

"It is Elle, is it not?" Her voice sounded like paper rubbing upon the sand. Charmant picked up a cup filled with watered wine and offered it to her. She shook her head minutely and he handed the cup to Lady de Noelles Marchand's personal attendant.

The elderly servant stood at her mistress's head, clearly distressed. Her grim face turned dark the moment Prince Charmant ordered them to evacuate.

Charmant refocused on Lady de Noelles Marchand. He wondered how much this woman knew. How much she had kept secret from him. He wanted to feel angry, to clench his fists and grit his teeth at her deception. But, gazing down at the sick woman, he was unable to direct any fury at her. Instead, he thought of Elle and her deceptions. If this woman had told him of her stepdaughter's true nature, he never would have believed her.

Keeping his voice even and gentle, he replied. "Yes."

Tears trickled from the lady's eyes. She made no move to wipe them. The elderly servant caring for Lady de Noelles Marchand sprang into action, wiping her tears. Gently, the servant propped her lady up and managed to get Lady de Noelles Marchand to sip the drink Prince Charmant had offered moments ago.

Charmant felt annoyance stir in his chest but tamped it down. The lady was being contrary, but she was ill, her daughters had been attacked, and now he was trying to make her leave a comfortable castle for the cold air outdoors. He needed to exhibit patience. Taking a deep breath, he listened as she said, "I knew Elle would be the death of me. She would not let us go, though she clearly wanted something greater than our small family."

Charmant nodded.

"Did you know we are the last of the de Noelles? If I and my children die, all of our titles and monies go to Elle."

The prince knew this, hadn't thought about it. Elle's dowry was so great that he did not covet the de Noelles Marchand's wealth. It had brought him relief to know that the girls would have their dowries covered and he would not need to spend anything on them.

"I suppose I did," he admitted.

The lady reached out grasping for his hands. Charmant took her frail fingers in his.

"Please, Your Highness, do not let that girl destroy everything my family has built."

"That is what I am trying to do, my lady. I am trying to save your life and those of your daughters."

Lady de Noelles Marchand shook her head.

"It is too late for me, and Adeline will not last much longer. Take Enora back home. Make sure she survives this."

"But you can be moved, my lady," he insisted. "I do not wish to save simply your daughters, but you as well."

She shook her head. "I will not live to see tomorrow. Elle has made certain of that," she gestured weakly to the cup, now resting on a nearby table. "She has poured tincture after tincture down my throat. I shall not last long."

Charmant's mind whirled in confusion. His face must have shown his shock and disbelief because Lady de Noelles Marchand's face softened.

"I am sorry to tell you, but your wife is a poisoner Your Highness. Only the lucky few went mad and are cared for by the monks. I have been careful for many years, but she took advantage of my vulnerability. The poison courses through me now. It is slow acting, but if it works as others have, I will die with my precious Adeline tonight."

The dying noblewoman fixed the prince with a hard look. Her voice grew stronger, brusquer. "You will do your duty as Enora's brother and ensure she is married to a good husband. The de Noelles line must survive."

"Of course, my lady. I will do everything I can to save you and your family," replied the prince.

Lady de Noelles Marchand nodded.

"Good, now leave and go attend to my Enora. I wish to be moved into bed next to my Adeline. I have nothing further to say," she turned her face away from him, addressing her attendant.

"Assist me. I must move to my daughter's side."

Prince Charmant watched for a moment, noting Lady de Noelles Marchand's shaking hands and trembling voice. He bowed to her and wondered at her strength. The woman was clearly terrified, marked for death. But she remained strong for the one daughter she believed could survive this turbulence.

If I were marked for death, he thought, *I do not believe I would be so sanguine.*

CHAPTER 61

S wiftly and carefully the Noamhites carved a hole large enough for Elle to squeeze through. She pushed through the crowd, grabbing one of their tools and a torch on her way into the cavern.

Stepping gingerly, Elle crossed the threshold from gray quartz through the ethereal chalcedony and calcite and into the sparkling interior. A lesser being would have immediately fallen to the floor far below, but Elle shifted her form to balance on the delicate crystals lining the interior of the cavernous space.

Her long, thin form clutching the walls, she lifted the torch high and watched as firelight glimmered off every surface. The enormous space was round and lined with purple and pink crystals, into which eldritch symbols were carved. It looked like the interior of the largest geode ever created.

Examining a nearby crystal, Elle read the language of her people written into the mineral.

Home, she read. Each crystal told a similar story, sharing the journey her people had made through time and space to this dimension and this planet. Finding the seeds of life here, they observed the development of plants and animals. Finally, funny little apes hopped down from the trees and walked on two legs.

When those apes armed themselves and showed signs of intelligence, many of her people decided to leave. They congregated in this place as well as other transport portals positioned around the planet, and they left. Most of them.

Elle remembered the stories from her own childhood back home. She'd heard how her great grandmother lived on Earth for millennia, leaving as the planet grew crowded. Her great grandmother's stories sounded wondrous. A planet filled with enormous beasts, delicious and dangerous foods, and enormous swathes of salt and fresh water. Elle had dreamed of dipping into those foreign pools. So, one day, she'd left home to adventure on her own. She'd risen from a portal below the surface of the moors and presented herself as a goddess to those simple tribespeople.

However, the women of the tribe were not simplistic. They'd learned about the monsters of the water from their ancestors, and they bound her tightly, destroying her portal and trapping her here, in this form, for more than a thousand years. She'd had to watch as these idiotic apes attempted to discover physics, math, science, constantly losing information and bumbling around like a bunch of simpletons. She'd come for a quick jaunt to frighten the locals and plumb the depths of the seas and swamps. Instead, she had become stuck in a form that could barely hold its breath in those waterscapes.

Fortunately, the woman did not know all. They could not bind her every form.

A small mouse extruded itself from Elle's body and went scampering off, climbing down the crystalline path to the darkness below. Her worshipers were the many times great grandchildren of the women who had trapped her. She would bring them back with her to her homeland. Her long absence would not be rewarded, per se, but at least she would come bearing gifts.

The Changed One in her group was her greatest accomplishment. She hadn't known if she could change human bodies and make them more like her own after the ancient druids bound her, but the Changed One was proof that she still had the power to force the atoms and molecules of another living being to change - even if slowly.

Her mouse-self encountered something at the bottom of the cavern, something she'd hoped to find. Scrabbling up, the little creature climbed to the top of a switch, then jumped down onto it, using its small weight to push down the lever.

The chamber shifted around Elle, long, low steps forming out of the crystal beneath her feet. A fierce joy warmed her, flames burning blue at each fingertip as she descended.

The long, steep, and slick staircase stretched to the cave floor. Though she wanted to dance down the crystalline path, Elle took each step carefully, as if she were walking down a waxed staircase in glass slippers. When she reached the bottom, Elle's mouse reattached itself, resorbing into her skin as if it had never been.

Lifting her torch, she peered around the cavern. Her heart filled with joy at the familiar surroundings. The glittering walls led to a broad, flat expanse of quartz flooring interrupted by one enormous black pool positioned precisely in the center of the room. Carvings etched the ground, artfully swirling toward the pool in neat, intricate rows.

Each scene told the story of her people's travels across the stars and galaxies. Worlds beyond this one glittered across the floor. Every image burst with life, the artisan clearly displaying to any traveler that, though they were leaving this world, the next would be filled with adventure.

Elle found the carvings depicting her home world and followed their circuitous route to the midnight pool. The black, still expanse of basalt-like substance stuck to the floor of the cavern like glue. A deep obsidian when viewed from far away, clusters of light and swirls of color appeared in the darkness upon her approach. Once activated, it would transform into a portal, shooting her through space to her home planet.

The journey would kill many of her followers, as they were not genetically adapted to traverse cold and airless space. But she and possibly the Changed One would survive the journey - once she returned to her natural form.

Crouching in front of the black substance, Elle hovered a hand over it. A deep ache filled her and her eyes fixed on her home solar system. She wished she could dive in now, dive in and go home. Her still-human appendage almost touched the icy stone. Almost, but not quite. She stood up suddenly, fighting temptation. It had to be done properly. She must return to her form to survive the journey.

Bracing herself against longing, she turned and walked up the crystalline steps. It was time to gather her followers, the book, and the key. Once they were all inside the cavern, she could begin.

CHAPTER 62

The setting sun sent fiery rays over the western castle wall. Rough tents were erected across the courtyard and around the many small buildings that populated the castle complex. The tents and surrounding buildings burst with servants preparing to bed down for the night.

Three tents stood out against the setting sun. Each were set up for the nobles still in residence at the castle. The largest tent with flowing cloth walls sat open, awaiting the prince. The tent to the right of this was smaller, though no less ostentatious with its colorful cloth walls set against the drab brown and gray shanties the servants had managed to erect for themselves. This was designated for Princess Elle. The final grand tent stood behind the princess's and, while it was larger than both the prince and princesses' tents, it was less grandly appointed, the walls made of snug wool rather than flowing linen. This was the medical tent set up for Lady de Noelles Marchand and her two daughters.

The first two tents stood unoccupied. The last housed Enora.

Inside the castle, the halls echoed as Charmant paced in front of his comatose sister-in-law's door. His mother-in-law, along with her attendant, had barricaded herself and the young woman inside.

"You must come out, my lady," he called through the door.

No reply.

Two strong men stood respectfully at the end of the hall, awaiting orders.

Heaving a huge sigh, the prince nodded to the men.

They picked up a large cord of wood and, together, pounded it against the door. After several tries, it was clear they could not get up enough momentum to break down the door, though their attempts dented the banded wood.

They dropped their battering ram, and the largest man kicked the door with his booted foot. The lock broke, but the door stayed firm.

"Has she blocked it?" asked the prince in dismay.

The largest man half nodded, half shrugged, sweaty hair falling into his eyes.

"No matter," declared the prince, putting his shoulder to the door. The second servant rushed up to join him and they all heaved together.

Something behind the door groaned and scraped along the floor as they pushed with all their might. Eventually, a narrow gap opened. The two burly men were much larger than Charmant, leaving him to push through the small opening.

One of the servants rushed to light a taper and handed it to the prince, who thrust the candle, along with his head and chest, into the dark room. Two shadowy forms lay on the bed, neither moving. The silent room seemed to oppress the candlelight, making it impossible to see the bed that lay beyond. All the prince saw from his vantage was an overturned cup, dark liquid bleeding into the fragrant herbs strewn across the wood floor.

"Oh no," whispered the prince. He sniffed. While lavender, mint, and rose sweetened the air, a foul smell lay beneath.

Pulling his body through the gap, he gained his legs. Thrusting the light forward, it revealed the sickbed. Warm furs and expensive linen covered his sister and mother-in-law. Their translucent skin, blue lips, and motionless chests revealed the obvious. The two women were dead. Behind him, the door scraped open a little further and one of the servants squeezed through the gap.

"Your Highness, I..." the man stopped.

"They are both dead. We must call for a priest."

"Of course," the man said bowing.

"Get the obstruction moved and then call a priest so he can bless the bodies. We must do this properly."

"Yes, Your Highness."

Prince Charmant turned and left the room, the numbness of grief adding weight to his limbs. He had failed these two noblewomen. They had died under his roof. His father was right, and he was wrong. The ladies de Noelles Marchand were slated to die, and the king had been wise to leave the castle to avoid the sight of the two dead women. And now it was left to the prince to deal with the aftermath.

CHAPTER 63

Gazing down at the sleeping Lady Enora, the prince decided not to wake her. This child was now his responsibility. Looking at her, he realized how little he knew about her. He hadn't truly seen her during his pursuit of Elle. She was likely twelve or thirteen, barely a marriageable age. He wondered if her mother would have kept her back another year or two if it were not for his father throwing those ridiculous balls. What an extravagance, and what heartache had ensued.

The prince vowed to care for this girl, to marry her to a noble family when she was ready to do so and, in the meantime, to keep her safe and her dowry intact. He would treat her as a sister. Tears pricked his eyes. She was the only sister he had left.

He thought of Elle and the creature she had been all along. He hoped she would leave his castle soon, leave and never return. One day he would marry again, but not for love or infatuation. He would marry a woman of noble birth with childbearing hips and provide her with the life she'd been brought up to expect. He would be gentle with her, but she would give him heirs aplenty.

Something shaved off his heart. He could feel it. Something

fundamental that had made him the sort of prince who falls for a beautiful woman the moment his eyes rested on her dainty figure. From now on, he would not be fooled by a woman's exterior.

Turning and leaving the tent, he instructed the girl's servants to keep her safe and breathe not a word of her mother and sister's deaths. He would inform her when she awoke.

The servants bowed. Every one of them looked confused. It was strange enough that a prince would deign to speak with them. But it was the least strange thing he'd done in the past days.

Charmant wondered if they all thought him mad. Perhaps he was. The monster his wife had shown herself to be would bring madness to any heart.

He strode over to the eastern side of the castle, the side he'd forbidden the servants to camp on. A slight breeze rustled through the orchard leaves, but he could feel a strangeness in the air. No bird-song broke the silence. The occasional rabbit or mouse did not bound from a nearby bush. Narrowing his eyes, he searched the grounds for a reason, but nothing appeared. The animals had departed with no sign as to why.

As he turned to the western side of the castle, he caught sight of a strange light glistening from between the trees. Squinting, he gazed into the orchard once again. Two luminous eyes blinked through the dense greenery.

Heart in his throat, Charmant backed into the shadows of the castle, pushing against cold stonework to watch.

Dark branches rattled and trees shook as something large pushed through them. Apples and pears, not yet ripe, battered the ground. Then, two trees fell with a resounding crash.

The thing from the lake slithered out of the orchard.

Charmant's lips clamped together, holding back bile as the tentacled monstrosity slimed its way to the castle terrace. The massive creature oozed along on four greasy tentacles, each ending in splayed, five tentacled extremities.

Hands? Feet? wondered the prince as he stared. The monster gripped each stone with sucker-covered finger-like tentacles and used that anchor to pull its mass up each castle step. Behind it, a trail of gray slime glistened in the dying light.

Losing sight of the creature when it mounted the terrace, Charmant stepped out from the castle wall, his limbs heavy with terror and his hands gripped into tight, white fists. He needed to see it, needed to make sure it disappeared into the now-empty castle and did not somehow climb the walls and fall upon him, devouring him with a yet-unseen mouth.

He watched as the creature made its way to the terrace doors. The lake monster loomed taller than the doorway, and its tentacles spanned wider than the entrance.

Charmant clasped a hand over his mouth to keep from screaming as he watched the abomination contract, pulling its waving tentacles close and flat, now resembling a giant slug. One sucker-covered tentacle hand reached out and grasped the lintel, pulling the slimy horror through.

The monster disappeared into the castle's gloom.

Charmant uncovered his mouth and retched, throwing up the contents of his stomach onto a lavender bush. He clasped his knees with his hands, crouching and heaving until there was nothing left.

Face flushed and hands shaking, he wiped his mouth with his sleeve and peered back into the shadowy castle. His home. That thing now squelched its way through his home.

He had to follow it. Had to make sure it left with Elle or, if it didn't...he shuddered.

If it doesn't leave with Elle, I have to kill it.

Standing up straight, he pulled his everyday knife from its place on his belt. It looked dull and ineffectual in the gloaming, but it would have to do. Returning it to his belt, he glanced around once more. The oppressive quiet gripped his heart.

Go, he told himself, *go go go go go.*

Stepping cautiously, the prince followed the slime trail up the stairs and into his castle.

CHAPTER 64

The ballroom smelled of murky lake water and something else. Something Charmant could not easily identify. He took a deep sniff of the tenebrous ballroom, stepping into the gloom further, trying to determine that unknown fragrance. The scent of putrid, briny water filled his nose. It was as if he were transported out of his castle, his home, and into the marshlands described by old Marchand in his letter.

Looking around, Charmant realized this place no longer belonged to him. It had been marked by the monster and by Elle. He didn't recognize the dank ballroom. It was not the same extravagant, well-lit place in which he'd danced with queens and noble daughters. Instead, evil lurked here.

It is now the residence of monsters, he thought.

It reminded him of stories his mother used to tell of giants. She would begin with the bible story of David and Goliath. Then, as each of his brothers would fall asleep, he would lay awake as she spun tale after fantastical tale about the giants of the wood, giants of the lake, giants of the mountain. Finally, seeing the youngest prince still awake and listening, she'd quietly tuck his wool blanket around him and

whisper "and they all slumber, deeply, in their domain. None shall
wake unless someone deliberately disturbs them. And you, my son,
shall never do so. Sleep well."

Charmant's guts twisted. He'd awoken the giant of the lake. He
or Elle, what did it matter? They'd awoken a monstrosity and it was
his duty as prince to send it back to its slumber.

With an effort, Charmant moved his legs. Stepping deliberately,
he walked forward on careful feet. The well-worn ballroom floor
creaked and groaned faintly, each sound so loud in his ears that he
was convinced the monster ahead could hear him coming. Looking
down through the stygian gloom, he noticed that the slime trail
glowed faintly. His fingers twitched as he wondered if this slime was
truly like that of a slugs or made of some stickier substance.

Gripping his hands together, he suppressed the urge to touch it.
Perhaps it could glue him in place, trap him and never let him go.
Maybe it would eat through his hands like lye through human flesh.
Perhaps touching the slime began your transformation into that
horrific lake creature.

He did not want to find out, so he placed his booted feet beside
the slime, avoiding it as much as he could and using the blue-green
glow of the gooey path ahead to light his way.

The trail wound through the ballroom and covered the entire
ballroom entrance. Charmant jumped over the threshold, a game he'd
played long ago when his brothers had convinced him that it was the
only way to keep evil spirits from chasing him into their home. The
jump from ballroom door to hallway may have banished evil spirits,
Charmant could not tell. But it did not prevent him from jumping
right onto the slime trail. The repulsive substance coated the hallway,
goo covering the floor, walls, and ceiling.

He tried to step thoughtfully, avoiding pools of the substance, but
even as he tried to step around the gunk, occasional globules splashed
down from the ceiling. As he walked, slime sprayed his hose and
seeped into his cloak, soaking him to the skin.

At the end of the trail stood the open cellar door, dripping with shining goo. Charmant sighed. He should have known.

Peering down the steps, he wondered if he should traverse the tunnel, to see what his wife, a different kind of monster, was doing down there. Curiosity tugged at his chest, making his heart beat faster. He took a step, then faltered. What if he got down the steps and walked right into that horrifying lake monster? Elle had warned him to stay out of her business. What if she went back on her word and killed him for intruding?

He looked around the hall. He could hear no fluttering bird wings. Perhaps all of her little minions were down there, with her.

Or, perhaps, Elle and her followers were leaving, and he could learn something to prevent her from ever returning. His duty was to his people, and a creature like Elle could never be suffered to exist in his land again.

Straightening his spine and shaking out his hands, he checked that his knife was still strapped to his side. Then, he stepped onto the first slime-smeared stair, then the next, walking steadily down into the bowels of the castle cellar.

CHAPTER 65

E merging from the staircase, Charmant blinked in the bright light. Rushlights or torches lit up the empty cellar and the tunnel beyond at regular intervals. While the flames revealed the room's emptiness, they also lit the trail sliming its way through the room and into the bright tunnel beyond.

Seeing it in full light made the substance appear even more menacing. Charmant had encountered thousands of slugs and snails in his lifetime. He'd played with them, killed them, rescued them from drowning. He'd watched in reverence as snail trails glistened in the morning sun like dew-soaked spiderwebs.

This trail sucked in the firelight, a slick of blackness coating the floor of the otherwise bright room. Seeing it opened a hole in Charmant's stomach, making his bladder feel full and his bowels ache.

It is a mark of death, the true mark of the Beast, he thought, his mind spinning as he stared. He would not be surprised if the trees this monster had touched sickened and died over the next days and weeks.

At that thought, he looked down at his boots and hose, feeling the viscous substance on his own skin. Stygian blackness covered his lower extremities. A shiver ran across his skin at the thought of traversing that tunnel of slime, risking his life every time he touched the black, tar-like substance. He looked behind him and realized he would have to move through the slime again if he backed out now. And by doing so, he would learn nothing.

Steeling his spine, he took a step forward, then another, and another as he followed the slime trail into the tunnel.

CHAPTER 66

The Changed One squeezed through the cavern opening and oozed down the steps to the flat ground below. All of Elle's people gathered around the pool, watching her expectantly. A fierce grin lit her face and her body flamed with enthusiasm.

"My people!" she shouted. "My faithful Noamhites. We join together in a final ceremony before I take all of you to my home, for you to live your days there in wonderment and joy."

She lifted the book and the key in triumph. They sparked in her hands, each contact burning her skin. Ignoring the pain, Elle shook the two objects for emphasis. The Noamhites bowed, even the Changed One.

"Rise, my people, and follow me in the ancient song and dance written in this book by your wise ancestors. Sing the words and dance the four patterns and you shall free me of the shackles here on earth, and free yourself of this earthly plane."

The Noamhites stood.

Elle cried out "Anns a 'chumha tha ar maighstir a' feitheamh!" Then, opening the book, she carefully sketched out a simple four-stepped dance.

Her people called after her, repeating her words. They sang the words again and again, dancing as she did, shaping the letter of power which opened the portal.

They stepped and sang again and again until Elle felt her bracelet grow hot on her wrist. She pressed the key against it, fitting it into a slight depression in the metal. The key clicked into place and the bracelet that had held her in human form for over a century slipped off, falling to the ground.

Elle exploded into her full form and her people paused in their song to watch, mouths open in wonder.

CHAPTER 67

Charmant peered down from the cavern entrance, watching as the flashing metal fell from her wrist. He gripped the wall, unable to tear his eyes away when her human body burst open, shedding any aspect of the beautiful woman he'd married. In its place stood a brilliant, glowing shape, amorphous in its moment of transformation, then solidifying into a tentacled monstrosity.

This being, this monster that was his wife, was formed purely of brilliantly white tentacles. Each seemed interconnected with no solid middle. From the tentacles sprung eyes in place of suckers, but those eyes would blink and become tiny mouths, which would close and then become suction pads. The tangle of tentacles was both horrifying and beautiful as its amorphous shape glowed with varying degrees of light. Some areas were impossible to gaze upon, while others refracted into crystalline colors like a rainbow.

Elle's beautiful and disturbing original form transfixed the both the prince and her Noamhites. Her people stared up at her incredible form, forgetting about their chant and the dance.

Charmant yanked his eyes away from Elle's form and onto the patch of pure black floating in the cavern's center. The flat stone slab he'd seen when he first peered into the cavern now rippled, filling with pinpricks of light. They were tiny at first, but as he stared, they grew in brilliance and clarity.

Stars, it is filling with stars, he thought, smiling in spite of himself. Quickly, he schooled his face. *Devilry is afoot,* he reminded himself, tearing his eyes from the star-filled wonder below.

"Sing and dance, my people," called Elle's intoxicating, contralto voice.

The Noamhites took up their chant again, Charmant watching their strange movements. As he observed, he found his mouth forming the foreign words, his feet shuffling in synchronistic movement.

Biting his lower lip and grasping the wall's crystalline surface so hard that blood trickled from his palms, he stilled himself. The urge to dance, to shout those words came over him in spasms, his tensed muscles attempting to move without his conscious control.

Shaking, Charmant fell to his knees and opened his mouth to gasp. Instead, a torrent of words burst from his lungs. Clamping both bloodied hands over his lips, he crawled backward on his knees, trying to get away from the irresistible force coming off the monstrous crowd below.

Charmant watched as Elle opened the book and began her own chant, something that wove between the words of her people. He could hear the sounds coming from her strange mouths, but they seemed garbled. It sounded as if she said, "Fosgailte, an uairsin faic doimhneachd àite sìorraidh."

As she spoke, the patch of starry black below swirled slowly. Then, it picked up speed, lights swinging from one edge to the other until it became a raging whirlpool. At the bottom of the pool shone a brilliant light that grew in luminosity until it filled the entire cavern, reflecting off the crystal surfaces and making it almost impossible to see.

Charmant squinted, transfixed as Elle's form approached the pool. She shouted something incomprehensible, her voice ringing with triumph, then dove into the whirlpool of stars. Her recon-structed form stretched eerily as she traversed the pool, as if it was not filled with water, but with space and time.

Watching her body shift and spread hurt Charmant's eyes, but he could not move, could not blink, as Elle's new form turned chromatic, glowing a brilliant red, then blue, then green, then every color he could possibly perceive. He would have stared for the rest of eternity, mesmerized by a being who seemed to fill the void of space with her very presence.

The cavern gave a great lurch, causing Charmant to fall back-ward. Crystals broke off the walls and peppered Elle's followers below. The followers, including the giant lake monster, chanted louder, moaning and crying out as they were tossed about the room and pelted with crystals.

Charmant gripped a nearby tunnel wall, yanking out clods of dirt as he pulled himself up. Hugging the wall, he wondered if he should stand there until the shaking settled as it had done before. That momentary convulsion had terrified him, but this roiling of earth and stone seemed to last for much longer.

As he wavered, wondering what to do, an enormous tentacle rose up from the bottom of the whirlpool and grasped one of the Noamhites by the wrist. The man screamed, whether in religious ecstasy or terror, Charmant could not be certain.

Elle's tentacle flung the frog-like human into the void, his body stretching beyond the breaking point, bursting into a vapor of blood, powdered bone, and bits of flesh.

Another tentacle rose from the black pool, driving Charmant's limbs into motion. Terror fueled his lurching escape up the shaking passage.

CHAPTER 68

Bursting from the tunnel entrance into the once-solid cellar, the new reality of falling stones and liquifying dirt confronted him. Tumbling to his knees, he watched as a crevasse formed in the center of the cellar, the once-flat floor now an ever-expanding black pit.

The floor is falling into the cavern, he thought.

Glancing around frantically, the prince tried to discern a way across as the candles and rushlights guttered and flickered. Soon, there would be no escape. He would be trapped in the deep black for the worms to eat. If he was lucky. If he was unlucky, he would fall back into the cavern from which he'd just escaped, a mush of blood and bone for the black pit to vaporize.

The ground beneath him shifted and he grabbed hold of a cracked stone wall as the dirt below his knees became unsubstantial, a hole forming where he once knelt. His sweat-slicked hands gripped the rocks, his dangling feet finding purchase against the wall just in time. Clinging to the cellar wall like a spider, the prince cast about for a way out.

The stone walls ahead had partially crumbled, creating a

constantly moving, but climbable path. At least, he prayed it was climbable. With just three rushlights still lit, shadows and moving stones made it almost impossible to clearly discern what lay ahead.

Climbing the uneven stones by touch, he made his way around the collapsing cellar, clinging desperately to the rapidly eroding walls as he went. Ahead loomed the dark stairway that led to the castle's main floor. He prayed he would get to the stairs in time to traverse them before they, too, collapsed.

His mouth moved, whispering entreaties to God as he gripped stonework with bloodied fingers and sweaty palms.

Ahead, a rumbling crash reverberated through the stairwell. Dust, dirt, and stone shards shot out of the opening, clouding the air and putting out the remaining rushlights. Charmant tried to cry out, inhaling grit and setting off a coughing fit that almost shook him from his precarious purchase.

Clutching the cracked wall, he peered through the gray and brown haze. It occurred to him that he could still see, though no candle or rushlight had survived that explosion. He spotted the source of the light, a hole in the ceiling on the other side of the now nonexistent stairway. It seemed impossibly far away as much of the cellar floor had turned into a murky, dust-spewing pit. Looking around, he saw no alternative exit. Only one avenue of escape remained.

Jamming his boots into uneven rocks, the prince imagined he was a goat, able to traverse the thinnest of paths. His fingers gripped the shaking stone, a hair's breadth away from becoming trapped in the wall , holding him there until his bones broke or stones knocked him from his perch.

It appeared that Providence watched over him, at least when it came to climbing walls. He managed to reposition his hands rapidly, finding footholds and handholds aplenty along the wall. The stairway entrance flummoxed him. Several of the stone steps had cracked and shifted so that knife-like edges lay exposed. The stone looked so sharp that he believed stepping upon one would slice his booted foot right open. Other stones had gone missing entirely, possibly thrown into the sucking abyss still spewing dust at the room's center. Below his feet, the last of the eroding dirt floor continued to evaporate into the void even as he gazed upon it. The rocks from the ceiling lay in a jumble at the other side of the former stairway entrance. If he could reach those rocks, he would have a way to climb up and out of the cellar.

Pausing for but a moment, the prince watched as the crevasse continued to expand, pulling more and more of the room down into it. His pathway to freedom would not be open for much longer. Soon, the castle would fall into the cavern, possibly into the sucking blackness below.

Charmant made a choice. He leapt onto the shifting ground, his booted right foot immediately sinking into the dust. Leaping from his uncertain purchase, he managed to avoid the sharp stones of the stairway and land on the first ceiling stone. His entire body hugged the stone for a moment before he got his knees under him. He could already feel his weight pushing the rock into the sucking dirt.

Scrambling to the next stone, and the next, he felt much like boulder-haunted Sisyphus, walking uphill eternally and getting nowhere. Each time he took a step forward, his makeshift ladder sunk lower.

At the last stone, he peered up into the weak light above. He cast about himself for more options, another exit, and saw none. Bending his knees, he made a desperate leap.

Sweaty, bloody hands grappled with the hole in the ceiling. His right hand found purchase as his left slipped. Dangling, he glanced over his shoulder. The cellar below sucked in the light, as if it were that starry pit, ready to destroy anything living. He pulled with all of his might, kicking his feet and managing to swing his left arm up.

Exhausted, straining muscles threatening to give any moment, he tried to pull his body up through the hole. It was useless. He had no strength left to give.

Looking down, Charmant tried to locate a wall or a stone he could use to provide leverage. Below his feet, he could see nothing.

A hand grabbed his left arm and Charmant's head snapped back around. He couldn't see who was above him in the dim light. Was it a Noamhite who had missed the homecoming? It felt as if the grasp pushed him back down into that sucking morass of dirt and death.

The prince opened his mouth to scream, to bite, anything to get that hand off of him. Then, a second hand latched onto his other arm with a firm grip and both arms yanked him up, out of the hole.

"Run!" came Yves' voice.

Charmant clutched his servant's shoulder, tears running down his face. Yves heaved forward, half dragging the prince down the crumbling castle halls.

CHAPTER 69

Standing outside of the castle, the prince and his servants watched as the structure crumbled inward. No one but Charmant understood that, below the castle, an enormous cavern now pulled his home into the ground. He didn't know if the entire building would fill the hole, or if it and the world around him would be pulled into the void through which Elle had disappeared. All he knew was that his servant, a man he barely knew, had followed him and saved his life.

He turned to Yves. The man watched slack-jawed; his eyes full of disbelief. Charmant wondered what his own eyes looked like. Jaded? Full of sadness? Empty and exhausted? He had no way of knowing.

The prince clapped his servant on the back and forced a smile. In the most jovial tone he could muster, he said, "I thought I ordered everyone who had family in the neighboring villages to go home tonight."

Yves turned to him; his dust-covered face haggard in the moonlight.

"I couldn't leave you, Your Highness. You needed me."

The prince nodded, his voice turning serious. "Thank you, Yves. I owe you a debt of gratitude."

The man smiled.

"There is something you do not know about me, Your Highness. May I share it with you now?"

Charmant nodded again.

"Long ago, my mother served at the castle. She came from a villein family, as lowborn as you can get. But she was beautiful and a hard worker. She met my father, the apothecary's son, and it was a true love match.

"My father's family was disgusted and refused to pay for her release. But my father went to the king - your father's cousin - and begged for her freedom. The former king did not care for the match, but your mother happened to be visiting at the time. She was young, as were my father and mother, and she believed in true love. Though she was but a visitor to the castle, she influenced the king to release my mother at no cost to her family, and she gifted my mother with a jeweled mantle worth far more than anything anyone in my family line has ever owned.

"Your mother's gift of a dowry allowed my parents to marry and gave my father the means he needed to support them.

"So, when the king, your father, called for servants, I asked to be selected. My entire family owes your mother a debt of gratitude and I mean to repay that debt."

Charmant listened, entranced, tears tracking through the dirt on his face. The sight of his monstrous wife and her wickedness, the loss of his home, and this beautiful story of his own mother's goodness overwhelmed him. He found he could not speak, but instead embraced his servant.

"Your debt is paid, my friend. You have saved my life and earned my trust. If it pleases you to leave, you may do so. But if you stay, I shall find a way to reward your kindness many times over." The prince pulled back, his gaze returning to the dust cloud over his ruined castle, sparkling in the moonlight. "Though, at the moment, I find I am without a castle."

Yves knelt before Charmant.

"I will serve you until the end of my days in any way that you wish, Your Highness," he said.

Charmant helped him up, touched by the display.

"Thank you," he peered around at the other gathered servants and spotted Octave. "Now, unfortunately, we determine the best course forward for this evening and over the next several months. My wise father is not here to advise me, and neither is his favorite counselor."

He waved to Octave.

"Let us camp here for the evening with whatever we have. Fortunately, it is a warm night. In the morrow, we shall take up temporary lodging at the Chateau de Noelles Marchand, which I believe I now own."

Octave bowed and herded the servants away from the ruin.

The prince and his servant got very little sleep that night. Yves stayed at the prince's side, as Charmant lay in silence, eyes firmly shut. The brilliant stars above dizzied the prince and reminded him of the view he'd witnessed in the black pit.

When he was a soldier, he loved sleeping rough on a summer's night. He'd even written poetry about the dark mantle above them, decorated with beautiful embroidery and pulled over the world as if to comfort it. But now, that vast expanse yawned deep with glowing eyes, watching him with callous coldness.

Dawn brought relief to his heart, its first gray light blotting out the stars before the sun burst forth with glorious color. The moment the sun showed its face, the prince led his castle staff to the Chateau de Noelles Marchand. The lady of the house, Enora, was carried on a litter at the end of the procession.

Reaching the small, but well-appointed chateau, Charmant felt his strength waning. The old butler, Perrin, greeted their procession with resignation. Trying to get his mind in order, Charmant stood, looking around at the solid-looking stone. His knees felt shaky, as if another earthquake struck, as if this house, too, would fall into a blasphemous pit from which no one could escape.

"Would Your Highness like a bath and refreshment?" asked Yves at his elbow, offering the prince a goblet of wine.

"Yes, thank you, Yves," he said absently. Just as he was about to take the goblet, Perrin opened the door and exclaimed, "Lady Enora!"

The lady of the house stood slumped and exhausted. She had been carried by litter the entire way to her home and now walked supported by two men on either side. Her dirt-smeared dress hung ragged on her petite frame.

As she stumbled in, she looked up at the prince, and his heart stopped. He hadn't really looked at the girl. Not closely. And the eyes that gazed at him now were a verdant, mossy green. Like those of her stepsister. The dim sunlight glimmered off her orbs, shadowing the bruised skin around them so that they looked as if they were floating in the hall, green eyes staring into him.

A horrified laugh welled up in his chest. He tried to keep it down, but the chuckle poured out of him. Clapping his hands over his mouth, he worked hard to tighten his ravaged lips and prevent the mirthless sound from spilling through his scabbed fingers. Instead, his chest heaved, and tears sprang from his eyes. Sucking in air through his nose, the noise burst out in a thin, screaming guffaw.

"Sire!" called Yves.

Charmant fell to his knees, the laugh toppling him as he leaned over and pounded the floor, gasping and laughing helplessly. Tears darkened the stone below him.

Strong hands grabbed him, pulling him down the hall as his panicked laughter echoed throughout the chateau.

CHAPTER 70

"Brain fever," Charmant heard a voice announce. His hazy mind could neither place the voice nor the meaning of the words.

Who is speaking? He wondered vaguely. Blinking through bleary eyes, Charmant saw Abbot Laurent, Yves, and another man who looked very much like Yves standing around his bed.

Am I in the castle? The prince wondered, trying to pick out a familiar object in the strange room. His eyes fell on Yves again, and he reached a thin arm out to his servant. Yves held Charmant's pale hand gently, as if the appendage might crumble to dust in his large, coarse palm.

"What..." started Charmant. His voice came out in a horrifying rasp, reminding him suddenly of Elle's men. Pain shot up from his eyes to his head, making him squeeze his eyes shut and moan. Tears trickled down his hot face, cooling his skin.

"Do not talk, Your Highness," hushed Yves. "Drink this broth and have a rest, sire."

Warm, savory liquid dribbled into his mouth, filling it as the prince tried to remember how to swallow. Somehow his throat had forgotten the trick, and Charmant let the broth dribble out the sides of his lips before someone squeezed his nose shut with a hard tweak.

Gasping and spluttering, the prince's throat rattled as some of the liquid went down, but most projected out of his mouth in a half-drowned cry.

"Try it again, Yves," said a firm voice.

"Yes, father," Yves told the man.

Charmant's eyes remained shut as he tried to roll onto his side, away from the broth-covered pillow. A strong arm lifted his head and placed the rim of a warm bowl to his lips.

"Try again, Your Highness," whispered Yves. "One swallow will make you feel ever so much better."

The prince took a sip, and this time, he could swallow. Once the broth hit his stomach, his fevered body remembered how hungry it truly was. Groaning in pleasure, the prince slurped and lapped at the small bowl, trying to capture every drop.

"Slowly now," warned Yves, a smile in his voice.

Charmant opened his eyes a crack, hoping to see his friend. The dark room made it hard to focus without straining, but Yves stood right next to him, propping him up and helping him drink the warm, soothing liquid.

"Thank you," rasped the prince.

An enormous grin broke across Yves' face, smoothing away the many worry lines that had carved channels into his skin since the last time Charmant had seen him. "You are quite welcome, Your Highness."

After the prince finished his broth, Yves lifted him up even further, flipping the pillow beneath Charmant to the dry side. Then, the servant eased his master down, allowing the prince's head to nestle in the cool softness.

In spite of this careful treatment, Charmant grimaced.

"We have prayed for your full recovery, Your Highness," murmured the abbot, still standing at the prince's left side.

Yves placed the back of his hand on Charmant's forehead.

"He is still quite hot," Yves told the other men.

"What happened? Am I ill? Is it... is it..." Charmant's body stiffened, and his throat locked up. He could not curse himself with the words. Instead, he lifted a shaky arm and examined his armpit for the telltale black and swollen buboes.

"No, it is not the plague, Your Highness," assured Yves.

Charmant slowly lowered his arm, tears pricking his eyes again. Yves turned away, then returned with a damp cloth for his forehead. It felt glorious. The prince sighed, licking his dry lips. He wanted to sleep for a hundred years, but he had so many questions.

"You had brain fever, Your Highness," the man who looked like Yves said.

Charmant cut his eyes to Yves, wordlessly asking for an explanation.

"My father, sire, Gabriel Joly. He and I have been treating you these past eight days. You collapsed in the chateau foyer. The king's doctor left with him, so I called the apothecary for aid. He and I have been bathing you, coaxing healing brews down your throat, and balancing your humors since you fell ill."

Closing his eyes and forcing his dry throat to swallow, Charmant took the information in.

Eight days, he thought. *Eight days since my castle's collapse.*

As if he could read the prince's thoughts, Yves continued.

"Your people have already begun to work on the castle. They have removed an impressive amount of stone, and Abbot Laurent believes their quarry can be put to service to provide anything additional needed to rebuild."

The words were supposed to have a calming effect, Charmant could tell. But the thought of unsuspecting townsfolk, farmers, and servants discovering that cursed cavern was more than he could bear.

Panic ripped up his body, from groin to throat, and he started shaking.

"This has all been too much for you, sire," said Yves, placing a calming hand on his chest.

"No, it is more than that," observed the abbot in a quiet voice. Leaning close to the prince he whispered, his words brushing the shaking man's ears. "You are worried the castle is cursed, that there is some demon or a pit to Hell. But do not fear, my, son. I have assigned three monks to the site. They are blessing every stone and we shall bless the very ground upon which the castle is built. If a pit to Hell has opened, our holy men shall do the work of God and close it once more."

"Yes," hissed Charmant. The words came without thought, "Close the pit."

"I shall, my son," the abbot reassured him. Straightening, Abbot Laurent drew the sign of the cross on the prince's forehead. Charmant's tremors ceased, and he sighed in relief.

"Sleep and recover, my son," said the abbot. "You are in God's grace, and he will guide these men as they make their healing tinctures."

Charmant took a deep breath and nodded slightly.

"Thank you, Father," he whispered.

He could hear the men shuffling around the room as his body relaxed. It did not take him long to fall back asleep.

CHAPTER 71

Prince Charmant lay in a stuffy room within the chateau all through the hottest days of summer. Yves and other servants fanned him with stiff cloth and feathers. They helped him drink fresh goat's milk or tepid broth. Someone helped him to a chamber pot. Then, he slept. Upon waking again, he ate a bit of well-soaked bread and some porridge.

Impatience stirred within him, and his exhausted body worried him. Ought he feel *this* tired simply shuffling to the chamber pot? He was still young; shouldn't he be able to lift a comb or put on his slippers without help?

Over the following month, Charmant pushed himself to regain his strength. Each day he walked a little farther until he managed to make it down the stairs. There, he saw a young woman so utterly unlike Elle that he wondered why the sight of her had driven him mad. Enora de Noelles Marchand was a tall child with dark auburn hair and changeable hazel eyes. She dressed richly but plainly, often in unadorned blue fabrics. She could not be further from his former wife.

The young lady gasped a frightened breath when she saw the wraithlike prince at the base of the stairs.

"I am sorry," he held up a hand that shook with effort. "I did not mean to startle you."

"Your Highness," she scolded in a light voice. "What are you doing out of bed? You must allow me to call your servant, Yves, to return you to your quarters."

"I am feeling much better, sister," he replied. "I am regaining my strength."

Charmant saw Enora straighten at the word "sister."

I should not have used that word, he chided himself. *She has lost her true sister and mother, and then I use the word "sister."*

"Of course," her voice changed to a high, tight tone. Similar to that of her mother. "I am pleased to see that you are recovering, Your Highness." She sketched a quick curtsy, then excused herself.

Sitting on the bottom stair of the staircase, Charmant stared at the spot where the girl had stood. She'd been through so much, lost her family, and here he was, stealing her home and calling her "sister."

He needed to do something, to get out of the chateau, to give the girl some peace. Not long ago, it was he who had lost his family, but he still had a father. He'd had hopes for the future, and a parent to make them a reality. This girl had nothing and no one. Something in his chest hitched and he realized tears were falling down his face. Swiping at them with an arm, he propped his chin on his fist and stared out into the empty room blankly.

"Your Highness," Yves startled the prince. "You made it quite far today!"

Charmant turned to his smiling servant. "I want to visit the castle, Yves," he said.

"Of course, in a week or so I am sure you will be recovered enough to go."

"I wish to go tomorrow. Prepare a litter. If I must be carried, I must be carried. But I will see my home tomorrow."

Yves bowed again.

The following day, Charmant laid eyes on the rubble that was once his castle. After a bumpy litter ride that left him pale and exhausted, he sat on solid ground in great relief. His guard, Pierre, offered him a chair to sit on, but the prince waved him away. He was not sure he could stand without help, and showing weakness in front of his people made his stomach squirm. Instead, the prince sat in the dust and rubble, watching as servants, villeins, soldiers, farmers, and townsfolk moved rocks, recovered valuables, and tackled the massive project in front of him.

The orchard and lake beyond lay unbroken, as the castle had crumpled down and to the North, smashing the chapel and training fields as it fell.

A monk walked over and bowed to the prince.

"Your Highness, Abbot Laurent guessed you might come. We have been blessing every stone, helping your treasurer to collect the recovered valuables, and praying over all who seek the Lord's guidance in this endeavor."

"Thank you, Brother," replied Charmant, continuing to watch the work progress. Something about the disfigured castle stone was both unutterably sad and strangely menacing.

The monk waited for a moment, bowed again, then walked away.

Are there others like Elle? wondered Charmant. *Others walking among us, glowing with health and beauty, fooling mortals into doing their bidding?*

He had been raised to believe in the devil but had always felt the menace was abstract. Real horror was inflicted on the battlefield, by other people. Now though, evil could be lurking anywhere.

Pierre reached down and offered Charmant a hand. The prince startled, staring at the work-roughened appendage.

"It is hot; you may like refreshment," the guard stated.

Gripping the solid hand, the prince took a deep breath.

"Yes, I believe I would," he replied as Pierre pulled him to standing. They waited, Pierre keeping a hand on the prince's back as a servant poured him a drink from a bladder marked with the apothe-cary's seal.

Another tincture thought the prince. *There may be monsters, even demons, but there are good people who care about me, too.*

The thought made him smile as he sipped.

Feeling refreshed by the brew, Charmant scanned the sweating workers. One man lifted something over his head, waving to the trea-surer. Charmant squinted, trying to identify the treasure at a distance. The item was not a rock or bar of gold, but a book. Excite-ment made him lightheaded and brash.

"The library!" he shouted. Without realizing it, he took several steps toward the man. As he got closer, something nagged at him. The scene did not look quite right. Charmant cocked his head this way and that as he continued to stumble closer. The book in the man's hand did not look like one of his father's library books, all of which were covered in fine red leather. The dust-covered book in its discoverer's hand appeared blackened. Sun glared down from the midsummer sky, making every surface bright except that of the book.

Even as the prince observed the book's strangeness, he reached toward the man holding it. The servant bowed, awkwardly kneeling with his head down and handing the book over with both hands.

Charmant grabbed the book, blowing the dust off and staring down at the stomach-churning swirls of Elle's book. Forcing his eyes away, he tucked the thing under his arm and walked as steadily as possible back to Pierre.

"I will be coming here every day from today forward to help with the search," he informed the guard. A wave of dizziness hit him, and he grabbed hold of the litter. Pierre helped him in.

"Your Highness will return tomorrow," the guard agreed, tucking a blanket around the prince's legs.

CHAPTER 72

C harmant kept his word, heading to the castle each day and helping where he could. In the early days of the excavation, he could only manage an hour or two of labor. Afterward, he would return to the chateau and pore over the book, puzzling out the words within. One day, about a week into his studies, Yves interrupted him with good news. His wardrobe had been discovered intact.

Heart hammering with excited anticipation, Charmant asked for it to be brought up. Four servants struggled to lift the solid wooden box up the stairs to his room, setting it down with a loud "thump." The prince grinned and rubbed his hands together, itching to escape into the many memories this old box held.

His haggard body forgotten; he flung open the doors.

"Your Highness," said Yves.

The prince turned. His servant had set out a cushion for him to sit on.

"Shall I present the items of your wardrobe while you continue to rest?" asked Yves.

Charmant's muscles groaned, telling him to take a seat. His body was unused to the hour of labor he'd put in at the dig. The rush of energy that had originally brought him to his feet waned.

'Yes," sighed Charmant, sitting.

Yves began pulling objects from the wardrobe. Some items were no longer intact, like his mother's favorite porcelain vase. But others remained in one piece. Charmant cried over the delicate laceworks and embroidered flags his mother and sister had presented him as a going away present. He smiled as he went through his army kit, laying out each chord, knife, and spare bowstring as if they were long beloved treasures.

When Yves brought out a grime and dust-covered spare shirt jammed into his brother's old boot, Charmant chuckled.

"I believe that needs a cleaning before I can wear it again," he said, and Yves smiled.

While the servant unfolded the shirt to see if it remained whole, something fell out, tinkling musically as it hit the flagstone. The object almost sent Charmat back into demon-haunted madness.

The tiny silver slipper.

Should I pick it up? Toss it in the lake? Give it to a priest?

That gleaming object shone with an ancient evil, daring him to find a way to rid himself of it.

Yves reached down to retrieve it.

"No!" yelled Charmant, launching off the cushion and grabbing the tiny shoe. He half expected it to burn his hand, to flame into the Lady Elle monster he'd seen sucked into space.

That image gave him an idea.

What if I sent it through the black whirlpool?

Charmant glanced at the book, filled with arcane knowledge.

I might be able to, if I had the right tools.

"Do you need help, Your Highness?" asked Yves, holding out a hand.

Charmant, lost in thought, took the proffered hand and stood.

"Yves," he started. Then stopped. He'd have to do this himself. He could not let on that he was going to perform an arcane, possibly a cursed ritual. "Yves," he started again, "I need to speak with the foreman at the dig site. I must relay an order about their findings."

"Yes, Your Highness," Yves bowed. "I shall have him fetched at once."

"No, no," Charmant put up a hand, "I will talk with him at dinner. Make sure he is invited."

Yves bowed again and left.

Charmant placed the tiny shoe next to the book, then opened the arcane tome once more. He made a mental note of all the elements he needed to send the shoe back to its mistress.

CHAPTER 73

The summer days swept by, Charmant gaining strength as the season wore on. He continued to help at the dig, sweating and shoveling, eating and praying with his people.

He knew that townspeople murmured about his visits, both admiring his diligence and wondering why he would put his hands to the labor. They knew of his soldiering days, that he was the youngest, and perhaps thought he had not been brought up to be served in the same way as his siblings.

The prince wished that were true. Instead, he simply wanted to be there when they found all of the pieces he needed for the spell.

The townsfolk and laborers spent a few hours each day unearthing the castle, then returned to their harvesting and work in the fields. They were good souls, salt of the earth. If he shared the arcane origins of the cave, his wife's loathsome nature, and the blasphemous powers she'd harnessed, they would never again come near this blighted spot.

So, Prince Charmant dug with villagers and villeins, shifting stones with calloused hands and piling them into barrows for the monks to bless and the masons to sort out. His people kept a lookout for valuables and any rocks that differed from the usual castle limestone.

He found the final item he needed on the last warm day of October.

Using a rod to lever out a particularly stubborn stone, Charmant stepped back onto something unexpectedly smooth. His footing faltered, but he caught himself, dropping the lever to stay upright. The stone crashed back into place.

Stepping aside, Charmant searched for the object that made him slip. There, covered in rock dust and crushed crystals, a stygian, round circle sucked at the crisp autumnal light. Kneeling, the prince picked up the object.

Elle's obsidian bracelet.

He fingered the woven metal, his work-roughened skin finding the embedded key that now melded with the bracelet.

Standing, he placed the bracelet and key into a small pouch strapped to his side and glanced around. Workers swarmed the area, excavating castle stones, and moving barrows upon barrows of masonry. His heart glowed with excitement.

A man with a freshly emptied barrow walked to the prince's side. He put the wheeled contraption down and bowed.

"Your Highness?" he asked, "Can I help you with that stone?"

The prince nodded and smiled distractedly. His mind was on the key, along with all of the other pieces he had collected. He thought he might have what he needed now. The idea twisted his stomach with fear and excitement. He wanted to leave at that moment, to run to the chateau and examine every item in detail and to read through the book again.

"Yes, I..." he started, then shook his head again. "Let us remove this stone, then I must be going."

The servant, a good-natured young man named Georges, bowed slightly.

"Of course," he said.

Once again, the prince set to his work, his hands sweating and his mind racing.

After Georges helped him move the stone and the man trotted off with his barrow, Charmant climbed out of the excavation pit and mounted his horse. Though he wanted to gallop away from the dig, to return to the chateau immediately, he kept his steed to a trot during the entire return journey. Lost in thought, it wasn't until he reached the chateau that he realized he'd left without his guard.

A goblet of spiced wine and a basin of warm water waited for him, along with a small loaf of white bread and some almonds, and freshly sliced plums.

Stomach rumbling, Charmant paused to refresh himself, washing and eating rapidly. Yves attended him, then walked with him upstairs. They paused on the landing, the prince aching to continue up into the vault room.

"I will change my clothes in a few moments, Yves. First, I must visit the vault. I have found something that should be stored there."

Yves bowed. Charmant felt a strange urge to return the gesture to this man who had twice saved his life. Instead, he adhered to decorum and strode away, leaving the servant to do what servants do when their master does not need them.

At the vault, Charmant nodded to the guards, who bowed in their turn. Opening the door, he was met by the many splendors found during the excavation. Gold goblets, now crushed and misshapen, sat on a shelf above sacks of silver coins. The few actual diamonds they'd used during the prince's wedding had been found and now rested in a small chest, accompanied by a few other jewels so far recovered. The two intact tapestries they found hung in the room, along with several of his father's leather-bound books.

The wardrobe and other items associated with Elle were nowhere to be found in the main vault room. Instead, Charmant had moved his wardrobe into a special back room and refused to allow anyone, not even the displaced castle treasurer, into it.

The castle treasurer was currently at the dig site along with the monks and four guards. The guards prowled the ruined castle, making sure peasants turned any treasure over to them. The prince, for his part, did not begrudge a few peasants their recovered riches. He had more than enough with Elle's dowry and the recovered jewels and money they'd found so far.

No, the prince's interest lay solely inside his personal treasure room.

Striding through the glittering vault, the prince unlocked the door and squeezed into the small back room. Closing the door behind him, he turned and lit two rushlights, bringing illumination to the stuffy space. Opening his wardrobe, he gazed at the items he and others had found. The book, the shoe, several pieces of purple crystal, and a sliver of black basalt. He emptied his pouch and added the bracelet and key to the collection.

Reluctantly, Charmant picked up the shoe. The silver thread flashed in the rushlight, sending sparkles of color across the ceiling. The tiny shoe was strangely warm and had an odd weight to it.

An iron shoe, he thought, remembering the fable of the young woman forced to dance by means of iron shoes and hot coals. It was difficult to tear his eyes away from the object. His heart wanted to mourn the loss of his wife, and this was one of the few things that remained of her.

But his mind reminded him that Elle was never his wife. She was a demon, something otherworldly come from Hell to plague humanity. And now she was gone.

He put the shoe down and picked up the book. Though small, it was quite thick. Runes and images scrawled across heavy velum pages. After careful inquiries, he'd found out that the thing was written in Britannic with runes and symbols of the Druidic people. Fortunately, someone, perhaps Marchand, had added a pocket to the back of the tome and included several sheets of velum with rubbings of many of the symbols, along with French annotations and translations. Additionally, the book was brilliantly illuminated with powerful drawings depicting circles of women pulling a tentacle beast from the water. They snapped a girdle around the thing, and it transformed into a beautifully rendered doll.

With the help of the translations and illustrations, Charmant could understand much of the book. It was an instruction manual for trapping a beast and had some vague mention to sending one back to Hell where it belonged.

Additionally, the words of the cultists and the process they had used was etched into his memory.

They'd cried out, "Anns a 'chumha tha ar maighstir a' feitheamh!"

Elle had responded, "Fosgailte, an uairsin faic doimhneachd àite sìorraidh."

The odd dance that had begun with the cultists, and infected his legs as he watched, was burned into his every nerve. When standing still, he had to lock his muscles to stop himself from shuffling a few of the repetitive steps. It had tainted him like the brain fever.

All of these elements gave Charmant an idea. A forbidden idea. An idea that brushed cold fingers down his spine and whispered in his mind.

He put the book down and stared at his collection.

"I should give all of this to a priest," he said aloud. "I should give it all to the abbot and be done with it."

But the idea in his mind told him otherwise.

You regain your power, your control, it said. *It's not witchcraft to follow a recipe and send that damned shoe back to Hell. You will feel better if it is no longer in this world.*

Those thoughts are not what convinced him. It was the last one.

What if more things like Elle exist? You need to be able to protect yourself, your father, your future family.

Charmant knew that all of the "should dos" of a dutiful, God-fearing prince could not compete with that last thought. He needed to understand how to protect himself and his family. He could not sit around and wait for another monster to attack and destroy something more precious to him than his home.

With shaking hands, the prince closed the wardrobe. Tomorrow, he would send that shoe back to its mistress.

CHAPTER 74

Charmant's eyes opened at daybreak. While he no longer experienced the strange dreams distinct to the creeping madness imparted by Elle, his sleep was often light and filled with shadows.

Nervous energy flooded his limbs as he rapidly bathed and put on simple clothing. He only kept one clothier available these days as he constantly wore the rough garb of a working man.

Once dressed, he ran up to the treasury, bringing the half-asleep guards to alertness.

Inside, the rooms were yet unlit as the treasurer hadn't returned to his duty of cataloging and counting. Charmant strode through the familiar space by the light of one taper. He lit the two rushlights in his back room and opened the wardrobe once again.

Pulling out the now-familiar book, he wrapped the leather cover in cloth, muffling it and keeping it safe. He wrapped the basalt piece, a crystal, and the bracelet/key combination in their own pieces of cloth, then put the whole pile in a sack.

Snuffing the lights, he locked the door to his small portion of the treasury. The main vault gleamed yellow and silver around him, the tiny light of his candle magnified by the precious metals gleaming on high shelves. The prince rushed through the glimmering gloom, his stomach churning and his treacherous mind superimposing another shining cavern, this one filled with crystals and liquid blackness.

Charmant ignored the panic clawing up his throat as he dashed through the treasury. Once at the other side of the door, back into the dim and solid halls, he gave the quivering candle to a guard. With sweat-slicked hands, he locked the door firmly, then hurried out of the chateau.

Outdoors, the prince took a long, slow breath of cold air. The weather had turned overnight with cold and mist permeating the predawn. He let the chill seep into him as he stared up at the blank sky. Others, he knew, might feel disconcerted at the cloud-covered predawn sky. He, on the other hand, felt grateful for the blackness. The naked sky, dark and full of stars, reminded him too much of that swirling ebon pit, pricked with changing lights. A stygian pit that stretched men until they burst into fragments of blood and bone.

Calmed by the cold, cloudy morning, Charmant strode to the stables with new vigor.

The stables were used to his early rising, as was Yves and his personal guard.

"Shall we join you, Your Highness?" asked Yves hopefully. Charmant had not allowed him to join the dig. Instead, he gave Yves daily tasks here at the chateau. But the young man always asked to go.

"No, I need you here, Yves. You will assist the treasurer in his work. I believe the excavation is almost complete and he is needed at the site. With your help, he can perform a full accounting of the treasury the moment the dig is complete."

The young man nodded and bowed.

The prince's guards stamped their feet and shivered in the early morning cold. Pierre, in particular, looked annoyed, shooting sidelong glances at Charmant as he readied his horse. The prince had unintentionally given his guards the slip the day before, but Pierre likely thought his actions were deliberate. Ignoring Pierre's frustration, Charmant mounted.

"Off we go to the castle," he announced.

As he rode, the prince watched the sky grow light, brightening from complete blackness to a moody gray. The mist cleared, but the air remained damp. Today hearkened the end of the warm months and the beginning of true autumnal cold.

Arriving at the excavation, he saw an unexpected hubbub. Jumping down from his horse, he rushed to the men running about the cratered center of the site.

"What is it?" he asked.

"Oh, Your Highness," said the man in charge of the site. "It appears we have gotten to the bottom of this strange opening in the earth and, we found gems beyond imagination!" He gestured to the site beyond. The crater glittered in the morning light.

They had found a few crystals before, but his people had assumed they were part of the treasury, turning them over to the guards. This was different. They'd discovered the cavern.

The prince stood and stared for a moment, the roof and tongue of his mouth sticking together, his throat dry as sand.

The man smiled, thinking the prince stunned.

"There are cartloads of gems, and a strange black rock that we have not seen before. Perhaps that is valuable, too?"

The man offered the prince one of the crystals and Charmant forced his shaking hands to take it. He angled it this way and that, not really looking at it. Instead, his eyes glazed, and his mind spun. Had they reached the end of their excavations? Now what? Rebuild over the cursed spot?

He knew this day would come, but the efficiency of his people boggled the mind. It was now harvest season and he had expected many of them to spend their entire days in the fields. Instead, they had split their time between castle excavation and harvest. Perhaps because of his order to remove all of the servants from the castle and saving their lives, they were grateful to him.

People depended on him and trusted his wisdom. That weighed heavy on his heart. He felt inadequate to making this one decision, much less showing leadership and responsibility for the many looking to him.

"Oh, careful Your Highness," warned the man.

Charmant looked down. His finger bled a little where he'd pricked it with the crystal.

First, I will find out if I can protect my people. Then it won't matter if we rebuild over this spot, because I will have the means to protect them all.

He handed the crystal back to the man and took a swig from a bladder of wine he'd attached to his horse's saddle.

"Recover anything that has broken from the ground. Leave any crystal or black stone still rooted in place. Load anything loose that you find into carts and take it to the chateau."

The man smiled, bowed, and turned to the workers, calling out the new instructions.

"Tell the masons to examine the site when they arrive," the prince told one of his guards. "I believe it is almost time to rebuild." He squinted up at the cloudy sky. "I believe I am going to take a swim at the lake this morning. Today is likely my last opportunity before it gets too cold to do so."

With that, he pulled the sack of wrapped objects off of his horse's back and walked around the dig site, heading to the orchard.

Two of his personal guards tried to follow him. Charmant could feel them hovering behind him. He turned again.

"I am within the castle walls and safe. I would be alone."

The men nodded, their eyes darting to one another.

"If you are bored with your work, the dig would be glad of more hands."

The guards bowed to hide their eye rolls. They never joined

Charmant on the dig, and he assumed this time would be no exception.

"Get our horses stabled. I will return before sundown."

The men raised their eyebrows and bowed again.

Charmant turned and marched to the orchard, his sack banging against his back.

CHAPTER 75

The air turned from brisk to biting beneath the trees. Above his head, final figs, ripe apples, and yellow pears hung on low branches, awaiting eager hands and open mouths. Some men and boys labored among the trees, picking ripe fruit and storing their bounty in woven baskets.

Charmant took a deep breath, his nose stinging with cold as he took in the comforting scents of loam and overripe figs. The orchard and the lake beyond had long been his sanctuary, and he was grateful his castle had crumbled downward and to the north. The angle of the fall caused the death only of those inside the castle. All who had evacuated, along with much of the valuable food, horses, outbuildings, orchard, and lake had been spared. They'd lost the chapel, a grain storage building, and the treasury. Because the collapse had happened at the beginning of summer, the grain harvest had yet to come in, and the treasury was mainly filled with metal, most of which had been recovered. Several valuable tapestries, books, and scrolls had been destroyed, but many more were recovered. Even now artisans were examining all damaged valuables to determine which could be restored.

Lost in thoughts of castle recovery, the prince stepped past the last tree and found himself lakeside. A low mist coated the water in an impenetrable film. Charmant was reminded of the stories his brothers told him about water sprites, all of whom seemed intent upon drowning little boys. Even though he knew the lake's true danger - Elle's monster - had left, he kept well away from the misty water's edge.

"Time to prove out my ideas," Charmant told the empty lake. "Time to send the cursed shoe back to Hell."

Casting around for an appropriate stone on which to unpack his bag, he muttered under his breath, "Hell, Elle, doesn't matter which, really, does it?"

Spotting a small stone near the boulder under which he'd originally buried the key, he chuckled sardonically.

"I must truly be going mad," he muttered, beginning his unpacking. Pulling out the basalt, crystal, bracelet and key, book, and the shoe, he carefully rested his sack on top of the stone, placing the ancient book on the dry cloth. In this way, he protected the book from the early morning damp.

Taking a deep breath of cold lake air, he opened the book to an illumination. Etched in red, gold, green, and blue, a woman floated above water, her arms outstretched and her body straight. Below her, tentacles writhed and reached.

Dry, shaking hands turned thick vellum.

On the next page, the illuminator broke the sheet into four squares. The very top showed a compass with each point clearly defined in runic text. The first showed a man stepping northward. In the next, he stepped at a northeastern angle - to the right. The third had him stepping back to center. In the last, he stepped to a southeastern angle.

The illuminations were alive with movement. The ink or paint used by the illuminator now shimmered in the wet air, causing the man to look as if he were repeating the steps, over and over.

A series of runes decorated the very bottom of the page. Though they were not written in any language known to Charmant, he knew what they said. He hadn't needed old Marchand's rough translations to understand the text. The chant coursed through his mind the moment his eyes rested upon the runes.

"Anns a 'chumha tha ar maighstir a' feitheamh!"

"In the firmament, our master waits!"

Charmant blinked rapidly. This page was the hardest to look at, and when he did, his feet moved, and his mouth formed words without him realizing. Quickly, he turned the page to find a sheet of blackness.

At first, he hadn't understood. Why would one waste valuable vellum, only to paint it black? But now, having studied the book many times, he saw the details etched in gray-black paint over the deeper blackness of the page. In the middle pulsed the symbol the man in the previous page had sketched with his movements. All around the symbol, the same shimmering substance had been used to create ever moving, ever-blinking eyes funneling down to that letter.

The key to the entire puzzle lay in the second-to-last page. Apparently, the druidic tribes who created this book had also wanted to close the portal once opened. This page showed the woman from the beginning of the series tapping a hunk of crystal against a piece of basalt with one hand, while placing the bracelet atop the dark stone with the other. Below her were the words, poorly translated, but etched in Charmant's mind.

"Fosgailte, an uairsin faic doimhneachd àite sìorraidh."

"Open, then see depths of everlasting space."

The final page showed how it all ended. The crystal was no longer held by a hand. Instead, it lay on top of the circlet-enclosed basalt. A slender, feminine hand hovered above them, and two runes floated below the scene. Behind this page, Marchand had tucked in the translation. He'd written the two runes boldly, etching them repeatedly until the vellum wore thin, ripping in some spots. The words were not only translated, but pronunciation was included.

"Glasadh an cumadh."

"Lock the firmament."

Charmant assumed that this page showed the end result of the chant. If he performed the spell, the window into the other world would eventually close, locked from his world. Just as the portal in which Elle traveled eventually closed on its own, though not before destroying his castle.

Flipping the pages back to the beginning of the section, Charmant looked around him. The mist had receded a bit, revealing the gray autumnal waters below.

Glancing behind him at the verdant orchard which would surely help to feed him and his people this winter, he considered the many blessings he'd been granted by God, all of which had brought him to this moment. He knew he could be blaspheming. Or he might be doing the Lord's work. He hoped it was the latter.

Rubbing cold, dry hands briskly against his fine, woolen hose, he glanced up at the cloudy sky.

"Please, Lord, let me be correct. Allow me this, a blessing among blessings. Let this strange, blasphemous ritual work. For surely, I must remove the scourge of Elle from this world."

He wished the skies above would part, sending a shaft of light through the clouds above. Instead, all remained gray and dull, cold and biting. Charmant nodded.

"Time to get to work, then."

He removed the book and replaced it in the sack, moving the whole parcel so that it rested beside the rock. Then, he placed the basalt and shoe on the low rock. Pushing the bracelet onto his own right wrist, he was surprised by its size. It seemed quite big now that it no longer clasped Elle's dainty wrist. Lastly, he picked up the crystal.

"I am ready," he told the mist.

CHAPTER 76

Tracing the steps in the lakeside sand and gravel, Charmant recited the words.

"Anns a 'chumha tha ar maighstir a' feitheamh," he whispered, stumbling a bit.

Again, he traced the steps and said the words.

A bitter breeze began blowing from the lake in front of him, pushing the mist toward him.

He stepped and recited again. Then again, staring at the basalt.

Nothing happened.

With heavy limbs he made the motions, muttering the words. His throat felt dry, his tongue cracked. Mist crept forward, swallowing shoreline as it came.

Charmant looked down at the basalt to see it deepening, darkening. His heart dropping to his stomach, he sketched out the steps once more and forced the chant out of a fear-constricted throat.

In front of him, the sliver of basalt transformed into a deep, stygian portal. On the other side, colors from beyond the spectrum winked up at him, swirling in a sickening dance. Slowly, a gray cloud engulfed the colors, leaving traceries on Charmant's eyes.

Dazzled for a moment, the prince mourned the lost color. He leaned forward, toward the pool, hoping the sight would reappear. Instead, the gray cloud swallowed more and more, covering sparse dots of light as it came.

It is pushing its way up to me, he realized with a start.

Charmant cried out, then dropped his crystal and slammed frigid fingers over his mouth. As if the thing inside the ebon pool could hear him, it swallowed up the last of the wild color and expanded, thrusting itself ever nearer.

His mind screamed at him to run. But another, darker urge told him to jump right in and see what happened.

As if hypnotized, Charmant reached out toward the onyx pool. His hand brushed the surface and intense, bone-aching cold burned his fingertips. Crying out again, he tried to move his hand, but it stuck to the surface, the whirlwind below trying to suck him in. Frozen in horror, pulling against the overwhelming force of the black whirlpool, Charmant watched as the gray cloud inside the portal continued to consume everything in its path.

Sound rumbled through the abyss, speaking no language Charmant had ever heard. He felt its meaning in his bones.

Kill, kill, kill.

Screaming with effort, pain, and terror, Charmant tried to stumble back. The blackness sucked at his fingers, trying to yank his entire body in. Planting his feet, Charmant glanced about for the crystal. His eyes landed on the tiny silver shoe, the reason for this ill-fated experiment. His wild heart slowed as hot rage coursed through his veins. This shoe, that woman, they were the reason he stood here, stuck, and about to be annihilated.

Using his free hand, he batted the tiny object into the pit.

The tiny shoe fell into the blackness. Its silvery flashes bright against the surrounding dark, until it smacked into the cloud far below. Wind whipped up through and out of the portal, blowing Charmant back while his fingers remained locked to its black surface. He watched in disbelief as the shoe spiraled back and forth, no longer dropping, but supported by that gray mass. If anything, it seemed his offering provided further power to the demonic beast that lived in that gray cloud. It doubled its speed, rushing toward him.

Reaching down with his free hand, Charmant fumbled through sand for the crystal. Clammy, gritty fingers scrabbled until he felt the sharp edge of the crystal. Pulling it up, he dipped it toward the portal, shouting "Fosgailte, an uairsin faic doimhneachd àite sìorraidh."

Nothing happened.

CHAPTER 77

The gray mass pushed toward Charmant, and an icy wind whipped out of the portal. He could now see it was a mass, not a cloud. And that mass sparkled with all the colors that had entranced him earlier, along with a few more outside of any spectrum he could imagine. As he stared, his mouth open in a silent scream, the colors blinked and re-formed into eyes.

Charmant tucked the useless crystal between his right armpit and his arm. He cast about for the book, safely tucked away a few steps from the rock. As he looked, his eye caught on the bracelet, hanging from his right wrist.

Pushing it down to his right palm, he held it with his two free fingers, his pinkie and his thumb. The bracelet now hovered over the deep blackness, a circle of sanity above a place of pure chaos.

Next, Charmant grabbed the crystal and shouted the words again.

"Fosgailte, an uairsin faic doimhneachd àite sìorraidh."

Nothing changed. The gray mass advanced, the shoe still dancing, mockingly, on top of the gray beast. Almost all of the blackness had been consumed by this monster, which, Charmant assumed, meant that it was close.

In desperation, he shouted the words on the final page. Words he had believed to be instructions, not an incantation.

"Glasadh an cumadh!"

The portal flattened, its icy cold still holding the tips of his fingers, but now they were frozen to the top of a small basalt piece, not a tunnel into space. In his left hand, the crystal blackened and crumbled, turning into a fine powder that coated his palm.

The prince panted, staring at the blackness, waiting for that gray mass to reappear, to grab his trapped right hand and drag him to the depths of Hell. Nothing happened after a breath, then after two.

It took him a moment to feel the stillness in the air around him. Gazing at the lake, he saw the mist receding once again, uncovering more of the luminous water below. A laugh bubbled up from his chest, spilling out of him. Not the high-pitched laugh of panic nor the wild laugh of madness, but the true hearty chuckle of a man who'd just accomplished the impossible.

Picking up the warming basalt with his left hand, he pulled it lightly and freed his fingertips. A film of dry skin came off, along with some of the pliant skin on his right ring finger. A single drop of blood soaked into the stone, warming it further as if to remind him of the rock's magical properties.

Before he could drip more blood onto the basalt, Charmant put his finger in his mouth and tasted copper and sand while he sucked his damaged digit. Pulling it out, he stared at the pad of his finger, watching for more blood. None came.

Carefully wrapping the stone, the bracelet, and the book in their cloths, he restored them to their sack.

Then, he walked out to the lakeside, removing his boots and wading ankle deep in the cold, clean water. Rinsing his hands, he gazed at the chill blue expanse and wondered if any of Elle's kind or her monsters remained.

They must be out there. But he now had the means to protect himself, his people, and his family from their monstrous ways.

Breathing in the scents of lake water and greenery, Prince Charmant glanced at the sky just as a shaft of light laddered its way through the clouds.

I can protect us, he told himself and smiled.

The End

EPILOGUE

THE WOLF

The huntsman's assistant stumbled into the chateau, his wild babbling disturbing the entire household.

Prince Charmant ran down the stairs, Yves a step behind him. Enora walked onto the landing above them and began to make her quiet way down.

"Enora, please stay behind Yves and me," instructed Charmant, shooting the girl a worried smile.

She drew her eyebrows together and nodded, catching up to the group and staying just behind Yves.

At the base of the stairs, Perrin and Octave backed away from the huntsman's assistant. When Charmant caught sight of the disfigured man, he stopped and grabbed Yves' arm.

"Send Enora back upstairs," he instructed in a hoarse whisper.

Then, in a louder voice, he asked, "What seems to be the trouble?" He searched his mind for the man's name, "Thomas?"

Thomas stood, hands on knees, panting. He looked up at the prince and Charmant bit his cheeks to keep from screaming. The man's face was a study in dichotomy. Tanned and well-formed, the left half of the man's face accented the ruin of the right half. Gray and spongy, the right side of the man's face looked as if fungus had taken hold, leaving white-spored rot in its wake.

"Your Highness," Thomas slurred. "It is Master Chasseur. He killed the wolf, but the wolf bit him and scratched me in its final convulsions. It, he, well," the man gave up trying to explain, but instead extended a withered arm covered in gray and white patches. "Come, and you shall see. Bring a doctor. No better not. Bring a priest. The Master will not live much longer, and neither, I fear, shall I."

Charmant stepped down to the bottom stair.

"Better do what he says, Octave. Fetch Father Audibert. We shall visit the huntsman together."

"But Your Highness mustn't put yourself in danger, sire," protested Octave.

Charmant clapped his faithful steward on the shoulder.

"If accompanying this young man to his master's home will put me in danger, then we are all in danger. Are we not all exposed to his malady right now?"

Octave nodded; his eyes downcast. He bowed to the prince and walked away to find the priest.

"Thomas," said the prince gently, "how did you get here?"

"I walked, Your Highness," croaked the young apprentice.

"Fetch him something to drink," the prince instructed Perrin. "And give him some pottage."

"Begging your pardon, Your Highness," rasped the young man, "but I am not hungry. I am not thirsty, either, though I have had naught to drink but rainwater since that monstrosity scratched me. You needn't trouble yourself, my Lord."

A gasp and a retching sound came from the hall's entryway. Prince Charmant glanced at the priest. Doubled over a decorative vase the man clutching the porcelain as if his life depended on it.

"Get Father Audibert something to drink, then," the prince told Perrin.

After a few moments, the white-faced priest joined the prince at the bottom of the stairway. Father Audibert's eyes were so transfixed on the young apprentice's disfigurements that he almost forgot to bow.

"We are going to visit the huntsman, Master Claude Chasseur," Charmant told Father Audibert. He paused as Perrin returned to the room with goblets of watered wine. Thomas refused the offer, but Prince Charmant and Father Audibert took long gulps. "He has killed the wolf which has plagued our lands for many months, and it appears he and his apprentice paid for this honor."

"Get a scribe, Octave," instructed Charmant. "I will bring him and my personal guard along to the huntsman's home and we will..."

"Master is not at home," interrupted Thomas in a slurring rush. "He is in a shack inside the wood. Along with the wolf. We put the wolf in our slaughterhouse shed. Then my master collapsed in the hunting shack. I walked. To bring back. A priest."

With that, the young man's leg gave out. It was then that the prince noticed that the strange rot had spread to his right leg. In fact, white and gray mold covered the man's entire right side.

"Please put young Thomas in a wagon. And have a man don the beekeeper's gloves and mask so that he can safely move Master Thomas to this hunter's shack without fear of infection," the prince nodded at Perrin who scurried from the room.

"We shall depart immediately."

Outside, Charmant's personal guard, Pierre, stood ready beside his and the prince's horses. The stable boy saddled a pleasant mare for the priest, and each man mounted up. A burly servant dressed in gloves, a hood, and a beekeeper's face covering pushed a wheelbarrow holding the huntsman's apprentice. A blanket covered most of the young man's deformities, another blanket swaddled his head, leaving only his good eye visible.

"Thomas, tell us the way to this place so we may help the huntsman."

"It is not far," Thomas croaked, "when we exit the chateau grounds, take the first path you see into the wood. The path winds into a shaded thicket that feels like walking into twilight. Stay your course and you will reach a bright meadow. The shack is on the far side of the meadow, near a sweet spring."

The prince nodded, and the travelers turned their horses toward the gate when one more horse, laden with provisions, trotted up beside them. Yves sat on the horse, gripping its mane for dear life. His uncertain seat always made Charmant smile.

"Ah, Yves, ensuring we have enough to eat and drink. That is good of you," sighed Charmant.

"I also brought your kit, Your Highness," Yves replied as he turned his horse toward the front gate.

Charmant nodded slowly, going through the motions of steering his horse onto the correct path as he thought about the contents of that kit.

After banishing the shoe two weeks ago, he had shared a brief account with Yves, telling his servant only that Elle had used some kind of power residing in the basalt and crystals they found below the castle to transport herself elsewhere. He told Yves that Elle was not what she seemed, that she consorted with monsters, and because of this, he, Prince Charmant, had kept the tools necessary to banish any further monsters to wherever Elle had gone.

Together, they built a kit of crystals, basalt, the bracelet, and the book so that the prince could take it with him at a moment's notice in case monsters threatened his kingdom again. Yves had brought this collection of eldritch tools with them.

"You are a smart man, Yves," Prince Charmant told his servant as they got on the road. "Thank you for bringing everything we might need."

Yves smiled and bowed his head slightly. Charmant could see the young man's white knuckles and shifting seat, so he stopped talking and instead watched for the trail cutting through the autumnal woods.

It did not take long for the men to find the path. The servant pushing Thomas' wheelbarrow looked concerned.

"Look, there are wheel ruts worn into the trail," Pierre pointed them out to the servant, who nodded his woven mask and adjusted his grip on the wheelbarrow.

Charmant looked at their arrangement, seeing that the servant would slow them further as he bumped along the rutted path.

"You will have to take up our rear," the prince told the servant, and the man bowed his hooded head. The prince led the group, guiding his horse to place careful steps upon the well-worn path.

Ahead, red, gold, yellow, and brown adorned the trees, a light breeze causing the leaves to flash and drift. A few evergreens rustled in the brisk air, their dark green needles contrasting against the fiery colors of fall.

Each man trotted into the woods, their noses catching the dusty scents of dry leaves as they road. Behind them, they heard the bump, bump of the wheelbarrow. The man inside made no sound.

Prince Charmant looked behind him, straining his eyes to see the small group. The trees above shaded the world around them, the flashing leaves causing light to come and go throughout the forest. Facing forward, he kept the path ahead in sight, trying to maintain his focus as the entire wood flickered and rustled. Above him, squirrels chattered, and birds chirped, adding cheerful music to the pretty scene.

Following the trail deeper and deeper into the trees, the world quieted and darkened by degrees. As gloom closed in, Charmant's nerves began to fray. His eyes darted from the path as the occasional fern or bush rustled.

It is merely rabbits and foxes, mice and other little creatures running away from us, he told himself, *loosen your hand and do not spook the horse.*

His stallion snorted and shook his head, sensing the prince's feelings as they pushed forward. Trees closed in on each side, turning the early autumn afternoon to twilight. Ferns crowded the path, causing the servant behind them to swear as he pushed the wheelbarrow without pause. Vines climbed trees, choking out the breeze and making the air still in this dark place.

Silence reigned with only the occasional shaking fern as a small animal ran from the sound of their invading hoofbeats.

Charmant's stomach squeezed at each small sound. It was all he could do to keep a steady hand and consistent pressure on his horse. He wanted to gallop the animal out of there, to burst into the meadow beyond. Instead, he focused on the dwindling dirt path, making sure he followed it scrupulously as they moved through the darkness.

Breaking out of the trees, the wide meadow full of golden grass came as a bright relief. Charmant paused, letting his and his horse's eyes adjust to the clear autumn sunlight pouring down from above.

"Thank goodness," sighed Yves from beside him.

The prince nodded.

"Now we must find this shed," he said to no one in particular. Leading off to the right, he trotted around the wood's edge, looking for a rough structure.

Following the tree line, Prince Charmant almost led his horse right into the shack's wooden wall. Roughly hewn of tree branches and mud, the structure stood as tall as a man and about the length of two fallen trees. The long and narrow hovel spanned a small clearing. Large blocks of dried mud mixed with rocks and bits of wood made up the walls along the width of the structure and trunks and branches made up the length. An additional small shed stood at the end of the construction, presumably for preparing meat after a long hunt. The small fire pit in front of the rude shack sat cold and black, an empty spit sitting expectantly above the dead coals. Leaning against one side stood a rough-hewn door that would perfectly cover the gaping hole cut into one wall of the small hut.

Charmant backed his horse away from the huntsman's shelter and dismounted, then led the horse back up the tree line to meet the rest of his party. They all dismounted when they saw him, Pierre gathered up the horses and tied them to nearby trees as Yves, Father Audibert, and the prince waited.

Once the horses were situated, the party heard the wheelbarrow as the servant made his way out of the trees.

"Over here," called Yves before the man had to decide which way to turn. The tall, golden grass blocked a clear view across the meadow, so Yves waved a hand above his head.

They stood in silence while the wheelbarrow bumped closer to them. Finally, Thomas and the servant stopped. Prince Charmant's heart went out to the poor servant wearing the beekeeping gear. Even on this brisk day the man's sweat darkened the thick cloth.

"Where is the huntsman, young Thomas?" asked Charmant.

The pile of blankets moved, the young man pulling himself up with his left arm. The blankets dropped, revealing his withered right appendage. Stick thin, the arm was now covered in scaly white lichen. Though the young man could not move his arm, the mass of white seemed to move and spread as they watched, coaxing each man to lean closer for a better look.

Charmant's stomach dropped, and his bowels tightened when he realized he had taken a step forward. Glancing around, he saw the other men in his party had also leaned in.

"Step back!" he commanded.

Each man straightened in shock.

"Please, Thomas, cover your arm."

The young man seemed to understand what was happening. With his good arm, he pulled the blanket over his infected skin, covering the spreading mass.

"You must take me into the shack to be with my master," rasped the sick man. "Push me in and burn it. Then burn the slaughter-house. That is where the wolf lays. There is nothing here for you."

His eyes turned to the priest.

"Please, Father, bless us and then burn us. There will be no bones for our resurrection, but this thing that has happened, this rot, this curse making its way through our skin, it must burn up with us."

The priest looked down on the boy.

"Wheel him into the shack. I shall see the state of his master, and we will decide from there," Father Audibert spoke in a shaky voice.

Yves sidled up to the prince and handed him the bag. Each item within was thoroughly wrapped in cloth and packed tightly so that nothing clanked or moved. Hoisting the small, heavy parcel over his shoulder, reassurance flooded the prince. He would be able to face anything with the arcane knowledge he possessed here.

"Follow the Father's instructions," Charmant told the servant in the beekeeper's gear. "Once you have placed young Thomas in the shack, leave and remove the beekeeper clothing. It will burn with the shack - if that is Father Audibert's instruction."

The servant bowed, then hefted the wheelbarrow, clearly ready to complete his task and be on his way.

The group filed to the hovel, Prince Charmant, Father Audibert, Pierre, and Yves walking past the open doorway, allowing the servant to push Thomas inside. They heard rustling as the man removed his gloves and hood, then an earsplitting scream.

Pierre rushed in first, pulling the screaming servant out of the structure and pushing him into the grass. The man collapsed, screaming and sobbing.

"What is it, my son?" yelled the Father over the man's sobs. "What did you see?"

Pierre poked his head into the room, then quickly drew his ashen face out again.

"I can tell you, or you can look for yourself, Father," he said through clenched teeth. Then he clutched his stomach and panted, his visage turning from white to green.

Prince Charmant tapped him on the shoulder.

"What is..." he started. Pierre shook his head, turning away from the prince and throwing up in the fire pit.

Charmant and Yves looked at one another. The prince took a step toward the doorway.

"Let me come with you, Your Highness," Yves whispered, walking beside Charmant.

Gripping his friend's shoulder, Charmant caught Yves' eye. "I have seen the horrors of battle. Are you certain you are ready for this, Yves?" asked the prince.

Yves stared down for a moment, his mouth a thin line. When he looked back at the prince, he nodded.

Both men squeezed in through the doorway.

Inside the dim hovel, the wheelbarrow sat against the far wall, leaving just enough room for the two men to enter. They looked around the small space, eyes adjusting to the gloom. In the far-right hand corner, near the wheelbarrow, an enormous pile of white lichen grew against a wall. It glowed slightly, making it easy to spot in the dimness.

Prince Charmant opened his mouth to say something to Thomas and Yves, his mind searching frantically for comforting words. Then, the white lichen growing into the far wall moved.

"Master, Master Chasseur?" asked Yves in a shaky voice.

The pile moved again, this time, a long tendril of white stretched out toward them. Both Yves and Charmant stumbled back, knocking into an arm of the wheelbarrow, and pushing the implement into the dirt. Young Thomas tumbled out. He made no sound as he fell. His blankets fell back to reveal why. The white lichen had taken hold of his entire body. Only his left eye and a small portion of his nose and mouth remained uncontaminated.

"Oh, Thomas," whispered Charmant. He reached toward the young man, but the desiccated body shook as the boy managed to move his head from side to side in a "no" gesture.

Charmant understood and stepped away, tears filling his eyes. He could do nothing for the young man.

Thomas opened his lips a crack, his voice hissing through as he whispered, "Fire, Highness. Burn us with fire."

Yves gasped, gripping the prince's arm. Charmant's head whipped up in time to watch as the mass in the corner moved again.

A long, iridescent tendril reached toward Charmant and Yves. It stopped in the middle of the room and then let out a hiss. A spray of spores dispersed into the hovel's still air. One word seemed to resonate below the hissing. As if the mass said, "Please."

On the floor, the decaying form of Thomas yelled as best he could.

"Run!"

The two men turned and bolted out of the room, squeezing through the door and into the sunlight.

All four men who had entered stood outside in the cleansing sun, white-faced and gasping. Finally, Charmant said, "Father," right as Pierre said, "I need a drink."

Both men stopped and stared at one another. Then they grinned, their eyes wild.

"Father, fortify yourself to bless those men. Then we must burn this place and that meat shed to the ground."

Yves, ever prepared, detached a wineskin from his belt. All five men drank sips of potent wine, the liquid calming ragged nerves. Then, Charmant sent the servant and Pierre on horseback to the chateau to return with wood, pitch, torches, and any other help they could find.

Charmant and Yves stood with the man of God as he made the sign of the cross at the shack's doorway. They waited respectfully while he prayed and blessed the diseased men as best he could, from a distance. With the priest's work done, they all pulled the makeshift wooden door over the hole in the wall, then jammed dry leaves and grass into the wooden structure.

The three men approached the small slaughterhouse structure. There, another makeshift wooden door closed off the entryway. Two large boulders held the covering in place.

Curiosity itched at Prince Charmant as he and the other two men jammed all the tinder they could gather into cracks and crevices. He wanted to see the wolf that had killed his huntsman, but fear clenched at his guts.

Before his thirst for knowledge completely took hold of him, Pierre and several more servants arrived carrying pitch, torches, and more tinder. Additional men carried buckets that they hauled past the prince to a nearby stream. No one wanted the dry, autumnal forest to go up in flames.

Squinting up at the sky, Charmant saw light limning leaves with gold as the sun dropped below the tree line. Fear gathered in his hands, making him shaky. He did not want to be caught under the star-strewn night sky. Not after the things he had witnessed.

It is now or never, he thought, staring at the slaughterhouse shed.

"Yves, I want to look inside before we go," he told his servant.

Yves stared up at the prince, eyes wide. The man stood about half a head shorter than him, but the way he shrank away told the prince that his faithful friend had known this request was coming and had been dreading it. Charmant walked to the slaughterhouse door before his nerve could fail him. He could hear Yves dragging his feet behind him.

"Grab a torch and some pitch. We will look inside, throw in the pitch and torch, then close the door again."

Standing at the door, Charmant watched as Yves scampered away, coming back quickly with two other servants in tow. Both held buckets of pitch. Yves carried the torch.

Charmant and Yves nodded to each other, then instructed the servants to move the door. The men pulled away the small boulders holding the door fast, and then slid the wooden covering over.

Yves thrust the torch into the small room.

Inside, scaly lichen coated the mud and wood structure. Long tendrils stretched out, seeking to grasp onto something new.

"Pitch!" called Yves in a shaky voice.

One of the servants thrust a bucket of pitch inside, and Yves dropped the torch. Stepping back, Charmant stared as the tendrils curved back, away from the fire. Then, in a final agony, they released a hoary mist, sending out puff after puff of those strange white spores.

The cloud glimmered in the firelight, dazzling Charmant. He stared open-mouthed as it drifted toward him.

"Close!" shouted Yves, pushing the prince aside and enclosing the brilliant haze. He pushed the door shut, then instructed the second servant to paint the building with pitch.

"Thank you," gasped Charmant, coming to himself.

Yves pushed a boulder against the door. Charmant moved to the second boulder, belatedly realizing how close he'd come to infection and death.

"Of course, Your Highness. I would give my life for you," Yves stated, a grim smile on his lips.

Standing, both men watched as the servants painted the buildings with pitch. They watched as the fire caught and the structures lit up the early evening air.

Moths swooped around the fire, attracted by the light. Bugs buzzed near the prince's ear, reminding him that winter had not yet arrived.

He looked up at the sky, watching with relief as clouds covered the first star of the evening.

"It looks as if it will rain," said Yves from beside him.

"Yes," replied the prince. "I suppose we should leave before we are caught in the downpour."

He looked back at the fire blazing in front of them. A fire that consumed a good man, his assistant, and the wolf that had terrorized his people. Clapping his hand on Yves' shoulder, he squeezed as his heart filled with gratitude for good people like Yves, like the boy Thomas who had warned them of this horrendous place.

Relief and grief flooded him as a fat raindrop hit his nose. More drops pattered down, sizzling in the crackling fire. A few drops of his own trickled from his eyes. He made no effort to wipe them away.

The End

Author's Note

Thanks for reading *Macabre Fairy Tales, Book 1: The Cult of Elle*. I hope you enjoyed it!

You may be wondering if there will be a book 2 in the series – and the answer is yes! This is a four-book series that will be released over the next few years. I know some authors release a book every month or two, but that is not me.

So, if you are interested in joining Prince Charmant on his next adventure, you can either a) subscribe to my author profile on Amazon, b) subscribe to my newsletter by visiting my website: jsdouglaswrites.com or c) keep an eye out for my next release in the summer of 2024. I will just mention that, if you take the newsletter route, you will get a free novella and the occasional free short story – as well as a chance to read my books early.

What fairy tale comes after this macabre version of Cinderella? Why, Snow White of course. This series was inspired by my love of fables and fairy tales, and my daughter's love of princess movies. After watching *Cinderella* and *Snow White* with her for the millionth time, I got to thinking, "How did Prince Charming marry both Cinderella and Snow White?" *Macabre Fairy Tales* books one and two are my answers to that question. And, because I am physically incapable of writing a story without a monster, ghost, or at least some existential dread, all books in this series are horror stories/weird fiction.

Thanks again for reading my story. I hope you enjoyed it and will enjoy the other books in the *Macabre Fairy Tales* series.

If you are looking for another book right now, you might enjoy my novella *Terror at Twll Du,* available as an ebook on Amazon. Here is a brief excerpt:

Terror at Twll Du

by J.S. Douglas

INTRODUCTION

The house lounges at the end of a tidy cul de sac. It's in a good neighborhood. Not great, but not terrible. Centrally located. Low crime rate. The type of neighborhood where a scampering of kids rides their bikes during spring break or play basketball on the street in the summer. There are no hoops on this block, though. No kids, either. No dogs barking. Cats rarely stay for long. Each yard is so orderly that drivers making a wrong turn onto the street often feel as if they've driven into a mirage. Most do a U-turn at the mouth of the street, instead of coasting down to the end and using the loop to return to the right path.

The house at the end of SE Pardee looks benign. Pretty, even. The spring green grass is evenly cut, and a border of daffodils pops with yellow brilliance against the light blue siding. It looks as if a caretaker comes by and gardens regularly. There are no weeds.

Someone – a former occupant perhaps – painted the mailbox. One side of the white receptacle is bright with green numbers; the other says "Twll Du" in swooping spring-colored letters. It's as if the painter felt the house deserved a name, much like a British home. Perhaps the painter was a Brit, trying to make their mark on these foreign shores.

The listing says that Twll Du is a 2-bedroom, 1 bathroom ranch home sitting at 1,600 square feet. "A Great Starter Home!" and at only $299,000 it's "Priced to Sell!" The listing doesn't say why it costs less than a Portland condo. If a potential buyer asked the listing agent about the price, he'd tell them that the owners live out of state and want a quick sale. He wouldn't go into the deaths that took place in the home if he thought the buyers were squeamish. He wouldn't have to. Oregon state law doesn't require that the realtor disclose a death in the house – he'd double-checked.

Continue reading *Terror at Twll Du* by downloading the ebook on Amazon.

Made in United States
Troutdale, OR
09/28/2023

13265631R00176